LINEAR TACTICAL SERIES
REDWOOD

D1509693

USA TODAY BESTSELLING AUTHOR
JANIE CROUCH

REDWOOD: LINEAR TACTICAL

This book is dedicated to my Gra...
Crazy Auntie Lisa
Bestest sister-in-law
I always love to hear your voice

Plus the chick on the cover looks like you. 🤍

1

Lexi needed a mark.

She felt eyes on her as she crossed the lobby of the midrange hotel in the middle of Wyoming, walking toward the bar in the rear. She was used to eyes on her. At one time, her presence here in a hotel she'd never heard of would've done more than cause a few stares—it would've caused a commotion.

A commotion was the last thing she wanted tonight.

She kept her head down, letting her thick blonde hair cover most of her face. Demure, shy damsel in distress—that was the role she was playing tonight. Someone who needed to be rescued. She might be a good actress, but it didn't take any theatrical skill to play someone in trouble. All she had to do was be herself.

That was the hardest role to play lately.

She glanced around as she walked, looking for the man she would use to help her out of this mess. Her gut churned at the thought of resorting to this. But she didn't have any choice.

She couldn't believe she'd gotten so close to finally

escaping the nightmare she'd been living for the past six months only to stall out, literally, in the last few miles.

She couldn't believe she had no other option besides using someone else, in whatever way she could manage, to get the cash she needed.

She clutched the purse she'd bought at a thrift store a few months ago—a pitiful knockoff of a brand she'd used to own in every size and color—against the black silk dress that hugged her curves. A Carolina Herrera dress also bought at a thrift store, still available because of the rip in the seam she'd repaired herself.

All those years sitting around in wardrobe fittings had rubbed off on her.

She slid onto a barstool at the end of the bar, keeping a look of dejection on her face, and quietly asked the bartender for a glass of water. The clock was now officially ticking.

She'd picked this seat for a reason. Between the location on the corner and the mirror up over the bar, her perch allowed her to see nearly everyone in the facility without it seeming like she was looking.

The bar itself she'd scoped out earlier today when her tire had punctured and she'd ended up at an auto shop a couple blocks away. She liked the bar not only because it was part of a hotel, which meant people wouldn't be in a hurry to leave, but because the bar had multiple darkened booths in the back. They were set up to view a small stage when there was live music. But tonight they would just provide a little privacy.

Lexi's stomach turned a little at the thought.

This wasn't the greatest plan ever. There were a lot of things that could go wrong. But all she needed was a hundred dollars—enough money to get her tire replaced and buy another tank of gas.

She was so close. And she'd spent every last dime, plus

more she still owed, getting to this place with an ID in her pocket that said Lexi Johnson. The guy who'd made the ID— and set up the electronic trail connected to it that made sure it would pass a cursory inspection—had assured her that Johnson was a more popular name than Jones or Smith. He'd also advised her to stick with her real first name since she'd be less likely to accidentally answer to the wrong name.

So she'd become Lexi Johnson.

And Lexi Johnson was who she would have to stay if she wanted to remain alive. All she had to do was make it to a small town about an hour from here where there was a job and a tiny apartment waiting for her. Not much, but hopefully, she'd be safe from the hell on her heels.

She nodded at the bartender as he slid the water in front of her. Time to put this not-terribly-brilliant plan into play. Step one: look pitiful. Step two: get someone to approach her. Step three: move the party over to one of those booths and flirt until she was able to get some money from the guy. Maybe by using her nimble fingers to pickpocket. But who knew? She'd seen guys pull out their wallets and hand it over to a woman to go buy a round to impress her with how much money he had.

Of course, those had been millionaires, and showing off a few thousand dollars in cash was nothing to them.

But hopefully, it wouldn't be too difficult to get the relatively little amount of money she needed. Two hundred at most. Yeah, she'd probably have to kiss some stranger she had no interest in. But she'd kissed a lot of people she'd had no interest in over the years—usually very handsome guys who'd also been some of the biggest jerks on the planet.

She wondered what most of them would say if they could see her now. Stooping so low for a couple hundred dollars. Nobody from her old life had ever tried to reach out to her.

Not that she blamed them. Everyone had condemned her for what she'd done.

Including the judge who'd sent her to prison.

She took a sip of water and a deep breath. The past wasn't what she needed to focus on. Only now. The *now* was all she could live for.

She glanced around the bar using the mirror. She couldn't be too overt in her approach in order for this to work. But there were things she could do to draw the right guy's attention.

The best option was probably the man a few stools over from her at the bar. Businessman, possibly late forties, slim build, in a suit with his tie loosened. Probably here in Reddington City for a computer conference or cattle convention—whatever kind of stuff they had in Wyoming. He seemed manageable.

He was watching the game on the TV but had already glanced at her a couple of times. All she had to do was make eye contact, and that would probably be encouragement enough.

There was another guy though, one already sitting in one of the booths she wanted. He looked a little more . . . *slick* than the guy at the bar. More product in his hair, suit fitting him a little better. He was frowning at his phone. Maybe someone had stood him up? It might be worth seeing if she could get his attention.

But God, she didn't want his attention. She didn't want either man's attention. Wanting attention was what had led her to this very place. And she'd had enough attention to last a lifetime.

Careful not to meet either man's eyes, she let her gaze wander further down the bar. Two women chatting. A couple huddled close to one another. An older woman scrolling through social media on her phone.

She accidentally met a man's eyes across the bar. They both happened to catch each other's gaze. But then she couldn't look away. She tried. She glanced down at her water to let the moment pass, but when she looked back up, his eyes were still on her.

Holy hell. It was like something out of a movie, where everything and everyone else faded away. What was it about him? She'd been on the arm of more beautiful men. This man wasn't beautiful. His face was too rugged, too rough cut. He was certainly attractive, but he wasn't beautiful.

He was a warrior.

And she really couldn't force herself to look away, despite the warning signals blaring inside her mind that she was drawing too much attention to herself. That this man was truly noticing her.

She wanted him to notice her.

Two years ago, she would've let him know that she wanted him to notice her. Would've walked right over to him, gotten much closer to that chiseled jaw and broad shoulders.

Her fingers tingled with the impossible urge to touch him, to run them through his thick, brown hair. She wanted to know what color those intense eyes staring back at her were.

She sucked in a breath. When was the last time she'd felt the urge to touch a man? When was the last time she'd thought about anything more than mere existence?

He was sitting on the opposite side of the bar—the corner, his back to the wall like hers was. He was also able to study the room.

The thought forced her to jerk her eyes away—he definitely wouldn't be studying the room for the same reason she was. She was here for a purpose. She had to keep that in the forefront of her mind. She couldn't afford to let an attraction, even one as visceral as this, derail her.

There was no way she could use him for her mark. He was too big, too strong, too sexy.

Far too aware.

This really wasn't the time for her libido to start working again. It had been in hibernation for eighteen months and needed to stay that way, at least for tonight.

But she wished the situation was different. Wished she was just a woman sitting in a bar with no agenda. Not one running for her life. Not one most of the world considered a selfish bitch who'd cried wolf.

Suddenly, it was much easier to keep her gaze off the too-aware, too-sexy man. Lexi had forfeited the right to have a relationship, maybe forever.

That was part of her penance—a penalty much longer than her jail time.

She forced herself not to look at the warrior again. She shifted her gaze back to the other two guys. The man in the booth was looking her way, so she glanced down at her water. Demure. It was fake, and she didn't like to do it, but she was beyond morality now.

Most people would argue she'd been way beyond morality for quite a while.

The other man, the slim man a couple stools down, glanced her way, and she gave him a small smile before looking back down at her water. Now was the waiting game. Looking approachable but not desperate. See who took the bait.

She couldn't resist one last look up at the man directly across from her. His eyes immediately found hers once again.

Shit. He was going to be the one to come talk to her. She

could almost see the alpha male in him establishing a claim on her. He was definitely going to scare away the other two.

And for a second, she almost didn't care.

But then she remembered what it felt like to be lying in an alley, crying and bruised, terrified for her life. What it felt like to never be able to sleep, to not have enough to eat or anywhere to live.

She needed to stay the course. Make it to a town she'd never been to called Oak Creek, take the job and place to live that had been offered in an act of kindness from someone who had every right to withhold kindness forever.

And just *survive*.

A handsome man in a bar who made her feel more alive than she had in years had no part in that equation.

When she glanced up and found his eyes once more on hers, she deliberately turned away from him. Gave him a cold shoulder, international sign for *I'm not interested*, and hoped it would be enough.

He was getting up. *Shit, he was getting up.* And if her goddamn heart didn't stop fluttering like she was some maiden being courted, she was going to rip the thing out of her chest.

But God, another part of her wanted him to come over. She didn't want to steal from him. But maybe she could ask him to borrow it or something. He looked like he was capable of handling anything.

His phone saved her. She watched as he pulled it out of his pocket and frowned at whoever was calling. And she was definitely not disappointed when he turned away from her to answer it.

It was better this way.

Right.

"Excuse me, miss?" The bartender slid a drink in front of

her, then pointed to the slick guy over in the booth. "The gentleman over there would like to buy you this drink."

Well, that solved that problem. The choice had been made for her. Now she had a role to play. "Did he now? What is it?"

"Vodka tonic. It's what he's drinking. I think it's what he hoped you were drinking too." The bartender kept his face carefully neutral.

She raised an eyebrow. "I see. Frugal too. If I turn him down, he'll just take the drink himself."

The bartender gave her a half smile. "Yep. Those were my instructions."

"Is he on his way over here yet?" She could look up in the mirror and find out herself, but she didn't want to be too obvious.

"Getting up now. Do you want me to get rid of him for you?"

"No. I'll give him a shot. Thanks though."

The bartender looked a little disappointed before schooling his features into a blank canvas again.

That's right, buddy, I'm a disappointment. Get used to it.

"I see you got my drink."

The bartender turned away with a little nod, and Lexi spun to face the slick guy from the booth, forcing a small smile. "I did. Thank you."

"It looked like we might both be drinking the same thing, and that it must be a sign that you wanted me to come talk to you."

There was nothing about this guy she found attractive. From the way his hand was already touching her where it rested on the back of her barstool to the smell of his cologne —which wasn't overpowering but too cloying nonetheless— everything about him made her want to back away.

It's a role, Alexandra. Play it. You've played much harder.

She smiled at him. "I have to admit, I'm a little glad for the company. It's been a rough day."

"I have a booth over there." His fingers trailed along her back as he pointed to where he'd been sitting. "Why don't you come hang out with me, and we'll see if we can get you cheered up."

She gave him a falsely grateful smile. "That sounds great, actually." She slid the vodka tonic toward him. "Here, you drink this one. I'll keep drinking mine." There was no way she was getting drunk around him. She'd stick to water.

He winked at her. "Let's go have some fun."

She didn't cringe as he slid his arm around her shoulder and led her to the booth. "Yeah, let's have fun."

2

An hour later, Lexi was definitely not having fun.

Evidently, she wasn't the only one who'd picked this bar because the booths gave a semblance of privacy. Vodka Tonic next to her, actual name Caleb, had evidently chosen it for the same reason.

They were on their third round of drinks—at least he was, she'd been nursing or dumping hers as often as possible—and he'd become more handsy as the minutes passed. And his wallet was nowhere nearer to her than it had been when she'd joined him in the booth.

His cologne wasn't nearly as bad as his conversational skills. She already knew that his watch cost more than a thousand dollars—something that evidently impressed most women, or so he said. She knew that he worked with a bunch of pricks—again his words—at an insurance sales office in Idaho Falls, and that said pricks couldn't open a door without his help. She knew this hotel was kind of crappy and that he would've been driving a BMW now if his two ex-wives weren't demanding such unreasonable alimony.

She should be thankful that Caleb was so busy talking

about himself that he hadn't asked a single question about her. That's what she needed.

But every second she spent with him pushed her closer to releasing the scream building inside of her.

This shouldn't be so hard for her. She was *acting*, it was a role, but every time he touched her, her skin crawled. Every laugh that came out of her mouth was so obviously fake, she couldn't believe Caleb hadn't caught on.

When he slid his hand under her skirt—*again*, the third time in five minutes—she knew this wasn't going to work. She might actually be sick.

And she was no closer to achieving her goal than she'd been when she'd first sat down with him. Even though Caleb liked to talk about his money, he kept a very tight fist on his wallet.

He smiled at her, unperturbed by the fact that she'd forcibly removed his hand from her thigh. "How about I get us one more round, and then we take this upstairs to my hotel room where you can pay me back for all the drinks I've bought you tonight."

She stared as he gave her a wink as if he hadn't just implied she was a prostitute.

There had to be another way to get to Oak Creek. Maybe she could ditch her car for a few days and hitchhike. Come back for it once she had a little bit of cash. It wasn't optimal but—

A shudder ran through her as Caleb's hand ran so far up her thigh his fingers actually touched her underwear this time. She jerked back.

Yeah, this wasn't going to work.

"You know what?" She grabbed his hand and yanked it back out from under her skirt. "I had a good time, Caleb. But I've got to go."

He laughed and inched closer. "Don't play hard to get. We're finally getting to the fun part. I know you don't want to leave now."

"Sorry, but I'm going to have to. I just remembered I have a . . . thing." She slid away from him until she was at the edge of the booth. "Thanks for the drinks." That she hadn't drunk. "And for the . . . company."

Caleb didn't look like he planned to give up this argument easily. Lexi used what weapons she had at her disposal and knocked over one of the glasses on the table straight into Caleb's lap.

"Fuck! The hell?"

As he frantically wiped at his crotch, she slid the rest of the way out of the booth and made her escape. Shit. If Caleb followed and made a scene, she wouldn't make it out of the bar and across the lobby without drawing way too much attention to herself.

She turned to the right instead, toward the marked patio doors connected to the side of the bar. It was dark out here, probably for use during the summer, and she let out a sigh of relief when she saw it was empty. She could hide here until Caleb left.

She breathed in deep gulps of the night air, welcoming the October chill. At least there were no Vodka Tonic hands on her here.

She walked over and leaned on the banister railing. She couldn't see much in the darkness, but she could breathe the cold air. She welcomed the cold. Welcomed the isolation. It matched what she felt on the inside: frozen and alone.

This weather was so much different than California where she'd spent most of her life. It was more similar to western North Carolina, which she'd called home for the past five years.

She'd convinced herself she hated it there. But it hadn't been the place she hated. It had been her own life.

"I should've known you were playing me, you little bitch."

Lexi spun at Caleb's voice behind her. *Shit.* In trying to avoid a confrontation, she'd put herself in actual danger. Caleb was just drunk enough to be a problem.

She shook her head. "No, it's not like that. I really do have somewhere I need to—"

She hissed as he reached over, grabbed her upper arms, and yanked her forward. "Don't lie to me. You bitches are all the same. Act like you're interested then refuse to make good on what you promise."

Lexi didn't pull away. She needed to talk him down from this if she could. If she had to scream, that was definitely going to draw attention she didn't want.

"Caleb, I'm sorry if you thought I was promising you anything. I was just looking for someone fun to talk to."

"I'm sick of all of you thinking you can lead us on. You're going to give me what I want. What you promised." His fingers dug in to the skin of her arms.

She forced herself to stay calm. "What did I promise you? You bought me a couple of drinks. Do you want me to pay it back?" Not that she had the money to do that. "I thought we were both just spending time with each other."

He yanked her against him. He stank of alcohol and sweat and that god-awful cologne. "We had an understanding. Don't act like we didn't have an understanding. You're all the same."

This had nothing to do with her. Whatever he was talking about now was some sort of residual issue with some other woman. But that didn't help Lexi now. She didn't want to draw attention to herself, but she also wasn't going to stay here and be sexually assaulted.

"You need to let go of me, Caleb." She'd never learned any

self-defense. She'd had her own security team, so she hadn't needed to. But she knew how to scream her head off. She looked him dead in the eye. "Back off."

She knew she was in trouble when he sneered. Before she could let out a yell, he spun her around and pushed her up against the wall, his hand covering her mouth and his body pressed up against hers.

"You know this is what you really want." His whisper was more terrifying than his volume had been.

Lexi pushed back against him, twisting, yelling from behind his hand, not caring who heard them now.

But he used his body weight to hold her there, grinding against her. She couldn't get a sound out. Couldn't breathe. "We can have a good time here if you don't want to go upstairs."

Oh God, she was going to be sick.

"I think the lady has made it abundantly clear she's not interested in spending any more time with you."

Both she and Caleb stiffened at the deep, masculine voice coming from the darkness.

"Stay out of it, buddy. My friend and I are just having a little fun." Caleb's hand tightened on her mouth.

Please don't believe him. Please don't believe him.

"Given you have your hand over her face and her body pressed up against a wall, I'm going to argue that maybe your *friend* isn't having quite as much fun as you are." The man stepped closer. "You need to let her go, right fucking now. Then if she tells me she wants to be here with you, I'll be on my way."

"Whatever, man. This bitch isn't worth the trouble. None of them are."

Lexi sagged, sucking in air as Caleb released her. He turned and walked back into the bar without another word.

do with the past five minutes with Caleb and much more to do with everything that had led up to this point. How she'd screwed up her life and brought on her own demise.

But she didn't have to say anything. And when he opened his arms and stepped toward her—slowly, respectfully, making sure it was what she wanted, the very opposite of Caleb's behavior—there was no way she could stop herself from moving closer to his strength.

He didn't ask her questions, didn't offer any false words of encouragement. He just held her, strong, steady.

She let the tears out but didn't sob. She'd learned quite a while ago to cry silently. But it felt so good not to be alone. Just for these few minutes to have someone to lean on, even if it wasn't permanent. Even if he wasn't hers.

She wasn't sure how long he held her there in the cold Wyoming night. Much longer than she had the right to expect. But she was too greedy, too emotionally needy in this moment to pull away.

But finally, she forced herself to.

If she didn't leave now, she was going to end up asking him for help. He'd want to know why, to dig deeper. And if he found out the truth, any concern or interest she'd seen in those big brown eyes would disappear.

She forced herself to step back. "I guess I did need a babysitter. Christina Hemsworth and I are lucky you took that class."

He put a finger under her chin and lifted her face until she was forced to look him in the eye. "What can I do to help?"

Had she ever wanted to tell her side of the story more? All of it, from beginning to end, and pray that maybe this one man might be different from everyone else and consider believing her. Defending her. Protecting her.

But she couldn't take the chance. She'd risked it all to get to this point, and now she needed to get out of here and find some way to make it through these last few miles to her future. A future that did not include this man.

"I'm fine. It's been a rough couple of days, and asshole Caleb didn't help." She patted the man on his chest, forcing her fingers not to dawdle there like they wanted. Forced herself not to ask his name. She was better off not knowing. "I should give back your jacket and head on out."

She stuffed her hands in the jacket pockets to keep from touching him again and felt it.

His wallet.

Why? Why did it have to be the one man who'd actually been kind to her? Treated her with respect? Why couldn't it have been Caleb whose wallet had jumped into her hand?

But she would have to be an absolute fool to pass up this opportunity. Regret pooled in her belly again, bitter and sour.

"I don't want to leave you alone if you're not sure you'll be all right," he said, those brown eyes so intense. "I understand if you don't want to press charges against Caleb, but are you sure there's no one I can call for you? Are you staying at the hotel? I know for a fact that Reddington City has counselors you can talk to free of charge if you need to. I'm happy to help facilitate that."

She was so going to hell. If not for what she'd done before, which nearly everyone agreed was enough for a mono-grammed seat in Hades, then definitely for what she was about to do now.

"No," she whispered. "Really, I'll be fine. I just need a few more minutes out here to pull myself together. I really kind of love the Wyoming night air."

He smiled. Holy hell, everything about his face changed with that smile, became more gentle, more approachable. And it was obviously so sincere.

God, she wanted to trace her fingernails down that strong jaw.

"There's nothing in the world quite like Wyoming nights."

"You're from here?"

He gave her a half grin. "My whole life."

There was obviously more to that story, but she'd let him have his secret since she had a million of her own.

"Well, I like what you've done with the place." She started to slip off the jacket to hand it back to him, her fist already around his wallet. It was going to be tricky keeping it out of his sight, but she would manage.

He stopped her, pulling the collar of his coat back around her shoulders. "You wear it. I have a lot more body mass to withstand the cold than you do. Is your jacket up in your room?"

"No, I'm not staying here. I just stopped to get a drink before heading out of town." An idea came to her even as she hated herself for coming up with it. "I left my jacket in the booth inside. I was in such a hurry to get away from Caleb that I ran out without it."

Not true. Well, partially true. She didn't have a jacket, but she had been in a hurry to get away from Caleb.

"Why don't I go back in there and grab it for you?"

She closed her eyes, not at all proud of the fact that he'd taken the bait she'd laid out for him. "That would be great. I'm sure Caleb is gone, but I really don't want to take a chance on running into him."

The man's face hardened. He obviously wouldn't mind running into Caleb. "What color is it?"

"Dark gray." She did have a jacket like that, but it was in the back seat of her car, not in the booth. "Cream-colored collar and cuffs."

He nodded. "I'll be right back."

"I'll be right here."

He'd barely been out of sight five seconds before she had the wallet in her hand and was looking through it for cash.

Her stomach curdled further as she pulled the bills out, not stopping to count them. It was at least a couple of hundred dollars. He had credit cards and even a library card in there too, but that wouldn't help her.

She couldn't resist looking at his driver's license. It had a local address here in Reddington City.

Gavin Zimmerman.

She trailed her fingers across the picture. "I really wish we could've met under different circumstances, Gavin Zimmerman. In a different life."

She sighed, then stuffed his credit cards and ID back into his pocket, keeping the wallet and cash. She slipped the jacket off her shoulders and let it fall to the ground, ignoring the chill that surrounded her instantly.

She balled her fist around the cash and, without looking back, hopped awkwardly over the railing and into the dark, cold Wyoming night.

3

"If you keep staying in here and working all hours of the day and night, they're eventually going to elect you sheriff for real, you know."

Gavin grinned and looked up from his computer at Zac Mackay standing in the doorway of his office. "Would you vote for me?"

Zac leaned his shoulder against the doorjamb. "Hell, no. We need you too much at Linear Tactical. Plus, remember all the times you told me how you were never running for any sort of public office?"

Gavin leaned back in his chair, smile falling a little. "Reminds me too much of dear old Dad. I've got neither the temperament nor the stomach for politics."

Gavin's dad, Ronald Zimmerman, had been the governor of Wyoming for the past six years and in the state's legislature before that. Gavin knew exactly what was involved with politics and wanted nothing to do with it.

Zac nodded. "I hear that. I'll take being a soldier any day. At least that way we have a better chance of knowing who our enemies are."

"That's the damned truth." Gavin pointed at the chair in front of his desk for Zac to sit in.

Gavin had been the acting sheriff in Oak Creek for the past six months since Curtis Nelson, the actual elected sheriff, had had a stroke. Fortunately, Nelson had recovered and for the past couple weeks had been back at work part-time. He'd be back full-time by the first of the year.

"You need something I can provide in my remaining time as sheriff? Bodies hidden? Parking tickets taken care of?"

Zac grinned. "Both, probably. But the guys sent me over from the Eagle's Nest to get you. They said your brooding time is up and it's Friday."

Gavin raised an eyebrow. "My *brooding* time?"

"Yeah. We generally give you two days to recover from a visit to Reddington City if just your dad is involved, four days if it involves your ex. It's been five days that you've been buried in here."

"I did see both Dad and Janeen." Gavin let out a sigh. Neither of them was the source of his *brooding*. That dubious honor belonged to a wallet thief. "And that went about how you would expect."

"Janeen still planning to run for Congress?"

Gavin scrubbed a hand down his face. "Yep. Another couple of years in state politics and then she's heading for the big league. Like her or not, you have to admit she knows how to make a plan and follow it."

"She may be a bitch, but she's definitely an organized one." Zac gave a sympathetic nod. He'd been part of the group who'd helped Gavin get shit-faced drunk after Gavin had walked in on Janeen with another man five years ago. "And your dad still won't cut her loose?"

Gavin rolled his eyes. He loved his dad, he really did, and generally they got along very well. But Ronald Zimmerman had a long-term plan that involved the White House. Janeen was part of the plan, the ideal running mate: young, smart, female, and politically aligned.

"You know Dad. He's looking at a much bigger picture than just our divorce. I'm sure if I pressed it and made him choose, he'd pick me over her." Probably. "But honestly, I don't care. Janeen has remarried. She's someone else's problem now. And Dad's."

That was true. His and Janeen's marriage had been in trouble before he'd caught her cheating, and the speed of his subsequent divorce had been more a sting to his pride than any true emotional turmoil. Janeen definitely wasn't the reason Gavin had been cranky and keeping away from people all week.

"You okay, brother? I feel like this is something more than normal political family dysfunction. Generally by this point, you're back out in public. Maybe I should've gotten over here sooner, but I know you don't like babysitters."

Gavin eyed Zac. They'd known each other for nearly ten years now. He'd originally written the other man off because of his surfer looks—ridiculous wavy brown hair with some blond highlights. Blue eyes. Quick smile.

But the son of a bitch had proved himself shrewd and a strategic thinker. Zac had made an excellent team leader in the Special Forces and had made an even better friend over the years, both in and out of the army.

Gavin had never planned to be part of Linear Tactical when Zac and another teammate, Finn Bollinger, first started talking about it, but they'd made a place for him when Gavin's plans had blown up just as he'd gotten out of the service.

He shut off his computer for the night. If his friends were hunting him down, it was time to resurface. Time to stop thinking about green eyes and sad smiles. "So you drew the short straw to come babysit Broody McBroodster?"

Zac grinned. "I was always the first to volunteer for hazardous missions. You know that."

"Well, I'm not about to arrest anybody for no good reason, so I think we're safe."

Although he very definitely wanted to arrest someone. Or at least find her.

He'd been suckered, and he didn't have anyone to blame but himself. He'd sat at the bar and gotten all hot and bothered over the woman across the way. He'd been about to go talk to her but had made the mistake of taking his father's call, and when he'd looked up again, she'd been sitting with that asshole.

"Oh my," Zac said, eyes big. "What's that look about? You really are thinking about arresting someone."

Gavin rubbed his face. "It's a very short, humiliating story."

Zac stretched his legs out in front of him. "Those are always the best kind. You know you're going to have to tell me."

"I left Dad's house, tired of the political bullshit—Dad still can't understand why I don't jump at the chance to be in the same house with my ex. I decided to have a beer and watch the game for a few before driving home. Ended up at the Hilderbrand Hotel."

"This is not nearly humiliating enough."

He'd really been taken in. When he'd seen that asshole pressing her up against the wall, he'd been ready to beat the shit out of the guy, to forget he was a law enforcement officer. And then, he'd fallen for it when she'd cried—held her like the dumbass sucker he was.

Gavin rolled his eyes. "Let me summarize for you. Basically, I got fleeced by a cute blonde with big green eyes and a very practiced sad smile."

Zac sat up a little straighter. "Now we're getting somewhere. Fleeced how?"

Gavin shook his head. "I offered her my jacket, and she stole my wallet right out of the pocket."

Zac laughed. Not a small chuckle, a straight-up belly laugh.

Gavin let out a long-suffering sigh. "Glad my hardship amuses you."

"No wonder you're holed up in this office." Zac was still laughing. "Damn, Redwood, no good deed goes unpunished, does it?"

"Evidently not."

Zac tried to get his merriment under control but wasn't having much luck. "But seriously, having your wallet stolen is a hassle. Did you have to cancel all your credit cards and stuff?"

Gavin shook his head. "No, fortunately, she took the cash but left the plastic. Cash I would've given her if she'd asked. Two hundred and eleven dollars."

He'd come back out after searching for her jacket with the bad news that it wasn't in the booth and hadn't been turned in to either of the bartenders. Worst fucking thing? He'd been prepared to give up his own favorite bomber jacket to replace hers.

Because he hadn't wanted her to be cold. Wherever she was going, whatever seemed to make those ridiculous green eyes of hers so sad, he hadn't wanted her to be *cold*.

And that made him a fucking idiot.

"Damn," Zac said. "Did you turn the whole hotel into a crime scene? Drag people out of their rooms for questioning?"

Gavin could chuckle about it now. "No, I decided to let it go as a lesson in the pitfalls of falling for a pretty face."

But evidently not a very well-learned lesson, because he had dusted his credit cards for prints. Not because he planned to actually arrest her, but because he wanted to know who she was. To have a way and a reason to see her again.

Because he hadn't been able to get her out of his mind in the five days since they'd met.

So yeah, that made him a really big fucking idiot.

"If that lesson only cost you two hundred and eleven dollars, then I think you got off pretty cheap," Zac said. "Everybody's at the Eagle's Nest. Come have a couple beers. I'm buying since—"

"Don't you say it." Gavin knew what was coming.

"—you're broke." Zac stood up and grinned. "There's no way out of it for you now. If you don't come, I'll be forced to tell the guys what happened and why you're hiding here. But if you come with me, I promise not to say a word."

All he had to do was ask Zac not to say anything and the man would go to his grave with the secret nowhere near his lips. Zac MacKay had saved his life more than once during their missions with the Special Forces. Gavin had returned the favor a time or two.

But the fact that the guys had a system for dealing with him whenever he came back from Dad's didn't sit well with him. Gavin didn't want to be a burden. So he would go hang out.

"Well, when you put it that way, I think it's definitely time for a beer." He grabbed that very same bomber jacket and slipped it on, and they walked out of the office together. Everything he was working on here could wait until tomorrow.

He felt better as soon as he stepped foot into the Eagle's Nest.

Oak Creek got quite a bit of business year round. They were close enough to the Tetons to bring in all different types. Hikers and nature lovers in the warmer months, skiers and snowboarders in the winter.

Plus Linear Tactical itself brought in a steady stream of law enforcement and private security groups who wanted to train with the best. LT offered all sorts of classes from basic self-defense to weapons usage and management, from hour-long situational awareness seminars to week-long immersive wilderness survival training sessions. Gavin enjoyed them all.

He also enjoyed the unique mixture of small-town living and some of the amenities of a bigger city: a hospital, a local community college, and a number of shops.

The Eagle's Nest, the bar that sat at the south end of town and had been run by old Mac Templeton since decades before Gavin had ever set foot in Oak Creek, was like a second home for all of them. Tourists tended to flock to a couple of newer, trendier bars a little closer to the resorts. The tourists could have them. Gavin and his friends weren't looking for trends.

Two of the Linear Tactical guys, Finn Bollinger and Aiden Teague, sat at one of the booths they tended to frequent. Kendrick Foster, a younger man who'd come into town a couple years ago to help with a kidnapping situation and never left, sat across from them.

All three men called out a welcome as Gavin and Zac walked toward them. Zac slid in beside Kendrick and Gavin pulled up a chair so he could sit at the end of the booth.

"Finally." Finn slapped Gavin on the shoulder. "When are you coming back to take over the beginning self-defense classes?"

"Depends. Male or female classes?"

Finn rolled his eyes. "I have not seen the inside of a female self-defense class since a certain five-foot-two blonde bombshell walked back into my life nearly two years ago. The only self-defense I'm going to need is my own if she hears I'm teaching them."

Gavin leaned back, crossed his arms over his chest, and nodded solemnly. "Then I guess I'll take one for the team and volunteer to teach the young, attractive coeds."

Everyone laughed. Gavin felt better. It was his nature to be alone—he had the nickname Redwood for a reason—but being with his friends was always a good thing. He needed to remember that.

"Who wants a drink?" Finn asked. "Mac hired a new waitress. Actually, I hear she's more like a manager. She's going to take over running the place for him."

Gavin nodded. "Good. With Mac's heart issues, he needs to slow down. Should've started backing off a decade ago. I'm surprised he's willing to give up the reins, even in his seventies."

"Me too," Aiden said. "But evidently this new girl is some sort of . . . family member."

The guys all let out awkward chuckles around the table.

"What?" There was obviously something Gavin didn't understand.

"Let's just say that if they're family, there's not much resemblance between the two. The new waitress is . . ." Finn faded off, glancing over at Kendrick.

"Don't stop on my account." Kendrick ran a hand over his dark head, hair cut so short he was nearly bald. "Mac is black and that woman is as white as they come. If they're blood family, it must be an interesting story."

"I'm glad Mac finally has someone helping him out," Gavin said. "Even better if he's going to be retiring."

Finn nodded. "Totally agree." He raised his hand to get the new waitress/manager's attention.

A few seconds later, Gavin stiffened in his chair as a voice behind him asked, "What can I get you guys?"

Oh hell no.

"Beer for me," Zac said. The other guys echoed the same.

Gavin turned slowly in his chair to face the green eyes he'd had on his mind for nearly a week. "I'll take a beer also. And maybe two hundred and eleven dollars."

4

G avin wasn't going to lie. The look of sheer panic that fell over her face as he turned around and she recognized him felt pretty damn good. Let her squirm.

Of course, the other guys had no idea what he was talking about and were all looking at him funny. Except Zac, whose jaw might actually have hit the table, but the other man didn't say anything.

Kendrick was the one who broke the silence that was heading into awkward territory. The computer expert was easygoing and charming. He didn't like awkward, especially when he obviously knew something odd was going on.

"Lexi, this is Gavin Zimmerman. He obviously has a weird sense of humor as you can tell." Kendrick turned to Gavin. "Sheriff, this is Lexi Johnson, the Eagle's Nest's newest member of the waitstaff."

Lexi gaped like a fish. "*Sheriff?*"

That's right, sweetheart, squirm. He gave her a smile that couldn't possibly be mistaken as friendly. "Technically, the title is acting sheriff, but the ability to arrest someone remains the same."

He almost felt bad for her when the color leeched out of her face. Kendrick kicked his leg under the table.

"Don't listen to Gavin." Kendrick gave her a friendly laugh. "He must have some handcuff fetish none of us knew about. Thus all the *arresting* talk."

Gavin gave her another smile, still not friendly. Both of them knew he wasn't joking.

"I—" She swallowed and tried again. "Should I get you your beers?"

One sentence from him could let her off the hook, but he wasn't ready to do that yet, so he said nothing.

It was Zac who finally spoke. "Yes, if you could bring us beers all around, that would be great."

She took off like she was on fire. He had to force himself to turn back to the table and not watch. Would she run straight out the door like she had in Reddington City? Was she truly concerned he was going to arrest her?

She should be. He wasn't, but she should still be concerned.

"Dude," Kendrick was glaring at him. "Do you have some sort of head trauma? What is wrong with you?"

He glanced over at Zac, but the other man was studying his fingernails, obviously not about to get involved in this conversation. Aiden and Finn stared at him, trying to ascertain what they were missing.

Gavin shrugged. "She doesn't seem very trustworthy to me."

Finn shook his head. "I've already been here a couple nights this week, and there's been nothing about the new waitress that struck me as questionable."

Aiden nodded. "Yeah, she seemed fine to me too. Although, granted, I do feel like I've met her before, but can't put my finger on where. I'm usually pretty good about that sort of stuff."

Gavin straightened in his chair. "All I'm saying is, what do we really know about this woman? As you guys pointed out, obviously she's not family to Mac. How do we know she's not taking advantage of him?"

Exactly the way she had taken advantage of Gavin a few days ago.

"You want to tell me why my new manager looks like she's going to hightail it out the door after one conversation with this table?"

Shit. Gavin glared at the other guys as he turned around to face Mac. This was why he didn't like to sit with his back to the rest of the room—too much of a chance someone might sneak up on him. The guys could've given him some warning the older man was coming up behind him.

He twisted in his chair so he could look up at Mac. Despite being in his mid-seventies, he really did seem pretty fit.

At least fit enough to be glaring at Gavin. "Just because my ticker isn't as spry as it used to be doesn't mean there's anything wrong with my brain, young man."

Gavin held his hands out in surrender. "I'm only looking out for you, Mac. I want to make sure you really know this woman before you hand over the keys to the kingdom."

Mac folded his arms across his chest. "I'm seventy-three years old. I've been running this bar since before your father first ran for office. He's been in here to have a drink more than once. Are you questioning my business sense?"

Double shit. Now he'd offended Mac, and that wasn't what he'd been trying to do at all. He looked back at the guys but they were all solidly on Mac's side. Zac gave a little shrug of support, but Gavin knew he was on his own.

Why not tell everyone what had happened with Lexi in Reddington City? Then they would all at least stop looking at him like he was tossing puppies into oncoming traffic. But for some reason—hell if he knew what it was—he was loath to do that.

He turned back to Mac. "I thought you had family coming to help you. Lexi is family?"

Mac raised an eyebrow. "Just because she doesn't look like me doesn't mean she's not family."

Great, he was making this worse. "Mac, you tell me that woman is one of yours, and I'll back off completely."

He would too. Hell, Gavin would be the first to admit that family wasn't always blood and blood wasn't always family. If Mac wanted to claim this woman as kin, then Gavin would let it drop. He would never bring up the $211 ever again, because he'd give that much out of his pocket for Mac any day of the week, and Mac would do the same for him.

If Mac told him Lexi was family, Gavin would go over right now and apologize to her for making her uncomfortable. Tell her she never had to pay back a dime of that money as long as she promised to let him know if she was ever in financial trouble again rather than pull a stunt like she had.

He wanted Mac to say the words, was honest enough with himself to know he'd be pursuing her like it was his full-time job if Mac said she was one of his own.

And he'd damn well be discovering why she'd stolen Gavin's wallet rather than calling Mac to come help her.

And why those green eyes, with their deep, dark shadows, were way too sad.

He wanted Mac to say she was family so that Gavin could let down his guard. Then he could look at her like a man looked at a woman, not like a sheriff looked at a potential suspect.

God, he wanted that.

"Tell me she's family, Mac." His words were almost a plea.

Mac was quiet for a long minute. "She's someone who needs a second chance, and she's welcome here."

Gavin could almost taste the disappointment that pooled in his gut.

Lexi wasn't family—blood or otherwise—to Mac.

Which meant Gavin wasn't released from his duty to protect the people of this town from potential harm—which she might bring.

Mac might welcome Lexi Johnson here, and she might need a second chance, but there was one thing Gavin knew for certain.

She was a woman with secrets, and secrets could be deadly.

∽

"THERE IS NOWHERE ELSE for you to go, so you're not going to run."

Lexi stared at her reflection in Mac's tiny personal bathroom attached to his office in the back of the kitchen. She swallowed the panic threatening to consume her.

Was it really possible that her luck could be this bad? That the man she'd stolen from in an act of desperation was the actual sheriff—or *acting* sheriff, whatever that meant—of the town where she'd had no choice but to make her home?

An unfamiliar face looked back at her from the mirror. Between the broken nose eighteen months ago that hadn't healed correctly and the makeup caked on that changed the entire appearance of her chin and cheeks, she was looking at a different person.

That was the point, wasn't it?

The only thing she hadn't been able to change was her

eyes, so distinctly green. She'd tried wearing contacts but they'd bothered her eyes so much she'd looked like she was crying, which had drawn more attention than her eye color ever would.

But the person staring back at her was a stranger in more than just appearance. It was the fear that permeated the air around her and leaked out of her pores that made her seem so unfamiliar, even to herself.

That fear was such a constant companion now that she should be used to it. But she wasn't. She'd spent her whole life being strong, and now she was terrified of damned near everything.

Especially that sheriff sitting out in the bar now, Gavin Zimmerman. She'd remembered his name every day, even when she'd wanted to forget it. Remembered his face. Remembered the warmth of his body as his arms had wrapped around her.

Everything in her told her to run now. But she couldn't. She couldn't afford the time it would take to reestablish herself somewhere else. She had money she owed that would cost her her life if it wasn't repaid.

Plus where was she going to go? Mac had given her a job here without any questions, based on his grandnephew's request. Nobody else was going to do that. And even though her ID was supposed to hold up through an electronic search, she didn't want to take the chance.

She couldn't run.

She gripped the sink in front of her to stop her hands shaking.

"You're tired. You know the crash is coming, but you have to hang on," she told her reflection.

She'd been pushing herself too hard, and her body was about to give out. This wasn't anything new. Her battle with insomnia had started more than a decade ago, and it wasn't something that had changed when her life had fallen apart a year and a half ago.

She wouldn't sleep until eventually her body shut down. But she couldn't let it happen here. "You've made it through worse, and you'll make it through this. You're not going to run. You're going to go out there and find a way to work the problem."

That was the full extent of her motivational speech.

She forced herself out of the kitchen bathroom and back out onto the main floor of the bar.

She didn't have any money saved up yet, but maybe she could offer Gavin the tips she'd made today. It might mean she only ate peanut butter sandwiches for the rest of the week, but maybe the peace offering would be enough. Maybe he wouldn't tell Mac what she'd done, wouldn't arrest her.

She was thankful that Amber, the other weekend-shift waitress, had already gotten Gavin and his friends their beers. Lexi went over to the other side of the room to take orders. Distance wouldn't save her if Gavin decided to get out his kinky sheriff handcuffs, but she could at least stay out of his direct line of sight.

Until she saw Gavin talking to Mac a few minutes later. Should she go over there and defend herself? Should she run out the door?

Honestly, she wasn't sure how much Mac knew about her. He hadn't studied her face when they'd first met, like he was trying to meld together who she was now with who she had been. Mac didn't seem like the type of man who watched a lot of entertainment news, so he might not be aware of her entire situation.

But then again, his grandnephew Markus, the one who'd arranged this job for Lexi, had been part of her life for years as a member of her security team. So even though she looked completely different, Mac had to have an idea of who she was.

But if he did, he hadn't said anything to her. And she'd been thankful for it. And honestly, maybe Mac truly thought she was just an old friend of the grandnephew he hadn't seen in years but had been willing to do a favor for.

She watched Mac talking to Gavin now, pressing a fist against her stomach, willing her body to calm down. If Mac told Gavin about her tie to Markus, she had no doubt Gavin would dig deeper. And if he put pictures of Alexandra Adams and Lexi Johnson side by side, there was no way he wouldn't be able to tell she was the same woman.

No matter how many times she broke her nose, no matter how skillfully she applied contouring makeup, there was no hiding it.

So much of her life was out of her control. All it would take was one deep breath and this house of cards would collapse everywhere.

But she was an actress. And she could at least *act* like she wasn't about to vomit and run out the door. She made the drink order for a couple who'd just come in and walked it over to their table. She forced herself to put on a smile and act like nothing was wrong.

She kept that smile on her face for the rest of her shift, staying far away from Gavin and his friends. When they finally left, with not another word from Gavin and no side-eye glances from Mac, she could finally breathe.

At least for tonight.

It wasn't until the end of her shift, as she was gathering glasses to run through the industrial dishwasher, that Mac caught her, helping her stack them in the crate.

"You're looking a lot less sickly since the Linear Tactical

boys left. I suppose you know they were asking about you. Gavin Zimmerman in particular."

Yeah, she knew. But she forced a neutral expression onto her face. "Was he?"

"He's afraid you may be taking advantage of me. May be trying to get control of the bar and cut me out of the profits or some such shit. Wanted to know how we knew each other."

She closed her eyes for a second before pushing the pan of dishes into the metal box and closing the door. She'd thought she was safe, but maybe she wasn't.

"Did you tell them about Markus?"

Did you tell them your grandnephew used to be my bodyguard when I was a face anyone would recognize? Until I almost got two people killed and ended up in jail myself?

That would end her stay in Oak Creek pretty quickly.

Mac leaned back against the counter. "No, I figured I didn't actually owe them any insight into my personal business, especially since they were insinuating that I couldn't make my own good decision. People around here are too damn nosy. And it's none of their business how I know you. So no, I didn't mention Markus or how he might have known you in a previous profession."

Her shoulders sagged as she slid the other crate of dishes that had just come out of the washer down the counter so they could cool. "That makes my life a lot easier, so I appreciate it." She shook her head. "You know they're just looking out for you, right? They're not trying to be nosy."

Mac let out a grumpy sigh. "I don't need looking out for. It's not like you're going to steal all the plates and glasses and run off."

"Of course not. That's crazy talk." She winked at him. "I'd take the silverware. That's much easier to carry."

He let out a laugh, but then it trailed off. "Look, I don't

know your story, and I don't need to know it in order for you to work here. Markus is a good man. I don't see him much, but I know he's always been honorable and hard working."

"Yes he is," she whispered. Markus had been a good friend to her when she'd least deserved it.

"I'm not one to keep up on Hollywood gossip, so I'm not exactly sure what happened in your situation. But the way I see it, it's none of my business. Markus said you needed a job and somewhere to lie low, and I had both of those things to offer, so here we are. You're helping me by taking some of the workload off, and maybe I'm helping you by giving you what you need."

She nodded. "Thank you, Mac. I promise I'll do a good job. All I want is the chance to rest. Just for a minute. A chance to catch my breath. Then eventually, I'll be moving on." She would have to. She wouldn't be safe here forever.

"Believe it or not, I said something very similar when I wandered into this town more than fifty years ago. Different time, different set of troubles, but I recognize that look in your eyes because I've seen it before when I looked in the mirror. I never planned on staying here, yet here I am. Better be careful that doesn't happen to you too. Oak Creek has a way of growing on people."

She hoisted up the tray of clean dishes and walked toward the door to the dining room. "I'm fairly certain that's never going to happen. Not that Sheriff Zimmerman would allow it anyway."

"Gavin is also a good man. He tends to take things a little too seriously—even his temporary job as sheriff. He's a protector, will fight tooth and nail against any potential threat to what he cares about, including this town."

Lexi walked out to put the dishes away without saying anything. That was exactly what she was afraid of.

5

"So that jacket does exist. Gray with cream collar and cuffs. I'd wondered if you'd made that up, too, after I'd spent twenty minutes inside the bar looking for it last week."

Two nights later, Lexi wasn't surprised to hear Gavin's voice as she came around the corner of the Eagle's Nest from the back door after her shift. He was waiting for her in the parking lot, leaning against his black SUV, long legs stretched out in front of him.

The only thing that surprised her was that he'd waited two more days for this showdown rather than having it out with her the first night.

Which was fortunate, considering her body had well and truly crashed after that night. She'd made it home, vomited everywhere, then fallen into one of her insomnia comas, sleeping for thirteen hours straight.

Everything about her insomnia was brutal on her body, but the hours right before the crash were the worst. At least she wasn't at that low place now.

Maybe tonight she was more equipped to handle him.

He folded his arms over his impressive chest and stared

her down with those deep brown eyes. God, he was so alpha male and sexy.

Maybe she wasn't any more equipped to handle him tonight.

She cleared her throat so she could talk. "Yep, this jacket does, in fact, exist."

He didn't move or say anything, so she studied him. Still as mouthwatering as he'd been in that bar. Strong jaw. Wide shoulders. An aura of confidence so strong it was almost palpable. It had been there in the bar and was here now too.

But he wasn't giving off the protective vibes he had been last week. Now he was polite, but guarded. Not going to let her fool him twice.

"What are you doing here, Lexi Johnson?"

She'd been expecting that question from the moment she'd seen him two days ago. Had known it would be coming. So she wasn't flippant—didn't blow him off with some sarcastic answer. "I'm working. I needed a job."

"And Oak Creek, barely on the map, was the only place you could find to do that?"

She shrugged. "Mac needed someone to help run the place, and I didn't want to be in a city anymore."

She waited for him to press. He was right. There was no logical reason for her to come to Oak Creek for a waitressing job, even if she didn't want to be in a city. Jobs like these were everywhere in every town.

But he didn't press. He just stood there, studying her in that calm, thorough way of his. Steady. She barely resisted the urge to squirm. She needed to see this out, or he was never going to leave her alone.

"You're quite the actress, you know."

She froze. Everything inside turned brittle, like a flick of a finger would shatter her into pieces. Had he figured out who she was? Did he suspect but wasn't sure?

She was careful to keep her face completely neutral. "So I've been told."

"Told by other people you stole from or folks in general?"

He didn't know. *Thank God.*

"Look." She took a step forward, knowing *closer* wasn't the safest place to be. She wished she'd driven here so she could get into her car and avoid talking to him altogether, but her apartment was only a few blocks away, so it had seemed pointless. "I'm sorry about last week. I had a flat tire, and I didn't have enough money to fix it and get gas for the rest of the way here. I'll pay you back."

He shook his head and pushed off from his car. "It's not about the money. Hell, I would've given you the money if you'd let me know you needed it, even though you were a stranger. Why didn't you call Mac and have him come get you?"

Because she'd never met Mac, but she couldn't tell Gavin that. "I don't have a phone."

He cocked his head sideways. "You don't have a phone?"

Shit. She was making it worse. Who didn't have a phone nowadays? Was she supposed to tell him that she'd deliberately run over hers with her car because she'd been convinced that's how a stalker kept finding her? That he was tracing her phone in some way?

That was going to lead to more questions.

She swallowed. "I thought I would wait until I got settled here and get one."

"I see."

He didn't see. Not at all. But that was for the best.

He was still standing there studying her, as if he could will her to tell him all her secrets.

Sorry, handsome. My secrets are my own.

"Are you going to arrest me, Sheriff?" she finally asked. "I sort of assumed you would've already done that if you were going to. Unless you like prolonging my agony—keeping me on edge."

He took another step closer. She should back away, but she didn't want to. He didn't scare her—she knew down to her bones Gavin Zimmerman wouldn't do her any bodily harm.

But that didn't mean he wasn't a danger to her. To her peace of mind.

She still didn't back away.

"Do you intend to steal anything else?" he finally asked in that deep, husky voice that did things to her she didn't want to acknowledge.

"No."

"Then, no, I'm not going to arrest you." He didn't sound entirely thrilled with the statement.

"Then I'm going to go home." Now she backed away. She needed some distance from him before she did something stupid, like close the space between them and kiss him.

"You're staying on top of the realtor's office, right? Mac mentioned it. I can give you a ride."

She took another step back. He might not have any intention of arresting her, but she wasn't a hundred percent sure he wouldn't drive her out of the state if she got into a vehicle with him.

"It's only a couple of blocks. I'll walk."

"I'll come with you then."

"It's not necessary, Sheriff." She started walking. "Most of the children are already in bed asleep, so I can't lure them into my stranger-danger van with promises of candy and puppies."

To her surprise, he let out a low chuckle as he fell in step beside her. "I'll stick around in case you find a bank you're tempted to rob. Not to mention, even in a town the size of Oak Creek, the buddy system is never a bad idea."

She glanced over at him. "Are you sure someone kidnapping me wouldn't solve some of your problems?"

"Nah. Too much paperwork."

Sexy, a gentleman, plus a sense of humor under all that gruffness? That didn't seem fair. They walked silently through the parking lot toward the main section of town.

"Will you tell me where you're from if I ask?"

She needed to handle this delicately. If she hid too much —information most people wouldn't mind sharing—it would just make him more curious. She definitely wanted to avoid that. She needed to tell him something.

She decided to go with the truth. The fewer lies she told, the fewer she had to remember.

"I've spent most of my life in either California or North Carolina."

"East and West Coast. Winter is going to be quite a bit different here than either of those places. I hope you have a heavier coat than that." He reached over and tugged on her sleeve.

She didn't but planned to outfit herself in more Wyoming-appropriate clothes as soon as she had the cash to do so. Getting anywhere financially was slow given the monthly installments she had to pay on the ID she'd purchased. She barely had enough left for food and necessities. Forget any sort of clothing splurge.

"I'll get one."

"Do it soon. Winter can close in faster than you think around here. We've been known to have snowstorms in November."

He was so bossy. Which both irked her to no end and

turned her on a little. She gave him a little salute. "Roger that, Sheriff."

His lips tightened—in irritation or in an attempt to ward off a smile?—so she kept walking. "You do know you don't have to call me Sheriff, right? It's a temporary title and the real sheriff of Oak Creek, Curtis Nelson, is taking back over soon."

"What will you do?"

"Go back and resume my work for Linear Tactical. Teaching self-defense classes, weapons training. We do some other type of work too. Basically we take what we learned about survival in the Special Forces and make it applicable for civilians."

He'd been a soldier. "Of course."

"Of course, what?"

"You're military. Or former military. I should've known it instantly by your awareness at the bar last week."

He scoffed. "I obviously wasn't too aware. You left Reddington City with the entire cash contents of my wallet."

"Yeah. Sorry." She grimaced.

"Was that guy Caleb in on it too?"

"No, he was just a bad choice." She shook her head. "Taking your wallet wasn't planned, I promise. You lent me your jacket, and it was right there in the pocket."

"Doing something like that could be dangerous with the wrong person, you know. Get you in trouble."

"Or arrested."

He cut a glance her way. "Or that."

"This is me." She pointed to the plain door attached to the side of the small realtor's office.

"You get to be right next to New Brothers Pizza. I'm surprised they didn't jack up the rent because of that."

"I'll admit, it does smell delicious."

"You haven't tried it yet?" The sheer disbelief in his voice made her smile.

She couldn't exactly explain to him why she hadn't tried any of the mouthwatering smells that had tempted her senses since she'd arrived. Right now, and for the foreseeable future, her meals consisted of what she could get for free at the Eagle's Nest or whatever was in a can and on sale at the grocery store. It wouldn't always be this bad—*she hoped*—but that was how it was for right now. And splurging on a pizza definitely wasn't an option.

She shrugged. "Too much working. But New Brothers is at the top of my list of things to try."

He didn't believe her. He stepped in closer, crowding her just the slightest bit. Not so much that she couldn't get around him if she wanted to, but enough that he was making a point.

He wanted her attention.

"Tell me what's going on, Lexi. Why are you here?" The words were soft, low.

She turned away from him. There was no answer she could give that would satisfy him since it wouldn't be the truth. She put the key in her door's lock, turning it and pushing it open.

At least with him here she didn't have that moment of panic where she was afraid she'd been found again and some masked freak was waiting for her. Opening doors in the dark had definitely become a trigger.

But like her or not, *trust* her or not, Gavin would step in front of her to protect her from danger if she needed it.

Of course, no one was going to protect her from him, and he might prove to be the most dangerous of all. He wasn't hunting her, stalking her. But he had already been closer—physically and mentally—than anyone else had been for the past two years. She leaned her head against the cool wood of the door.

"I'm just here for a job."

"Look at me, Lexi."

She wanted to say no. But more than that, she wanted to say yes. She slowly spun around.

He didn't demand answers. Those brown eyes, though as intense as ever, were gentle. He reached up and tucked a strand of hair behind her ear. When was the last time someone had touched her with any sort of gentleness?

He eased forward until she was caught between him and the doorframe. She didn't move as his lips closed the distance between them. Brushed hers in a feather-soft touch. Once. Again. A third time.

Then it was like something switched on in both of them. Their mouths melded together. Passionate. Hungry. And it felt so good. Gripping his waist she pulled him to her, sighing into his mouth as his tongue dueled with hers.

She wanted to stay here kissing him forever, but she also desperately wanted to drag him upstairs and take this much further.

"The heat between us at the bar was real." He murmured the words against her mouth. "I thought you were playing me, but you weren't."

"Yes," she moaned, as his lips took possession of her mouth. "Real. So real."

He kissed her again, hunger ratcheting up between them. He reached behind her and opened the door she'd just unlocked, allowing them to stumble inside.

His lips immediately found hers again. "I want to come upstairs with you. Is that what you want, Lexi?"

She nodded, clutching him closer. She didn't care if it was socially acceptable or not. All she cared about was that right now, she felt something. Something that wasn't fear. Something that wasn't loneliness. Something that wasn't frozen.

She was greedy for it, starving for it. Starving for *him*. It was almost embarrassing how much she wanted him, how safe and wild he'd made her feel in the past few minutes just with his lips against hers.

He would think she was crazy if she tried to explain it, but yes, *yes*, she wanted him.

"Yes. Come upstairs with me."

Her eyes fell closed as he kissed her again, his tongue playing havoc with her mouth, teasing, torturing. She was drowning in sensation, and she loved it. For the first time ever in her adult life, she didn't have to worry if a man was interested in her for her fame or money. She didn't have either.

Gavin wanted *her*.

"Tell me one thing first." His lips pulled away from hers.

"What?" She kept her eyes closed and tried to pull his head back down to hers. When it didn't return, she opened her eyes.

His brown eyes stared down at her, but they weren't filled with the same passion and gentleness they had been a few minutes before, when they'd been kissing outside.

These were the cold, focused eyes of the lawman. The soldier.

"I won't be a sucker a second time, *Lexi*. Not even for someone as beautiful as you. You want me to go upstairs with you? Tell me, *why are you here?*"

Every part of her that had thawed under the gentle touches and brushes of his lips froze solid again. She dropped her hands to her side and withdrew so no part of her was touching him.

She'd been wrong. He didn't want *her*, he wanted *answers*.

Interrogation hadn't worked, so he'd switched to a different tactic.

She pulled every bit of strength she could muster around herself and tilted her chin up. "I think I already answered that question, Sheriff. Mac had a job, I needed one, and this seemed like a nice enough town with decent people." She narrowed her eyes at him. "Although, obviously that last part wasn't fully correct."

He flinched slightly. "Lexi—"

"Thank you for walking me home, Sheriff, and making sure I stayed out of trouble. But now it's time for you to leave."

6

G avin had fucked up.

He'd known it the moment Lexi's door had slammed in his face, and he still knew it now a month later.

Things had gone completely off track that night. He'd wanted answers. Wanted to figure out her MO. Wanted to delve into all the reasons why her green eyes could go from feisty to haunted like they were on a switch.

He'd been prepared to use multiple methods of interrogation to get to the bottom of Lexi Johnson. Kissing hadn't been one of them.

Burning nearly to ash when their lips touched *definitely* hadn't been part of any plan.

Sitting here in a booth at the Eagle's Nest, at the thought of the heat between them, he still had to shift to make himself more comfortable. He'd never been that turned on in his entire life—especially not just from a kiss.

Yes. Come upstairs with me.

Those words falling from her sexy lips had haunted his dreams for the past month. The breathless way she'd said them. The little sigh that had accompanied her words.

The same little sigh she'd let out when he'd held her at that bar in Reddington City. That's what had snapped him out of his lust-induced haze to remember that Lexi wasn't trustworthy.

Knowing that, regaining his focus, and remembering why he was there with her had taken every bit of strength he had. For the first time in his life, he'd been tempted to forget about right and wrong, lies and truth, and just go with what he was feeling.

But he couldn't. That wasn't who he was. *Redwood*—his code name from the Special Forces, still used occasionally by the guys—didn't operate in the gray. Didn't ignore that there was a threat because said threat had a pretty face and gave kisses that blew his damned mind.

Lexi was lying, and he needed to know *why*. Needed to get to the truth about why she was here in Oak Creek.

But he could've handled it better. Not interrogated her in the middle of foreplay.

Gavin wasn't known for being friendly. He could fully admit he was gruff even on his good days. What he was known for was his solidness and consistency.

But there was something about that woman that shattered his focus.

They hadn't spoken since she'd slammed that door in his face. Every time he'd tried—because he admittedly owed her an apology—she'd turned and walked in the other direction.

She seemed to get along well enough with everyone else. Business at the Eagle's Nest had been steady and good. Mac looked more relaxed than he had in years. They'd even started serving lunch. Gavin knew because he'd been here every single day.

And every single day, he'd expected to find Lexi gone. Expected to hear some sheepish tale from Mac about how she'd grabbed the register's cash and split. All his gut instincts told him she was about to run and never be heard from again. And he trusted his gut—it had saved his ass way too many times for him not to.

But evidently, his gut was wrong when it came to Lexi Johnson because she hadn't run. She was here every day when he showed up for lunch and here most evenings when he couldn't seem to keep himself away.

"You're staring at her again," Zac said from across the booth as he took a sip of his beer.

"Fuck off. I'm not staring." He was so staring.

"I'm assuming Lexi never gave you your two hundred dollars back?"

"She offered. But said she'd have to do it in installments, so I told her not to worry about it."

Zac nodded, neither of them stating the obvious: that if someone couldn't afford to pay back two hundred bucks in one shot, then they were in definite financial distress.

"Does she look familiar to you?" Zac said, turned his mug around on its coaster. "Sometimes when I look at her from a certain angle, I feel like I know her from somewhere."

"Maybe." Everything about Lexi had Gavin all backward, so he wasn't sure he could trust any feeling when it came to her. "I ran her name through our network at the sheriff's office. Nothing came up. No arrests, no convictions."

"That's good, right? Nothing is good."

Gavin shrugged. "Just means she doesn't have a record. At least not one under that name."

"You think she has a fake name?"

Gavin scrubbed a hand over his face. "Hell, I don't know. Something about this woman doesn't add up. I don't know what it is or why I feel that way, but I do."

"Gavin, you've spent the better part of this year working in law enforcement. On our team in the army, you always did the questioning and interrogating. You were like a damned bloodhound, able to get to the truth of things."

"And?"

"And it's in your nature to be suspicious. That's how you come at things."

"But at least I used to give people the benefit of the doubt. Now I'm not sure I do that anymore."

Zac shrugged. "Considering Lexi stole your wallet in the first thirty minutes of knowing her, I think it's understandable that you don't trust her."

"But it's not just Lexi. I feel like I've lost my edge about everyone over the past month." Gavin looked over at where two of his friends, Baby Bollinger and Riley Harrison, were talking at the bar. "You heard Baby has a new love interest."

Zac nodded. "Quinn. I've met her. She's been working here at lunch, right? And teaches at the local college campus?"

"Yep. Like Lexi, Quinn showed up out of the blue, and I got all suspicious."

"Quinn didn't actually show up out of the blue. She's Riley's sister."

"I know. And she has every right to be here. But I was suspicious of her too. I talked Baby into leaving Quinn alone for a while, despite knowing how much he cared for her."

Zac shrugged. "Nothing wrong with taking things slow."

"But I did it because Quinn came to work *here*. I was convinced there was some sort of nefarious connection between her and Lexi. That they were in cahoots to scam the town or some such shit."

Zac let out a chuckle. "What would we do without you to protect our honor from these big bad criminals, Gavin?"

Gavin sighed and took a sip of his own beer. "Probably live longer, happier lives."

"Cut yourself some slack. You're protecting the town. It's what you do. Your means may be questionable, but your intentions are good."

He glanced over at Lexi, who was carrying a tray of beers over to a table on the other side of the bar. Zac probably wouldn't say the same if he'd seen what had happened between them a month ago.

The kiss had been an impulse, not a planned tactic to get info, but he could definitely see why she would take offense at the whole situation. He should've handled it better, backed off and kept the interrogation and the heat separate.

Except that heat seemed to pervade everything around them.

He was still itching to kiss her again, despite the fact that he couldn't trust her. He wanted to get close to her to find out whatever secrets she was keeping.

But he also just wanted to get *close* to her.

He sat back with a sigh. The place was filling up. It was midweek, but the women were coming here for a girls' night out, and the men were all *casually* hanging around to be their dance partners. Maybe focusing on them would help distract him from the fact that the next step in finding out about Lexi would be to run her prints.

That felt like a huge, *suspicious-bastard* overstep, even to him.

"Why don't you just enjoy yourself tonight?" Zac said. "Don't worry about Lexi. Don't worry about anything. The girls will be here in a few minutes. Everyone is safe and unharmed. Let's be thankful for that since it very nearly wasn't the case."

Gavin leaned back further in the booth. Zac was right. It had been a hell of a month for everyone. An accident that wasn't an accident at all had nearly taken out Baby during an adventure race. Then the team had had an unexpected mission to Egypt to stop a terrorist and save one of their own.

"The girls deserve their night out," Zac continued. "They may not want all us guys here, but given everything that's happened, they'll understand. Besides, I'm pretty sure Annie is going to be sharing our news. We decided to get married Valentine's Day weekend off the coast of California on one of the Channel Islands. Cade is helping us out by providing a jet to get everyone there as a wedding present. So clear your calendar."

Now that really was good news. Gavin grinned and held up his beer mug to clank it against Zac's. "Right on, brother. That's something to look forward to."

They drank a sip of their brews before Zac looked up across the bar and a goofy smile fell over his face. "It's very definitely something to look forward to."

Gavin didn't have to look over to see who had walked in the door. Probably a number of people, but definitely Anne Griffin. She'd been putting that goofy look on Zac's face for nearly two years now. And Zac had helped the shy, stuttering doctor come out of her shell.

"She's wearing her red boots, the same ones she did on our first date." Zac stood and slapped Gavin on the shoulder. "I'm one hell of a lucky man."

Gavin watched as Zac walked over to kiss his fiancée hello. Anne shooed him away, undoubtedly because this was supposed to be the girls' night out. But her laughter rang out as Zac yanked her against him and dipped her to kiss her passionately, to the delighted hoots of the women around them.

It was good to see Zac happy. Hell, this place had become a certified matchmakers' headquarters over the past couple of years. It had been amusing to watch all his fierce brothers-in-arms fall so hard and fast for their women.

At one time, he'd believed Janeen was his forever person. That was part of what had been so hard about her betrayal. The loss of that dream. He wanted someone who would tell the truth, no matter how ugly, including when he was being an asshole and needed to be put in his place.

He wanted someone he could trust.

"You doing okay?" Kendrick sat down across from Gavin and pushed an obnoxious-looking green drink in a highball glass—complete with a cherry—in front of him.

"You buying me drinks, Blaze?"

Gavin genuinely liked the younger man, despite the fact the two of them couldn't be more different in temperament and personality. Kendrick was talkative, outgoing, and fun. Gavin, on the other hand, well hell, he was pretty much stoic and cranky.

Kendrick gave him a big, toothy grin. "I'd gladly take credit, and will buy you drinks any time you want, but this one is from the bartender."

"Mac?"

"No, I think Mac went home. This is from your favorite new waitress." Kendrick couldn't seem to stop smiling. "She asked me to give it to you."

Gavin studied the green brew. "Do you think it's poisoned?" He was only half kidding.

"No," Kendrick said. "I think the present of this little gem is in its name."

"Oh yeah? And what's that?"

"Pain in the Ass. Lexi said to make sure you got it."

Gavin didn't try to stop his laugh.

Pain in the Ass indeed.

7

Lexi fought back a yawn, loaded up another tray of drinks, and rushed them out to the table near the door. At this point, she was basically running nonstop to keep up with everyone's orders.

It was a Wednesday night for crying out loud, generally their slowest night of the week. She'd sent Mac home a couple hours ago when it was still quiet.

It was generally her night off, but she'd seen at lunch today that he needed to go. The new heart medication he'd started this week had left him tired and weak as his body adjusted. He hadn't wanted to go, but Lexi had insisted. No point in both of them being here with nothing to do when he could be at home relaxing.

Who knew that the entire Linear Tactical crew and all their significant others would show up for a night out? They were dancing to all the eighties music, and the place was packed.

Lexi certainly didn't mind making the money—the tip jar on the bar was full to the top—but it was a lot of work for her and Amber to handle on their own.

But at least Lexi's new lunch-shift waitress, Quinn, was having a good time. The older woman wasn't much of a waitress, but she was nice and worked hard. Most importantly, Quinn didn't ask Lexi for any personal details about her life, so that made her a great employee and quasi friend in Lexi's book.

And right now, her quasi friend was out dancing with a man a decade Quinn's junior, who was head over heels for her. The man everybody called Baby—who very definitely wasn't one—couldn't stop fawning over Quinn. Quinn obviously felt the same in her older, more formal way. It was adorable to see.

Lexi spun to make her way around some dancers, ignoring the way it made her feel lightheaded, handed off the beers at the table, and took another set of orders.

She ignored the brown eyes watching her two booths over.

She should've gotten used to those eyes on her since they'd been there nearly every damn day for the past month. Should've been able to ignore them by now. But no. Her traitorous body reacted every single time Gavin came around. Made her aware of him with every breath. Every step.

She didn't talk to him. That stunt a month ago had cemented in her mind that Gavin Zimmerman was a danger to her. Not physically—she had no doubt he would never hurt her. But emotionally? Mentally? He was the walking, talking embodiment of danger for her.

She wished the not-quite-sheriff would leave her alone. But also . . . she felt some twisted sense of relief when he was nearby. Almost every night, he'd made sure she'd gotten home safely, although he'd been smart enough not to come anywhere near her while doing so.

And then tonight she'd seen him help Mac out to his truck. Gavin had carried the boxes Mac had wanted to take out to the trash, and he'd done it in a way that hadn't made Mac feel old or useless.

And her heart had thawed a little. Gavin might have been a jerk in his tactics a month ago, but she couldn't deny his intentions were good. He'd been looking out for Mac and didn't want Lexi taking advantage of the older man.

So she'd made him a drink as a peace offering, told Kendrick the name and to make sure Gavin got it.

She'd heard Gavin's laugh and now the glass was sitting empty in front of him. At least he'd had enough of a sense of humor to drink it.

She knew all sorts of obnoxiously named drinks. Maybe next time she'd make him a Duck Fart. Or a Flaming Gorilla Titties.

The next two hours went by in a blur as the DJ kept the eighties music going, and the women kept the dance floor packed.

Quinn pulled Lexi in for a hug as she walked by after delivering a tray of shots to the women. Lexi had to laugh. There was nothing about their personalities or work relationship that had ever lent them toward hugging. But the older woman was obviously having a great time.

"It's my first girls' night out," Quinn whisper-yelled in Lexi's ear. "I think I'm doing well."

Lexi laughed again. "I don't think you're being graded on it, Harvard. But I'm glad you're having fun."

"Are you doing okay? You look pale."

"Yeah. I'm just tired." Her body was closing down on her again. Too many nights with only a few minutes of sleep. She'd thought she had another day or two before it happened, but evidently not.

She just needed to hang on a few more hours. She would make it.

"Let's take a picture!" one of the gaggle of women yelled. "It's not officially a good time until we post it on social media. And we have to immortalize the day that Anne announced her wedding date."

"Yeah!" Quinn exclaimed with more giddy enthusiasm than Lexi had ever seen from her about anything. The strait-laced college professor tended to be quite a bit more subdued and serious. She grabbed Lexi's arm. "You come be in the picture with us too. Since this is your bar."

It wasn't Lexi's bar, but that didn't seem to matter to the women yelling their drunken agreement.

But there was no way Lexi could be in a picture they planned to plaster all over the internet. That was how she'd been found before, and she had no more resources to run.

She forced a smile. "No, no picture for me. I've got to get back to work."

"Awww, please?" Quinn gave her a pretty pout.

Lexi needed to quell this before it grew into some big thing. "Here, let me take the picture. Maybe we can start a picture of the week and hang it on the wall."

The women all started talking over themselves about that, forgetting her refusal to be in the picture. Someone handed Lexi the camera, and the women all grouped together for a shot, posing in the way only women can after they'd had a few drinks. Lexi took a couple of shots, handed the phone back to its owner, then escaped. Crisis averted.

Would she ever be able to take another picture without cringing in fear?

As the night wore on, exhaustion pulled more and more heavily on her. It wasn't long before she knew she was really in trouble.

Insomnia was a bitch. She knew the condition, at least at this point, was all in her head. She was no longer being given the substances that had caused such adrenaline surges and crashes. She was no longer being manipulated by people she should've been able to trust.

But her body had been conditioned to stay awake for days on end, to continue to operate long after a normal person would have been consumed by exhaustion.

It had helped her a great deal in her other career—she'd garnered a reputation for a strong work ethic. The first one on set and the last one to leave.

But right now, the insomnia had her on the verge of collapse. Every step took her closer to crumbling.

She pushed it back the way she always had.

Just a few more minutes. Hang in there just a few more minutes.

And when those minutes were up, she would tell herself to hang in there a few minutes more. It was the only way to make it through.

"Hey, can I help you deliver those drinks?"

Lexi looked up from the tray in her hands. She hadn't realized she'd stopped walking. She had no idea who these beverages belonged to. The last thing she remembered clearly was taking the picture of the women, but that had been a couple hours ago. Quinn had left with Baby not long after.

The friendly woman in front of her smiled. "I'm Wavy Bollinger. We've met a couple of times in passing. Finn and Baby are my brothers."

"Oh. Hi."

"I wait tables over at the Frontier Diner, and I know what it's like to have an unexpected rush. One time, the Linear guys forgot to tell us that they were inviting the entire Reddington City police force out for a training session, then bringing them by the diner for lunch. I was the only waitstaff there."

Lexi wasn't exactly sure how she was supposed to respond.

Was Wavy trying to tell her she was being too slow? She already knew that. "Oh. That stinks."

It was all her exhausted brain could manage to get out.

Wavy smiled. "All that to say . . . I'm gonna grab a tray and help you out. This is way too many people for two waitresses to handle alone."

"Oh."

Before Lexi could process anything further, Wavy had grabbed the tray from her hand and delivered the drinks where they belonged. Lexi walked behind the bar and was able to stay there fixing the drinks while Wavy and Amber delivered them.

There was no way Lexi would have made it through the evening without Wavy. And it wasn't just her who helped out. As the Oak Creek regulars realized Wavy had stepped up, they began helping more too. Kendrick took a couple loads of glasses to the back dishwasher. Zac and Anne bussed tables in between dances. Lexi even caught Gavin emptying the trash at the end of the bar when it got too full.

She didn't get the chance to say thank you because none of them came close enough for her to talk to them. They didn't seem to want or expect thanks. It was like this was home, and they were just doing their part. She would've been charmed if she hadn't been so busy putting all her energy into staying upright.

The night spiraled into a bigger and bigger blur until every breath was agonizing. She somehow managed to get the bar closed and locked. She paid Amber half the tips and would've paid Wavy too, but she was gone.

Despite the help, there was still a lot that needed to be done to close the bar for the night, but it would have to wait. Lexi recognized the final signs of collapse in her own body. Soon, she would be falling where she stood. She put on her best normal voice and told Amber to go home. They'd deal with the rest of the cleanup tomorrow. Amber agreed and left out the back. The girl was exhausted too.

Lex almost wished for one of the pills her aunt and uncle used to slip her to shock her out of this stage if it had happened at an inconvenient time. The stimulants, usually amphetamines, had been brutal on her body, but there had been no doubt she would stay awake. Now, she wasn't sure she would make it the two blocks back to her apartment.

She might not even make it out of this bar. She walked as steadily as she could back to the bathroom. She knew from experience that if she gave in to her insomnia coma with anything but a completely empty bladder, she'd wake up with an unpleasant surprise.

She needed to call Mac. Thankfully, they weren't open for lunch tomorrow, but she didn't want him shocked at the state of the Eagle's Nest when he came in for tomorrow night's shift. She had no idea if she would make it back in time to help. Usually when she crashed, it was for twelve to fifteen hours.

She went to the phone on Mac's desk, but her eyes wouldn't focus on the numbers to press. Everything was contracting down to tiny pinpricks in her vision.

Shit. This wasn't good. She needed to get home right now or she definitely wasn't going to make it.

She counted her steps as she walked to the back door. That didn't actually do anything but it gave her something manageable for her brain to focus on and kept her from panicking as the world closed in on her like a coffin. She got outside and managed to get the key into the door to lock it behind her.

Now, all she needed to do was make it a couple of blocks to her apartment.

She counted her steps again. One. Two. Three. Fou— The

ground in front of her was barely visible anymore. She couldn't see or hear anything through the cotton that had filled her head.

She wasn't going to make it.

She *had* to make it.

Rescuing her when she finally collapsed had been part of her aunt and uncle's manipulative games. They weren't here to manipulate her now, but they also weren't here to make sure Lexi found her way to a bed when the collapse came. She only had herself.

One. Two— She stumbled on a crack in the pavement, then couldn't seem to regain her balance. She could feel herself beginning to fall, and there wasn't anything she could do to stop it. She waited for the pain.

But strong arms caught her, helped her back upright. "Whoa there, Green Eyes. Been sampling some of your own drinks?"

Gavin.

"I—" There was nothing to say even if she could make words come out.

"Lexi? What's going on?"

"I—I have to get home." She took a few more steps, praying she was still going in the right direction.

"What's wrong with you?"

She couldn't answer, so she focused on walking, leaving him behind. She only got a few steps before she wobbled on her feet again. The ringing in her ears grew louder. She knew what that meant.

"Oh no," she whispered.

"What?" Gavin was standing right in front of her now.

"Move," she tried to warn him.

"Lexi, what the hell is going on?"

She vomited all over him. She couldn't move, couldn't stop.

She expected him to jump away but instead he moved closer. "Jesus, Lexi, are you sick?"

His arms wrapped around her and helped her to her knees on the pavement while her stomach emptied the rest of its contents. For a long minute afterward, she sat there trying to get in enough oxygen.

"Home." She pushed the word out with all the remaining strength she had. She only had minutes now before her entire system shut down. "Home."

Everything spun again, and she thought she was about to keel over, then realized it was Gavin picking her up in his arms. A few moments later, the world shifted again as he put her inside his SUV.

"Home," she whispered again.

If she could make it to her bed, everything would be all right. She would work everything else out once she woke up.

She counted the seconds as Gavin drove, using every bit of her remaining strength to stay conscious. When he came to an abrupt halt, she almost wept in relief as she recognized her apartment door.

A few more seconds, Lexi. You can do this.

"Goodbye." She was vaguely aware of how weak and hoarse her voice sounded. But there was nothing she could do about that now. She'd have to make up some excuse to him later.

She reached for the SUV's door handle, missed, and reached again, sighing in relief as her fingers found the handle and opened the door. She fell out of the vehicle, somehow landed on her feet, and stumbled toward the apartment door.

A few more seconds.

"Oh, hell no. I'm not leaving you like this." Gavin was right next to her again.

"No." He needed to leave her alone. She couldn't get full sentences out. She gritted her teeth against the roaring pain. "Goodbye."

"I'll help you get inside."

"No. I can do—" She didn't finish the sentence as the world faded to black around her and disappeared.

8

Gavin caught Lexi as she passed out in the middle of telling him she could handle whatever was happening to her.

He had no idea what was going on, but there was no way in hell he was going to leave her here outside on the ground. He grabbed the key from her hand and opened the door, then scooped her up in his arms and carried her right over the fucking threshold.

She'd worked too hard. Exhaustion—that had to be it. Her body had given out, but she'd be coming to any second now.

But she didn't stir a bit as he carried her up the narrow stairs to the apartment and laid her on the bed.

He'd never been up here. The studio apartment was tiny—the full bed and dresser took up most of the space. There was a small kitchen area with a microwave, miniature fridge, and a single countertop burner. A dining table that could maybe fit two people was pushed up against the window.

Damn it, she should've woken up by now, or at least be stirring. Even unconscious, she was pale and her features were pinched, like she was in pain. Maybe she was.

Did she have the flu? Food poisoning?

He had vomit all over him. She wasn't quite as bad, but if she needed to rest, he should at least get her out of those clothes.

He reached down and gently nudged her shoulder. "Lexi, wake up a second, and let's change your clothes. Then you can go back to sleep."

She didn't move. Didn't so much as stir.

That didn't seem right.

"Lexi." He shook her shoulder with a little more force this time, then brushed a strand of blonde hair off her forehead. "Hey, come on, Green Eyes. Wake up for me."

Nothing. She lay there, still as death.

For a second, panic pooled in his gut as he checked her pulse. Oh, Jesus, what if—

It was there. His breath leaked out in a hiss. Thank God. But it was way too fast for someone who was unconscious. Her heartbeat was thundering like she was running a sprint.

Shit. She was on something. That would explain so much —the big secret she was hiding. Why she'd stolen the two hundred dollars from him. Junkies did whatever they had to do.

He slid up her sleeves but found no sign of needle marks. That didn't necessarily mean anything, only that she either knew how to hide her track marks or used something that didn't require needles.

Damn it, was she overdosing? Should he take her to the hospital? He didn't know enough about drug use to make that decision. But he knew somebody who did.

He had Zac on the phone a few seconds later.

"What's wrong?" Zac skipped all pleasantries. The other man knew Gavin wouldn't be calling at this time of night if there wasn't something wrong.

"Is Anne sober enough to make a house call?"

"Are you injured?"

"It's not for me, it's for Lexi."

"Two-hundred-and-eleven-dollars Lexi? What's wrong with her? She seemed fine at the Eagle's Nest earlier."

"She's passed out and completely unresponsive. I think she may be on drugs or something."

Zac muttered a curse and a couple of moments later Anne's voice came on the phone. He explained his suspicions to her.

"Check her heart rate."

"It's racing. That's why I called. I thought maybe it was exhaustion, but this doesn't seem right."

"Okay, we'll be right over. Just stick with her. If she's having trouble breathing, call 911."

Gavin checked Lexi's pulse at least a dozen times before Zac and Anne arrived. It was stronger, and slower, but she still wouldn't wake up no matter how many times he tried to rouse her.

He took off his gross shirt and looked around for a washing machine. She didn't have one, so he thew his shirt in the sink.

She didn't have as much vomit on her, but he wiped off the little bit, then decided to slide her shoes off too. If she was going to be unconscious, she might as well be comfortable.

He rushed down the stairs a few minutes later to let Zac and Anne in.

"Any change?" Anne asked, bag in hand.

"She's still unconscious. Heart rate seems to be a little more normal." He led them back up the stairs.

"I'm not going to ask why you don't have a shirt on. I always figured you guys would eventually need me to help hide a body, but I never thought it would be straight-and-narrow Redwood first."

"Please." He forced a smile at Anne over his shoulder. "If we needed to hide a body, we could do that on our own. Your medical expertise would not be needed."

And they would never put Anne in that position anyway. She was too kind and gentle and it would weigh on her. Zac wouldn't allow that to happen.

As soon as they got upstairs, Anne walked to Lexi's bedside. Gavin took guard on the other side. Zac stayed near the door.

"She hasn't moved so much as a muscle since she passed out trying to get in the door and I carried her up here."

Anne listened to Lexi's heart with her stethoscope, then took her blood pressure. She pulled out a digital thermometer and took Lexi's temperature, then held her eyes open and shined a light in them.

"Is there any particular reason you think this is drug induced? When you talked to her last, did she show any signs of being high? She certainly seemed coherent at the bar earlier."

"I was waiting for her when she closed up the Eagle's Nest. When she came out, she seemed almost drunk. Then she vomited all over me."

Anne sat down on the edge of the bed. "I don't think she's high. Nothing about her resting state suggests that. Her pupils are responsive. Her blood pressure is normal. Her heart rate was elevated but it's lowered into normal range now."

"Then why won't she wake up?"

"I don't know her health history, so I can't say definitively, but she's young, and from what I've seen, relatively healthy. So unless I run some tests and they say differently, my first guess would be exhaustion."

"But if she's just tired, shouldn't she wake up if only to tell us to leave her alone?"

Anne shrugged. "Her body shut down. It's protecting itself. Did she give any indication that she knew what was coming?"

"She just kept saying that she needed to get home."

Anne gave him a gentle smile. "We don't know much about her, which Zac tells me causes you a great deal of irritation. But this could be somewhat normal for her. Or maybe not *normal*, but probably not due to illegal substances."

"So what should we do?"

Anne let out a little sigh. "I could admit her into the hospital, but even with insurance, that would be an expensive bill for her, especially if there's nothing wrong."

"You know for a fact she doesn't have a lot of money," Zac said from the doorway. Gavin nodded. She definitely wouldn't like spending the money.

But Gavin definitely didn't like this. Did not like how still Lexi was. It seemed so unnatural. He'd been watching her for a month, and she was always running in high gear. She never sat around, never wasted time. She worked hard.

She'd handled the unexpected crowd tonight without complaint. And of course, there was no way she had been able to stop and take a break. Maybe it was exhaustion and nothing illegal. Exhaustion could certainly incapacitate someone, he knew that for a fact.

Part of the SERE—survival, evasion, resistance, escape—training they'd gone through to become Green Berets had included some sleep-deprivation exercises. They'd spent weeks out in the cold without full meals and taken turns being held "prisoner" by enemy combatants. Uncle Sam had wanted them to have a taste of what imprisonment might feel like. And it had been hell.

But the torture of sleep deprivation had caught them all a

little off-guard. The way it tore at their minds, their emotions. Their sense of hope. Sleep was a necessity for the human body *and* mind.

He couldn't stand the thought of Lexi going through something like that.

"I'll stay with her."

"That will probably be good in case anything changes. And get her some food and fluids as soon as she wakes up."

"When will that be?"

"I'd be surprised if it's any shorter than eight hours, to be honest. Sometimes I sleep twelve or more hours after a long shift in the ER," Anne began packing up her bag. "I'll run a toxicology report to be sure, investigate a couple of medical possibilities. I can't share any of her private medical results, but we can at least know if we're dealing with something outside of the norm. I'll run it myself, so it will only take a couple hours. I can do it from her saliva."

Gavin reached over and took her hand. "Thank you, Annie."

The quiet doctor smiled. "I'm glad you're looking out for her. I was telling Zac on the way over that I've never once seen her outside of the Eagle's Nest. I know we're all happy for Mac to have the help, but it seems like Lexi deserves some time to rest too. This is probably her body making sure she has that."

That couldn't be right, could it? "I'm sure she's had some time off. Just because she doesn't hang out with any of our crowd doesn't mean she doesn't have friends."

"You would know," Zac said. "You've been keeping pretty close tabs on her, right?"

"Yeah."

Yeah, he had. And Anne was right. How had he missed that? In a month of watching her, he'd never thought about how damned easy she'd made it for him. She was almost always here at her apartment or at the bar. He'd only seen her go to the grocery store once, and her car rarely moved from its parking spot at the side of the building.

She'd never made friends with anyone, never gone out to eat, never gone shopping at the handful of stores they had in town. And he'd missed that because he'd been too busy watching for iniquitous actions.

He'd been too damned suspicious.

"I know you ran her in the system and nothing questionable came up," Zac said.

Gavin held out his hand toward Lexi, who was lying completely helpless on the bed. "But this proves secrets, doesn't it?"

Anne handed her bag to Zac, walked over, and touched Gavin on the arm. "Yes, she has secrets. We all do. I know you and she got off to a rough start, but maybe she's not trouble. Maybe she's *in* trouble. Maybe she needs your protection as much as everyone else around here does."

"Maybe." Gavin gave her a hug. "Thank you, Anne. I know this goes outside your job description."

She smiled. "I'm glad you called. And I'm glad you're willing to take care of her, even if you don't trust her."

He shook Zac's hand, and they left. Lexi still hadn't moved from her place on the bed, so he finished washing out his shirt and hung it over one of the hard plastic chairs before settling himself into the other one.

As he sat watching Lexi still lying there still as death, it occurred to him that maybe both he and Anne were right.

Maybe Lexi was both trouble and in trouble.

9

Lexi let out a soft gasp. She was awake. And Gavin could finally—finally—actually breathe again.

About damned time.

She'd been asleep for thirteen hours. He'd talked to Anne twice during that time: once for her to let him know that the toxicology report had come back clean, and once more a couple hours later when he'd felt sure Lexi should've already been awake. Anne had told him to trust that her body knew what it needed.

Gavin had gotten much less than thirteen hours of sleep. He didn't feel guilty that he had spent the past few hours going through her apartment. Not that there was much of it go through.

He hadn't found a damned thing. Nothing to suggest Lexi had any sort of hidden agenda of any kind. She had a few outfits in the closet. A bunch of makeup in the bathroom. But nothing unusual.

And not a single personal item in the whole damned place. No pictures. No knickknacks. No cell phone. Nothing.

"Why are you here?"

Her voice was hoarse. It sounded painful. He went and got her a glass of water and brought it over to her. "Drink first."

She took the glass and gulped the water down. Watching her, something inside of him eased further. She was back. She was able to talk, so obviously she had a fully functioning brain.

Those green eyes spit fire at him again. Like *he* was the one who'd done something crazy.

"You scared the shit out of me," he told her. He shouldn't be so gruff but couldn't seem to avoid it.

"How long have I been out?"

So this was something that happened regularly enough for her to know to ask that question. "Since you got off work last night. Almost thirteen hours."

Again, no surprise on her features.

But then she froze, hand flying up to her face. She stared at him like she was expecting him to pounce on her.

"What?" he finally asked.

She threw her other hand up in front of her face. "I have to go to the bathroom."

She shot out of bed, ran to the tiny bathroom, and slammed the door behind her. Evidently her large muscle groups were working fine too. And after thirteen hours, he wasn't surprised the bathroom was a necessity.

He heard the shower running and decided to make them both something to eat. Because while he hadn't been upset by anything he'd found in the apartment, he'd been fucking pissed at the state of her pantry and fridge. There wasn't a fresh fruit or vegetable or piece of meat in this entire place. Ramen noodles—yes. Discounted canned soup—yes. Bread and peanut butter—yes. But that was it.

It didn't take a genius to realize she was so broke she couldn't afford to buy decent food.

What the hell was that all about? Tonight alone she had to have made more than a hundred dollars in tips. Oak Creek wasn't the cheapest place in the world to live, but it definitely wasn't outrageous or close to living expenses in most big cities.

Definitely not so expensive that she couldn't afford a pack of chicken and some vegetables after a month living and working here.

The lack of fresh food had led him back to the drug-use theory. But he hadn't found *anything* in here that suggested drug use. No paraphernalia. No discards. And he'd searched pretty damned thoroughly.

So where was her money going? Hell, he'd even looked under the mattress to see if she was hoarding it away there. Or maybe she was saving for something and had it all in a bank account. There was nothing wrong with that. In fact, it was admirable.

He scrubbed a hand down his face. The way his brain jumped from one extreme to the other with this woman was driving him crazy. Did he expect the best from her or the worst? He needed to fucking decide.

As soon as the town grocery store had opened up this morning, he'd placed an order and had it delivered. He hadn't gotten as much as he'd wanted to, but at least there was now enough food here for him to make her an omelet with fresh ingredients.

She was still in the bathroom when he'd finished making their food fifteen minutes later. He could hear her putzing around in there so knew she was still conscious.

She finally came out of the bathroom, makeup flawless. Was that what she had been doing in there all this time? Did she really think he cared if her mascara was perfect? He'd bet she was every bit as gorgeous without any of that stuff on her face.

He slid a plate with the omelet across the table toward her. She stared at it, obviously aware that she hadn't had the food here for him to make it.

She cleared her throat. "You probably have questions."

He raised an eyebrow. "I'm pretty much made of questions at this point. But eat first. Anne said to feed you when you woke up."

"Dr. Anne was here?"

"It was either call her or take you to the emergency room. You were unconscious and unresponsive."

She flinched. "I—"

He pointed at the plate. "Eat first."

She closed her eyes in pleasure as her lips closed around the first bite.

Gavin bit back a curse. First, because he very definitely should not be finding that sight so sexy. But also because this confirmed what he'd already known to be true. She'd been surviving off the crap in her cabinet and tiny fridge for too long. She was halfway through the omelet in under a minute, and he stood back up. He slid his plate over toward her. "Eat this one. I'll make myself another one."

"But—"

He turned away before she could say anything else. She was damned well going to eat until she was too stuffed to eat any more.

She'd finished hers and most of his by the time he'd cooked his second omelet. She got up to make them both coffee in a tiny four-cup pot as he sat down to eat.

"I guess I owe you a thank-you. Seems like you're going to have to start a tab for stuff I owe you."

He didn't want thanks. He wanted answers. "What exactly happened to you last night?"

She turned back to fiddle with the coffee pot. Was she

going to answer him at all? She poured some coffee into a mug and handed it to him, then sat down across from him clutching her own mug. Still she didn't speak.

"Listen," he said finally. "Are you on something? Drugs? Honestly, I thought you'd overdosed and might be about to die last night. You scared the shit out of me. Nothing I could do would wake you up."

He could see her weighing what to tell him. How much of it would be the truth? "I suffer from chronic insomnia."

"Insomnia?" That didn't make sense. "Last night seemed like the opposite of not being able to sleep."

"Last night was what happens when I go too long without any real sleep. I can push through for a pretty long time, but then my body eventually completely shuts down."

He had to admit that lined up with what Anne had said. "How long has this been going on? Should you see a doctor or something?"

Once again she looked like she was trying to figure out how much to tell him. "I've seen a doctor, more than one actually, although it has been a while now. My insomnia originated because of some drug use. I'm no longer using the drugs, but my body is conditioned not to sleep well, so sleep and I have a very complex love/hate relationship."

That was perhaps the most honest sentence he'd ever gotten out of her. "Okay." It was time for him to be honest too. "Do you need me to help you find a doctor or counselor of some sort? Your drug use didn't show up when I ran your name, so I know you weren't arrested or in court-ordered rehab for it."

"You did a background check on me?"

"Yep, and found out Lexi Johnson has no criminal record or outstanding warrants."

She didn't look as mad as he'd expected. As a matter fact she looked quite pleased with herself. "There you go."

"You're not mad that I ran your name through the system?"

That perfectly made up face didn't flinch as she took a sip of coffee and studied him.

It was hard to believe this cool, composed woman was the same woman who had collapsed outside the door so help-lessly last night.

"I'm less mad at that than at your seduction-for-informa-tion technique a few weeks ago. Does that usually work for you? Quinn told me you were suspicious of her too. Did you try to sleep with her to get information since she's also new in town?"

He'd been an ass. He couldn't deny it. "Actually, I think Baby volunteered for that duty."

She rolled her eyes. "Well, thank God there are good soldiers like you guys willing to take one for the team and sleep with all the suspicious newcomers."

She got up from the table and walked over to the fridge. She pulled out some of the orange juice he'd ordered and poured it into a tiny juice glass.

She didn't offer him any. He wasn't surprised.

"That kiss wasn't planned. I didn't mean for it to turn into an interrogation. But I did think you were trouble. I thought you might be here to take advantage of Mac. It wasn't outside the realm of possibility. I still don't know why you're here."

"Maybe it's not any of your business why I'm here, Sheriff. Maybe you're going to have to accept that I'm not here to steal the Eagle's Nest or hurt Mac in any way. Maybe you're going to have to accept that I'm not going to spill my guts to you just because you've got a pretty face."

Damn it, he didn't want to fight with her. The time watching her last night had made him realize he wanted to help her. Protect her. Stand between her and whatever it was that sometimes put that terrified look in her eyes.

He didn't want to fight. Didn't want to add to whatever burden she was already carrying.

"You really think I'm pretty?" He batted his eyelashes at her.

She broke out in a huge grin, and for a split-second, she looked familiar. Like what everyone else kept saying.

"What?" she asked.

But then it was gone.

"I like it when you smile." He picked up his plate and walked it over to the sink, rinsing it.

"If you just let me live here in peace, Sheriff, then I will walk around smiling all the time."

She got up and walked her juice cup over to the sink, raising an eyebrow at him. Suddenly, this tiny kitchen in this tiny apartment seemed even smaller. He reached out and trailed his fingers down her arm. He couldn't help it, he had to touch her. He'd been very careful not to touch her all night as she slept except for medical concerns. Touching her while she was unconscious went against every personal code he had.

But now, she wasn't unconscious, and he wanted to touch her almost as much as he wanted his next breath.

"I do want to see you smile more, Lexi Johnson. But I don't know that I can leave you in peace. Do you want me to leave you alone?"

"I—honestly, I don't know."

He kissed her. What should have been their first kiss. He had no agenda, no ulterior motive. Just a need to feel her lips under his. When her fingers dropped to his waist, clutching him closer, he slid his hands into her hair at the nape of her neck. He kept the kiss gentle, easy. She'd opened up to him a little bit today, and he didn't want to do anything that would jeopardize that.

Besides, he wouldn't mind just kissing her for a few dozen hours.

Eventually, he pulled back. He leaned his forehead against hers. "Lexi, I want to help you. Whatever it is that scares you sometimes... that has you looking at the nearest door like you need to be prepared to run through it at a moment's notice? I want to help. Let me help."

Those huge eyes blinked at him, and for a moment he thought she was going to share whatever burden it was she carried. She was going to let him help her.

Then the shutters came down.

"I think you've got too much soldier on the brain, Sheriff." She pulled away so they were no longer touching, closing in on herself. "Not everybody is a damsel in distress in need of a white knight. Some of us are just ordinary waitresses with no fancy story to tell."

He didn't believe that for a second. "Lexi, please. Whatever it is, I want to help. Let me help."

She didn't meet his eyes. "I've got to finish getting ready and head over to the Eagle's Nest to clean up the mess I didn't get to last night. You showed yourself in, so I'm sure you can show yourself out. Thanks for your help."

She turned and walked back into the bathroom. The door closed firmly behind her with a resounding click of the lock.

Gavin turned, gripped the sink until his knuckles turned white. He'd pushed too hard. But damn it, he couldn't help her if he didn't know what was going on. He rinsed their plates and the coffee mugs, and was about to do the same with her juice glass when he stopped. Instead of rinsing it, he grabbed a paper towel and wrapped it around the tiny glass.

She was the only one who had touched it. It only had her fingerprints on it.

He slipped on his jacket and put the glass into the pocket. He could run it for prints and find out more about what was going on with Lexi Johnson.

He wanted to help.

10

Lexi avoided talking to Gavin about anything of consequence for the next week. She'd come way too close to spilling her guts the morning after her insomnia coma.

He'd said he wanted to help. That tune would change if he knew the truth. Sure, someone like him wanted to help the struggling lady and banish the fears in her eyes.

But she was pretty damned certain he wouldn't be interested in helping the convicted felon who'd brought her trouble on herself.

She wouldn't be able to stand the look that would come into his eyes if he knew who she really was. Disappointment. Disgust. Forget any more kisses, it would be back to watching her like she was the enemy.

Better to keep the sexy sheriff at bay. She couldn't keep him out of her fantasies—and he was damned well there every night, kissing her in her dreams—but she could keep her distance in real life.

Focus on work, on getting the money she needed to pay off

what she owed on her ID, and get some set aside in case she had to run again if her stalker caught up.

She hadn't remembered it was Thanksgiving Day until she got to the Eagle's Nest and saw the closed sign Mac had left on the door. He'd told her yesterday that he wouldn't be here today, that he'd be visiting family. He'd even awkwardly asked her if she'd like to go with him, to which she'd laughed lightly and said no.

At the time she'd thought he was kidding, because who would run this place if they both were gone? But now, looking at Mac's sign, she realized the intent behind his awkward invitation.

Happy Thanksgiving. There's a lot to be thankful for, but do it somewhere else.

Mac was nothing if not direct.

Thanksgiving had never been a big celebration in her life. It had generally been a break for the cast and crew, so she tended to fly somewhere international and hang out for a while. Always somewhere upscale and classy. Five-star hotels that catered to her every whim. But she'd always been alone.

Last year had been the most people she'd ever spent Thanksgiving with. The North Carolina Correctional Institution for Women definitely hadn't been a five-star luxury establishment, but they had served turkey, or something like it, on Thanksgiving Day. And for once, Lexi hadn't eaten alone.

Alone was preferable.

Lexi let herself in to the bar. Nobody being here would give her a chance to catch up on some other work—stuff she enjoyed but struggled to find time for. Who would've known she had such a head for business?

The Eagle's Nest had been doing fine under Mac's watch all these years, but he hadn't been interested in making it grow or attempting to turn a bigger profit. When she'd first mentioned her ideas for growth—opening for lunch, offering themed nights, sprucing the place up a little—he'd been hesitant but had agreed. Once he'd seen how well everything was going, he'd pretty much let her take over. He "liked having young blood" in the place.

Mac was tired, she realized. Ready to start thinking about retiring. She'd been here six weeks and already was wondering if maybe she could eventually save up enough money to buy this place from him. Mac didn't have any children, and as far as she knew, he didn't have any other family interested in the bar.

Maybe, just *maybe*, she could make this place work long-term. She didn't miss acting—not that anyone was going to let her go back to that. She didn't miss being in the limelight. But she did miss having something to put her effort and energy toward.

It would take a while to get the money, and it would mean a lot of days and nights of hard work, but she wasn't afraid of hard work. All she needed was a chance.

And now that Gavin wasn't hunting her anymore—he seemed to be taking her request for privacy at face value—maybe it could all work out.

She wasn't surprised he'd run her name through his law enforcement system and was glad that her new ID had held up. The man she'd bought it from had told her he'd built an electronic persona that would withstand a basic search, but she'd had no way of knowing whether that was accurate until it happened.

Evidently, it was accurate. Because a certain sexy sheriff had sat with her all night rather than arrest her. Or, at the very least, serve her with some very pointed questions.

And then he'd kissed her senseless. Again. Maybe once

more not to try to get information out of her, but because he wanted to help. Wanted to protect her.

She'd told him to leave and had fled to the bathroom. She'd studied herself in the mirror for a long time. She couldn't tell him the truth, but if she'd stepped out of the bathroom and he'd still been there, she would have dragged him to the bed and had her way with him. She wanted him with a ferocity she could barely recognize.

But he'd been gone. Of course, he'd been gone. He was a gentleman, and she'd asked him to leave.

And she didn't want to admit how much she'd missed having him skulking around and staring at her the past week and a half. She'd seen him a couple of times, but he'd obviously decided she didn't need to be under twenty-four seven observation. She should be happy. But she kind of missed him, her second stalker.

She spent a few hours getting the Eagle's Nest accounting books in order. Mac's system—stuffing receipts in a giant envelope and never looking at them again if it wasn't necessary—made her eyes cross. She was trying to drag the system into the twenty-first century, but it was slow going. Finally, she decided to head back to her apartment. It was already getting dark, and hopefully, she'd get a couple hours of sleep.

Maybe she'd stop by the Frontier Diner and grab herself a piece of their apple pie.

She'd been feeling better since she'd been eating the healthy foods that Gavin had bought for her. She'd been able to get a little more sleep and not feel so exhausted all the time. It had made enough of a difference that she'd picked up some fruits and veggies herself a couple of days ago.

She had six more payments on her ID, and she already had enough to make next week's payment, leaving her enough money for fresh food. She had enough money for a piece of pie from the Frontier without feeling guilty about it.

She swallowed her disappointment as she walked to the other side of town and found the diner closed. Of course. Thanksgiving in a small town. She should've expected it.

"I've got a shit ton of Thanksgiving leftovers in my studio if that's the sort of thing you came here for."

Lexi spun around. Wavy Bollinger. "Actually, I came for a slice of pie. But while you're here, I need to thank you for helping me out a couple of weeks ago during Quinn's girls' night out."

"No thanks necessary. I know what it's like to be expecting a quiet night at your place of business only to find yourself drowning."

"You took off before I could offer you a share of the tips."

Wavy smiled at her. "Definitely not needed. Look, I'm just getting home from the Thanksgria party, which is our town's unique blend of Thanksgiving and sangria, and it's been a crazy day. Why don't you come up and grab a couple of plates to take home with you? I'm sure I can find some pie that's nearly as delicious. Hang out with me for a little bit if you're not doing anything. I could use the company."

She shouldn't. Making friends only led to danger in the long run. But it had been so long since she'd just chatted with someone casually.

"Sure." Lexi smiled. "Anything for pie."

Wavy led her another block down Main Street then up over the hardware store.

"This is my studio. This isn't my legal address, but really I live here. We'll have to ignore the mess."

They walked up the outside stairs. "What kind of studio?"

"Art. Painting, more specifically. You'll see." Wavy unlocked her door, and they went inside.

This studio was five times larger than Lexi's apartment. It obviously wasn't meant to be a living space. A bed had been shoved into a far corner. Right next to it was the bathroom, although it was really nothing more than a toilet with a curtain wrapped around it. A little farther down the same wall was an industrial sink, plus a hot plate and a microwave set up on a table.

The rest of the massive room was taken up by canvases, easels, and paint supplies all over the place.

"Like I said, excuse the mess." Wavy stepped over a tarp and some brushes on her way to the refrigerator that looked to be at least thirty years old. "My art is still a hobby, doesn't pay any bills, but I'm hoping someday it will."

"Would you mind if I look at some your work?"

"Do you know anything about art?"

Lexi shrugged. "Honestly? Not really."

Wavy's face lit up in a grin. "Then be my guest. Would you like a drink while you're looking around? After today, I need one."

"Sure. Bad Thanksgiving?"

Wavy shrugged one small shoulder and brushed her reddish-brown hair back from her face. "Not bad, but very emotional. I'm sure you know my brother, Baby."

"Yeah, he's around the Eagle's Nest a lot because of Quinn."

"He had some unexpected news to share. Took us all by surprise. But it was good in the long run."

Wavy didn't seem to want to elaborate, so Lexi didn't push. "Well, I hope you guys are all okay."

Wavy poured a water glass half full of wine and handed it to her. "We will be."

Lexi took the glass and walked toward a group of paintings

near the fridge. As soon as she saw the first one, she knew this was going to take longer than she'd thought.

Wavy was *good*.

"Do you care if I do a little painting right now while you're looking around? I've got an image in my mind, and it's not going to stop bugging me until I get it down on canvas."

Lexi didn't look at her. She was too busy still studying the first painting. "Be my guest." She set her wine down on a bucket that was turned upside down.

She studied the canvas—a small oil painting of the Tetons surrounding the town. The mountains themselves were lovely in Wavy's creation, but it was the abstract colors floating around them that truly made the piece compelling.

The second canvas was more evocative than the first. An abstract cityscape this time, but still with a use of colors and textures that drew the eye. Lexi set that one down and was reaching for a third when another canvas halfway across the room caught her attention. This one was of Oak Creek itself, the view down Main Street including the wooden sign—all captured with near-perfect likeness.

Lexi hadn't been lying when she said she was no art expert, but she knew enough to know that one person being so well versed in two different styles like this was unusual.

"Did you do all these?"

Wavy looked up from what she was painting for a second. "Yeah. I'm more compelled by colors and the blending of patterns—not abstracts, that's too weird for my taste—but *life with more color*, I call it."

Lexi held up the Main Street painting. "This is pretty damned accurate."

"I can do realism if I force myself to be disciplined." Wavy grinned. "I'm not big on discipline."

Wavy went back to her painting, and Lexi looked around,

more and more in awe with each canvas she saw. Who knew there was such an incredible artistic talent hiding in a tiny town in Wyoming?

"Did you go to art school?"

"No. I was thinking about it a few years ago, but then Dad died and Mom needed me around. I've taken some online classes, but mostly I paint what comes to me. Nobody around here knows I do it, at least not to this extent."

"Wavy, I know you let me see this because I don't have any real art expertise, but, damn, girl, you need to send this stuff out. At least go talk to some art agents or dealers. Maybe something will come of it."

"I don't know. I've lived in Oak Creek my entire life."

"Look, I'll be the last person to tell you to leave this place considering I picked it out of everywhere in the world. But you've got a talent, and if you've got a passion, I think you should at least see where it will take you."

Wavy was painting so intently Lexi wasn't sure the other woman was processing what she'd said. But it really was a shame to hide all this talent away. The more Lexi saw, the more she was sure of it. She got her glass of wine and kept looking.

"What about you?" Wavy finally said. "What's your passion, Lexi?"

Surviving.

She didn't say it, but it was what instantly came to her mind. For the past eighteen months, that had been her sole focus. The only thing she could afford to feel passionate about.

Except what she'd felt for Gavin. Wanting him had been the only thing that had come anywhere close to cracking through the wall she'd built around herself in order to survive.

"Right now?" she finally responded. "I'm pretty focused on

building business at the Eagle's Nest." Hopefully, Wavy wouldn't push more than that.

The younger woman added a few more details to her painting before cleaning the brush she'd been using and setting it down. "And that's why you came here? To run a bar?"

Lexi smiled at her. "Not all of us have your artistic talent."

"Artistic talent comes in lots of different shapes and sizes." Wavy picked up the canvas and spun it around so Lexi could see it.

The painting had obviously been rushed and didn't offer the same level of detail that Lexi had been gazing at for nearly an hour, but its subject was crystal clear.

It was Alexandra Adams, famous television star, at a red carpet event in a gold silk dress, posing for photographs.

Lexi swallowed and fought to keep her glass from slipping out of her numb fingers.

It was a picture of her.

11

The world spun around Lexi. Looking at Wavy's painting, all she could think was that now she had to run again. And she had nowhere else to run to.

Why had she spent money buying fresh groceries when she should've been saving it? Why had she let herself get comfortable?

"Lexi!" Wavy's face was right in front of her. "You need to sit down. Take a breath."

She needed to run. "How did you find out?" Who else knew? Would there be other people looking for her? Was the press about to show up here?

"Lexi, please, sit down." Wavy led her to a folding chair. "Nobody knows but me. Something just clicked in my head when I saw you today. I'm a little upset that I didn't recognize you before now."

"But . . . how?"

Wavy shrugged. "I don't know. Blame it on my artistic eye —my brain sees things differently than most people do. And I was kind of obsessed with you on *Day's End*. You were my favorite Tia."

But there had been more than one Tia Day on the show because once Lexi had been fired and arrested, they'd needed someone else to carry on the show as the title character.

"Thanks," she murmured.

"I kind of wondered what happened to you after that whole stalker situation."

"I went to prison for a year for obstruction of justice."

Wavy waved a hand dismissively. "Oh, I know that. I didn't know what had happened since then. The press reported that you got out of jail, but then that was it. You sort of dropped off the face of the planet."

Lexi couldn't believe they were having this conversation so calmly. There was no look of disgust in Wavy's eyes for what she'd done.

"Why are you looking at me like that?" Wavy asked.

Lexi shook her head. "You're so easygoing about the whole thing. Usually the first thing people ask me was why I did it. How could I be so selfish?"

They weren't unreasonable questions. People rightfully wanted to know how she could've been so self-absorbed that she would trick security teams and police officers into thinking *she* was in danger when that wasn't the case. She'd trashed her own studio trailer and left false death threats for herself.

Why had she done it?

There was no good reason or excuse she could give. There wasn't one now, and there hadn't been one when the judge had asked her the same question before sentencing her to her year in jail.

Why had she done it?

She'd just wanted someone to be concerned about her the way the new security specialist, Shane Westman, had been concerned about the producer of the show, Chloe Jeffries.

Lexi had been immature, selfish, and reckless. She'd cried wolf, gotten everyone to surround her, and other people—the real people in danger—had almost died because of it.

Lexi had been tried and found guilty in the press every bit as much as she had in court. She had deserved to go to jail. Maybe she'd also deserved everything that had come after.

But Wavy was not demanding the answers that everyone else immediately wanted. Wavy wasn't looking at her like she was the biggest bitch on the planet. She wasn't looking at her any differently than she had when she'd helped out that night at the Eagle's Nest.

"I don't understand why I don't disgust you," she finally whispered.

Wavy walked over and poured herself a glass of wine. "You've been here two months now. I've seen how you interact with Mac, making sure he gets off his feet as much as possible and takes his medicine. I've seen you give Quinn a chance at waitressing when she was unbelievably bad at it. Hell, I've seen you give Gavin shit for being a suspicious, overzealous ass."

Lexi let out a small huff. "He is an overzealous ass."

"Those things are proof enough you're a decent person. I guess my only question is if you did what you did to try to get your coworkers hurt."

"No, I am—"

Wavy held up a hand. "But I already know the answer to that, so I don't really have to ask. You made a shitty judgment call. I daresay we've all made them once or twice."

Lexi had to swallow the well of emotion that threatened to swamp her. How could the words of one woman she hardly knew mean so much to her?

"Thank you," she managed to get out.

Wavy set down her wine and grabbed the canvas she'd just

completed. She took it to the far wall, turning it around so it couldn't be seen. "Nobody ever really comes in here, but we'll keep this out of sight just in case."

"I don't know if anyone would recognize me if I was standing right next to it."

Wavy studied her some more. "Your hair is much shorter, and blonde rather than the brown. You also have some pretty impressive makeup skills. Now that I'm looking at you I can see the contouring more closely. But that's not all, is it?"

Lexi reached up and touched her face. "Broken nose and cheek bone on my third day in prison. Someone decided they didn't like rich girls and gave me a shove into a wall. Since there were no reconstructive surgeons on hand in the correctional facility, the entire shape of my face was changed. Cheekbones no longer symmetrical."

"Jesus. Ouch."

"Yeah. Would've definitely ended my acting career even if I hadn't already successfully done that for myself. Makeup takes care of the rest—makes my cheeks look fuller, my jawline less pronounced."

"I'm surprised you don't wear contacts. Your green eyes are pretty noticeable."

"I tried, but I have some sort of reaction to them. They make my eyes water, and I look like I'm crying all the time. That drew more attention than the green."

Wavy was studying her, looking at her with an artist's eye. "Even with the eyes, it's a solid disguise. I don't think anyone would recognize you under most circumstances."

"That's what I'm counting on."

"Are you here in Oak Creek because of the press? Did they make your life hell?"

She gave a one-shouldered shrug. "The press and the

public haven't been very quick to forgive, not that I can blame them."

That seemed as good a reason to give as any. She definitely wasn't about to bring up the stalker who'd been hunting her, who'd found her and almost killed her.

It was one thing for Wavy to believe that she hadn't meant any harm when she'd cried wolf before. It was quite another to expect anyone to believe her if she said she had a stalker *again*.

The police certainly hadn't. She'd very quickly learned that her word meant nothing. It hadn't mattered when she'd shown them the bruises from where the stalker had caught her in an alley not long after she'd gotten out of prison. It hadn't mattered when she'd shown them the concussion diagnosis from the emergency room.

They'd called her a method actor and insinuated that a real stalker was no less than she deserved.

So she'd moved. When the stalker had found her the second time in a different city, sending her letters this time, she'd gone to the police *again*. They hadn't been as rude but had pointed out that the letters didn't actually contain any threats, so they couldn't help her.

They'd suggested she hire her own security. That hadn't been an option since she was broke.

When the stalker had found her a third time in a new city, she realized he'd been finding her by checking for mentions of her on social media. That happened everywhere she went. So she'd taken matters into her own hands and gotten a false ID and changed her appearance.

And come to Oak Creek.

"But why here?" Wavy asked. "There have got to be places you could go to, private islands or something, where you wouldn't have to work so hard but could also avoid the press."

Lexi very much wanted to rub her tired eyes but had trained herself not to in order to preserve her makeup. "I'm broke. And stupid. My aunt and uncle were my business managers, and they had full, unfettered access to my accounts since they'd been my guardians when I was younger. They took it all, then got in some trouble with some gambling mafia-type people and basically fled the country."

Lexi had no doubt Nicholas and Cheryl were, in fact, lying on a beach somewhere enjoying themselves.

Actually, the best thing to come out of all of this was not having her aunt and uncle in her life anymore. She didn't have any income, so they had no interest in being anywhere around her. They had their own problems with the mob, and Lexi was glad to be rid of them.

"Wow, that totally sucks," Wavy said.

Lexi shrugged. "A complete overhaul was probably what was best for me anyway. I'm not interested in going back into the limelight."

Especially with somebody out there waiting for her to do exactly that and then make her pay for it. If she could spend the rest of her life safe here in Oak Creek, even if she was alone, she would take it.

But that was up to Wavy now, wasn't it?

"But how did you end up here specifically in Oak Creek?"

"Mac's nephew, or actually his grandnephew, was a personal bodyguard of mine before everything went down. Markus arranged it with Mac."

Actually, Markus had been who the police had called when the stalker had found her the second time. They hadn't believed her but had at least put effort into it and called Markus as her previous head of security.

Markus probably hadn't believed her either, but he'd seen she was in trouble. He'd already known she was broke because she hadn't been able to pay him his last week's salary or the release bonus that had been a part of his contract. But he'd still helped her by asking Mac, a relative he hadn't really had much contact with, to give her a job and arrange for a cheap place to live.

It was a kindness undeserved, but it might've saved her life.

"And are you going to stay, or are you just passing through?"

"I'd like to stay, but if the press discovers I'm here—if anybody starts posting about me on social media or whatever, I'll have to leave."

She didn't know where she would go, but she knew the man hunting her would find her if anyone so much as mentioned her presence on social media.

Hadn't Cheryl and Nicholas been obsessed with that? Always looking up who had mentioned her and how to spin it to make more press and more money?

The internet made it very easy to hunt someone. All her stalker had to do was a focused Google search on her name and any mention of her, sightings listed by random townspeople, would lead him right to her.

Or if he really wanted to get more technical, he could do an image search for her face. That was why she hadn't wanted to be in the picture last week during Quinn's girls' night out.

There were too many ways she could be found if someone knew how to look—patience and persistence were all it would take. She couldn't even do a search on herself because there were ways to track those also. The fake-ID guy had told her that. So basically, she had to stay hidden and hope not to be blindsided.

But she knew the truth: he would eventually find her here. All she could do was hope it was later rather than sooner.

"Hey, don't look like that." Wavy rushed over and grabbed her hands. "I'm not going to tell anyone who you are or that you're here. The last thing anyone wants around here is a bunch of press, believe me."

Lexi wasn't a hundred percent sure she could trust Wavy, but what choice did she have? She had to stay here at least until she'd finished her payments on the ID and saved up some money.

Then she could start over. Again. Alone.

"Yes, I'm going to stay."

And pray it wasn't a decision that would cost her her life.

12

Thanksgiving weekend was generally a time to relax, eat, and be thankful, but Gavin would be thankful if he survived all the paperwork. It was his last few days as a full-time member of the sheriff's department, and all hell had broken loose.

Thanksgiving itself had gone pretty normally—football, food, sangria—but then Friday, Baby's girlfriend, Quinn, had been kidnapped by a psychopath. It'd all happened so quickly, there hadn't been time for law enforcement to help. If the Linear Tactical team didn't remain in a pretty constant state of readiness, it would have been too late for anyone to help Quinn at all.

But they'd almost been too late, and both she and Baby had sustained significant injuries.

They would be fine, thank God. But the amount of paper-work involved since Gavin had been the only official law enforcement officer on the scene was pretty staggering. Arrest reports. Injury reports. Damage to state property since this entire thing had gone down at the local community college.

There hadn't been much sitting around eating leftovers for him this weekend.

And no chance to see Lexi like he'd hoped.

After taking her glass, he'd run her prints, schooling himself for what he might find. When he'd gotten the report, he'd stared at it for a long time.

Everything was completely normal and matched his original search of her name. Lexi—not short for anything—Johnson. Twenty-eight years old, no arrest record or warrants. Prints were only in the system because she'd gotten her driver's license in California where they took a print as part of the driver's licensing process.

She was clean. Completely.

Between that, not finding anything in her apartment, and finally acknowledging that his friends were right about him being a suspicious bastard, here he was sitting in front of Lexi's apartment in his car first thing on a Monday morning. He was trying to get up enough nerve to admit that he'd taken her glass to run her prints. To knock on her door and tell her he was ready to trust her now.

Shit. That wouldn't sound good, would it?

I'm ready to trust you now that multiple avenues of investigation have proved that you are in fact Lexi Johnson, you have no criminal background, and you don't intend any harm to anyone.

When had he stopped giving people the benefit of the doubt? Quinn's kidnapping this past weekend might have been avoided if Gavin had been more willing to give her the benefit of the doubt over the past few weeks.

It was time for him to start trusting again.

He was going to explain all of this to Lexi and hope that it would make a difference when he came clean about running her prints. He was hoping the bag full of groceries, complete with everything he would need to make her a nice breakfast to start her day, including mimosas, would also ease the way.

Then he could ask her out for real. Because he might be a suspicious bastard, but he always tried to be honest with others and himself.

He wanted Lexi. He wanted to ask her out on a date. He wanted to kiss her without either of them worried about his intentions.

He wanted to get her into his bed and not let her out until neither of them could walk.

But first, honesty.

Just go in there and apologize like a real man, jackass, and admit what you did.

He was reaching for the door handle when Lexi came rushing out of her apartment door. She walked right by his SUV. If her head hadn't been tucked down inside the hood of her jacket, she would've seen him.

Shit, he was too late. She must already be on her way to work, although it was way too early for that.

But instead of turning toward the Eagle's Nest, she walked a little farther down the street to where her car was parked.

He'd never seen her drive her car. Hell, he'd never seen her go anywhere but work and back to her apartment.

When she started the car and headed south out of town, he slammed his hand down on the steering wheel and let out a blistering curse.

Then started his own vehicle to follow her.

He ignored all the voices of his friends screaming in his head that once again he was being a suspicious bastard. Lexi had the right to go wherever she wanted to, and just because she rarely drove anywhere didn't mean she was doing anything dubious.

But he followed her anyway, calling himself every name he

could think of and a few more that had never before occurred to him.

She ended up driving all the way to Reddington City. He was going to feel like a complete asshole if she went to some sort of clothing shop or shoe store not readily available in Oak Creek.

Maybe she was finally buying an actual winter coat. That would be a perfectly logical reason to be going to a larger city before work on a Monday.

He honest to God hoped that was it. Hoped maybe she had a doctor's appointment or root canal scheduled. But as she passed through town and ended up out by the cargo section of the airport—nothing around but warehouses and shipping businesses—his gut sank.

"Oh no. Why are you here, Green Eyes?"

He slowed down, staying close enough to keep her in sight but not close enough for her to notice him. Not that she seemed to be actively looking for a tail. She wasn't making sudden turns or doubling back. Wasn't waiting for a light to almost turn red before barreling through it. All of those would be classic signs that she was trying to lose anyone following her. It gave him a little bit of hope.

When she turned into a narrow road barely bigger than an alley, he kept going straight past. There was no way he could follow her there without being seen. At least in his car. A few yards down, he parked on the side of the road and jumped out.

Where the hell was she going?

When he got back to the alley, she had parked her car and gotten out. A car couldn't get much farther with the crates and boxes stacked along most of the alley. She was hurrying away from the main road, once again not looking over her shoulder to see if she was being followed.

He followed, unable to think of many good reasons why she'd be doing this. But able to think of a lot of *bad* ones.

When she stopped at a corner where two of the alleys intersected, he ducked behind a stacked pile of wooden crates.

He watched through the cracks as she paced back and forth at the intersection, obviously waiting for someone. Goddammit. He had really convinced himself that she was innocent. It certainly didn't look like that now.

Finally, some guy who looked barely more than a teenager stepped around from the other corner.

This was who she was meeting? Gavin was once again back to the drug theory. Especially when Lexi handed the guy some cash and the kid started counting it.

Neither of them was watching very carefully, so he snuck a few steps closer, behind a small dumpster. He lost the ability to see them, but he would take the tradeoff to hear them.

"Given his line of work, I would think your boss would take electronic payments," Lexi said.

"D is too aware of the pitfalls of all things electronic, I'm sure you understand. That's why he sends people like me to collect," the guy answered.

Who the hell was *D*?

"It's all there."

"Yeah, well, it's my ass if it's not, so I'll just double-check." After a few more seconds the guy spoke up again. "Okay, you're good."

"Then I'll see you next time."

"Boss wanted me to let you know that you were pinged."

"Shit." Lexi's voice rose in pitch. "By whom? How deep?"

Gavin had no idea what in the world they were talking about. What did *pinged* mean? And why did it have Lexi sounding so terrified?

"Boss said everything held like it was supposed to. He just wanted you to be aware."

"Does he know who it was? Where it came from? I need to know who exactly." The panic in Lexi's voice rose.

"I'm sure finding that out would cost you extra. Do you want me to ask the boss about it?"

Lexi hesitated so long Gavin thought she wasn't going to answer. "No. I can't afford any more."

"Whatever. Let me know if you change your mind."

Silence. Gavin stayed put, but there was no more discussion. He stayed hidden as Lexi finally turned and walked back to her car. Once she pulled away, he jogged back to his SUV.

What the hell had just happened? He had no idea whether it was illegal or not. Whether Lexi was in danger or not.

Every time he thought he had his questions about her answered, a whole new set showed up. Maybe he should've confronted them, but it didn't sound like the guy was giving her drugs or anything. And he obviously wasn't the person in charge, just the one collecting a payment, it seemed.

If she was making payments for something, it would explain why she never had money. Was she being blackmailed? Paying for security?

He caught up with her before she was back out of the cargo district then followed her again at a distance as she headed back to Oak Creek.

She parked her car in almost the exact spot she'd pulled out of. Then once again she got out, head tucked low in her jacket, and walked over to the Eagle's Nest.

He glanced over at the groceries on the passenger side next to him. His symbolic gesture of peace and apology for not trusting her mocked him from their bag.

Whatever was going on with Lexi, an omelet and a mimosa were not going to fix it.

13

The Eagle's Nest was insanely busy for a Monday. The entire town was still buzzing over what had happened to Quinn—the kidnapping and subsequent rescue. That was probably why so many people were here for the lunch rush. People Lexi had never seen in here for lunch even once.

That was a small town for you. They wanted to catch Quinn and get all the gossip.

She wasn't here, of course. It was going to take more than a couple of days for her to fully recover from what had happened. Her vocal cords might be damaged for weeks the doctors had told her.

Lexi hated that Quinn and Baby had been hurt . . . and that she'd lost her only other lunch waitress. But she was very glad to see that no one in town was looking any differently at her.

Wavy had kept her word and hadn't told anyone that she was Alexandra Adams. No one was looking at her sideways or giving her any winks or nudges. If anyone had known the truth, they would have given themselves away. They would've tried to take pictures, or maybe called the press directly to get their five minutes of fame.

The fact that someone had pinged the name Lexi Johnson was concerning. That meant someone was looking deeper into her identity, and if not for the electronic persona Deshawn had built, the Lexi Johnson ID would be blown already.

Her first thought was that it was Gavin, but he'd already admitted to running her name weeks ago. This was something different, deeper. Someone was suspicious and pushing at her ID in some way, or else Deshawn wouldn't have told her. The stalker? A reporter who thought they smelled a story?

But if so, wouldn't they have already gotten close to her? Wouldn't she have noticed? The only person watching her was Gavin. He was back in his booth again today, studying her like a hawk.

She had to admit she'd sort of missed him since the night he'd stayed with her at her apartment. She'd seen him around, but he hadn't been actively studying her like he was today. She'd missed seeing his face all the time.

Now he was back, complete with broody stare. It didn't annoy her nearly as much as it should. Those dark, hooded eyes following her every move should be a source of annoyance, but she'd missed it in some sick way.

But he was also sort of acting weird. He didn't say anything to her the whole time he sat in the booth, actually walked over to Mac directly to make his order. She'd thought they were past the point of suspicious glares. Evidently not.

But without Quinn here to work, Lexi didn't have much time to worry about Gavin. She didn't even have time to send him an obnoxiously named drink, although sexy Sheriff Proper would never do something so base as have a cocktail in the middle of the day anyway.

It was midafternoon before she had a chance to slow down. Usually, she liked to go home and rest for a few minutes, sleep if she could, before coming back and working the night shift. She was trying to keep from having a repeat of her insomnia breakdown, and resting in the afternoon helped.

"Mac, I'm going to take a couple of hours. You're going home early tonight. Don't forget."

Mac glared at her from over the inventory printout he was looking at on his desk. "You aren't the boss of me, Blondie."

She rolled her eyes and perched her hip on the corner of the desk. "Well, your cardiologist, a.k.a. the man keeping you alive, says no more than eight hours of work a day for you. Don't make me bring Dr. Anne in here as a second opinion, because you know she will back me up on this."

"I knew you were trouble the first moment I laid eyes on you." He let out a huff.

She grinned at him. "You and Sheriff Gavin both. You both give me that narrow-eyed glare all the time."

Mac laid down his papers. "I think you are a very different type of trouble for our Gavin. Looks like our Redwood might fall after all."

"Redwood?"

Mac smiled. "That was his codename or whatever in the army. Because he's so solid, from what I understand. Stands so firm no matter what the conditions."

"Yeah, that sounds about right." Definitely sounded like the Gavin she knew and could barely get out of her mind. She stood back up. "I'll see you at five and will expect you to be gone by eight so I don't have to call in the muscle."

"Be careful out there." Mac picked up his papers again, not responding to her threat. "They're vultures."

She was about to ask him what he was talking about but thought better of it in case it involved more stories about

Sheriff Redwood. That was the last thing she needed before trying to sleep. She headed out the back door and down the short alley leading to the parking lot. He was already in her mind enough without Mac bringing him up regularly.

Maybe she could come up with a drink that was a play on his codename—

All thoughts flew from her head as she rounded the corner and stopped in her tracks. The parking lot was full of press vans. Reporters and cameras were everywhere.

Oh God, Wavy hadn't kept her word. The press had found her. She needed to run. To get out of town. Did they know where she lived? Could she get to her car? Her stuff in her apartment? After this morning's payment, she didn't have much cash left over. Should she just run with today's lunch tips?

The panic crashed over her. She needed to get out before she was seen. She spun to escape, to run, to be anywhere but here.

But slammed into a chest instead.

"Going somewhere?"

Gavin.

"Reporters." She fisted her hands in his jacket. "There's a bunch of reporters out there." She would tell him everything if it meant he could help her get out of here without them finding her. "I can't . . . I have to . . ."

Bile rose in her gut at the sound of reporters talking behind her. "I saw someone around back."

"Quinn doesn't have blonde hair, Jacobs. It's not her," someone else responded.

Quinn. The name registered through the roaring in her ears. The reporters were trying to talk to *Quinn.* That made so much sense given what had happened this weekend with her kidnapping and all the brouhaha surrounding it. Of course the press would want to talk to her.

"I'm going to check it out."

Shit. They were still coming here.

Gavin's hands wrapped around her elbows. "What is happening right now, Lexi?"

She realized she was standing in his arms, clutching at his chest. That reporter might not be looking for her, but she still couldn't afford to let him get too good a look at her face.

She looked up at Gavin. What could she say? "I—"

She yanked him toward her and kissed him.

She'd meant it as a ruse. As a reason for why someone would be hovering behind a building when the reporter came to see what was going on.

But the moment her lips met his, all thoughts of subterfuge disappeared. It was fire. Just like every other time they'd kissed. Like her body had forgotten how much she was starving for Gavin's touch until their lips met, reminding her.

She wanted him. Wanted him to give her whatever it took to ease this clawing hunger inside her. One hand slid up his chest to wrap behind his neck and keep him anchored to her.

"Whoa. Oh, sorry." The reporter's words barely registered, definitely didn't stop them.

Somewhere in her subconscious, she realized the danger was gone. It was safe. The reporter was probably making a couple of crude statements about them but had confirmed there was no one around that corner that was of interest to the press.

She and Gavin could stop.

But they didn't. This heat between them was too powerful. When he started to ease back the slightest bit, she let out a needy whimper. She couldn't help herself.

"Jesus, Lexi. Do you know what that sound does to me?" he whispered against her lips.

Her only response was to pull him closer.

When his hands ran down her back and hips, cupping her ass and lifting her, she didn't resist. She wrapped her legs around his hips and kept her lips plastered against his. With hardly any effort at all, he walked both of them a few feet back toward the door so they were hidden by the empty supply cases stacked along the wall. He didn't stop until they were in the darkest corner of the tiny alley.

"Everything about you drives me crazy." He pushed her up against the wall. "And I can't seem to leave you alone, even knowing you've got all sorts of secrets and you're not being honest with anyone."

He was way too close to the truth, and his words should've sent a bolt of panic through her, but he took that moment to press up against her, tilting his hips and maneuvering hers to be exactly where he wanted them. He slowly rolled against her, and she didn't try to stop the shudder that coursed through her whole body. Then he did it again.

And again.

So many months without intimate contact with anyone had to be what was causing her to feel this way—this blistering need.

She'd never felt this way even when her life had been completely different than it was now. It wasn't about him; this was physical.

He rolled his hips again, and a low moan escaped her. "Oh, God."

He hadn't really touched her, yet she could feel the pressure building inside. Lava bubbling, ready to erupt.

"Say my name, Lexi." He pressed hard against her then

used his hands on her hips to move her in a way that had her gasping against his mouth.

"Wh-what?"

"This is *us*." Another thrust of his hips. Another kiss that seemed to touch her very soul. "You're here with me, not some random stranger. *Me*. Say my name."

She knew that, even if she didn't want to admit it. This wasn't about just a physical touch, as much as she might want it to be. She'd never been so out of control with anyone else. She only responded to him this way.

"Gavin," she whispered. "Only you. *Us*."

The possession that lit up his brown eyes should have scared her. Should've had her running for cover. Driving to Reddington City to make the payment on her ID this morning should've reminded her how precarious her *normal* life here really was.

But she didn't care. Right now, all she cared about was being close to Gavin. She wanted to be possessed by him.

He gave her what she wanted.

His fingers clenched her flesh under her jeans as he pulled her down atop him, thrust upward again. His hips forced her legs wider, opening her for him, the friction of their bodies driving her higher and higher.

She wanted them to be naked, but that wasn't possible. But this was enough. More than enough.

When his lips moved down her jaw to her neck, her head fell back against the wall. His mouth left tiny, painless bites against the side of her neck, and all she could do was melt against him with a little whimper.

"That's right. That's what I want from you. Let go, Green Eyes."

He slid his hand between their bodies and cupped her over her jeans, pressing firmly right where she needed it.

And she did let go. Groaning his name in a long, sobbing breath, she ground herself against his hand and let the waves of pleasure wash over her.

He kept her pinned against the wall, kissing softly along her neck and cheeks and hair as she came down from the waves of pleasure. He lowered her back to her feet but kept his arms around her. Good thing, considering she wasn't sure she could stand on her own.

But it didn't take long before her senses returned, and she couldn't stop the tension that flooded her body. Oh dear God, what had she done? She'd let him dry hump her against a wall in the middle of an alley, and she'd *loved* it. What could he possibly be thinking about her?

She tried to pull away from him, but he wouldn't let her. He was still pressed up against her. Still obviously aroused.

"You absolutely wreck me, woman. Obliterate all my control. I hardly recognize myself when I'm around you."

She relaxed slightly, since she felt the exact same way.

They stared at each other for a long minute. When he reached up to tuck a strand of hair behind her ear, she could still feel him hard against her.

Her hands slid to his waist, trailing along the top of his jeans. "Do you want me to—"

"Jesus, no." He stopped her hands with his and brought her fingers to his lips. "I'm damned near ready to get arrested for indecent exposure just watching you come apart in my arms. If you touch me, those reporters you were trying to avoid will definitely have a story. Maybe not the one they wanted, but one nonetheless."

She had to smile a little at that.

"Why were you hiding from them?"

Her smile slipped. "No reason. Just don't like to get all mixed up in that mess."

His eyes narrowed, and his hands moved to the wall on either side of her shoulders. She wasn't going anywhere unless he decided to let her go.

Redwood, indeed.

"I came by your apartment this morning to apologize, but . . . you weren't there."

That definitely wasn't what she'd been expecting him to say. "You did?"

"I wanted to make you breakfast. Had some groceries, including champagne and orange juice to make mimosas."

She ignored the way her mouth watered at the thought of one of her favorite beverages, one she hadn't had in so long. "Why? When?"

He finally put some space between their bodies and pulled something out of his jacket pocket.

Her juice glass.

"To return this."

She took it from his fingers. "I've been looking for that. I only have two. I thought I was going crazy because I couldn't find the second one anywhere in my apartment. Why do you have it?"

The answer came to her just as he said it. "I took it on purpose the night I stayed with you."

"To run my fingerprints."

He nodded.

That explained the pinging of her ID. Gavin had been the one suspicious enough to poke at her ID. Thank God it'd held. He obviously didn't know who she really was.

Part of her was relieved it was him. Not the press. Not the stalker. The other part was pissed.

Every single time she really thought he was attracted to her, every time she let herself get close, it wasn't her he really wanted at all. It was her secrets.

"So we're back to this, are we, Sheriff? Was this little seduction routine so you could get a retinal scan? Or maybe you were going for a vaginal swab but didn't quite achieve your mission since my clothes didn't come off."

"Lexi—"

Why did she keep thinking these physical encounters with him were meaningful when they obviously weren't? At least, not to him.

She held up a hand to stop him. "But I came up clean, didn't I, Sheriff Redwood?"

At least she knew that. She wouldn't be thrown into a panic about whether he'd discovered who she really was. Suddenly, every dime she'd paid for this ID was worth it. Every payment she still had left to make would be money well spent.

"Lexi." He bent his knees so that they were face to face, eye to eye. "I don't know what is going on with you, but whatever it is, I want to help."

He said it with such authenticity that she almost believed him. Or maybe she wanted to believe him. *Again.*

But she couldn't.

She pushed at his chest. She couldn't stand to be near him anymore. What they'd done seemed so tawdry, knowing the attraction wasn't authentic for him. She felt cheap.

Even when the press had called her a heartless harlot, she hadn't felt this cheap.

"This was a mistake. Stay away from me, Gavin."

She slipped around him and headed back down the little alley, back inside the Eagle's Nest. She'd stay here. There would definitely not be any rest today.

14

"Who would've ever thought we'd see Christmas decorations at the Eagle's Nest?" Finn said.

Gavin was back at his usual booth. Except it was starting to feel more like the doghouse.

At least today, he had friends with him. Gavin and Finn were on one side of the doghouse, er, booth, while Kendrick and Gabe Collingwood sat on the other.

"You know that has to be Lexi," Gabe said. The former Navy SEAL turned businessman had moved into the area and never left. "Mac would rather shoot himself in the foot than put up Christmas decorations in this bar."

Of course, it was Lexi. Everyone knew it was Lexi. Everyone knew that last week's ugly Christmas sweater contest, which had hilariously mimicked a wet T-shirt contest, had been Lexi's idea also.

"She's talking about doing a drunk white elephant next week." Finn grinned. "Everybody orders a crazy drink but doesn't say what's in it, hides it under a gift bag, and then everyone picks one, like a normal white elephant."

Kendrick took a sip of his beer. "She's definitely doing

wonders for this place. Steadier stream of customers while getting Mac to do less work."

The guys were still trying to talk Lexi up to him, sell him on her. It wasn't necessary. He'd already bought in one hundred percent.

If only he could stop fucking it up every time he came near her. She still wasn't talking to him after what had happened against that wall behind the bar a couple of weeks ago.

Not that he'd forgotten it. Her moans—those sighs as she came apart in his arms—had been playing on repeat as he'd lain in bed thinking about her every night since.

But she was back to not talking to him.

He took a sip of his drink, and the guys snickered. The Duck Fart had been delivered not long after he'd sat down, much to the delight of his howling friends.

"Shut up," he told the guys. "At least this one isn't too bad. Kahlua, Irish cream, whiskey—what's not to like?"

Okay, so he'd personally like more whiskey and less of the other sweet stuff, but it was still pretty tasty despite the name.

He'd drink it regardless. He'd drunk every sip of every obnoxiously named drink she'd given him. Partly in penance.

But mostly because if she was sending him the drinks, no matter how terrible they sounded—Dirty Whore's Bathwater, Windex, Buffalo Juice, Alligator Sperm—she was at least thinking about him.

He needed to believe that meant he hadn't screwed up every possible chance with her.

"Charlie wants to come here all the time now." Finn sipped his neat whiskey while Gavin watched, a little jealous. "Not just for girls' night out."

Gabe nodded. "Jordan too. All the girls do. They say it's better than most of the places, including the ones in Reddington City. Again, thanks to Lexi."

He rolled his eyes. "All right, you guys I get it. She's good for the Eagle's Nest. Good for the town. I'm not trying to run her off anymore."

He wasn't exactly sure what to do about her. Still had no idea what had happened that day he'd followed her to Reddington City. He'd gotten all the footage he could from security cameras in that alley but hadn't gotten a clear enough image of the guy's face to run through facial recognition.

Which didn't matter because that kid had only been the middleman anyway. Middleman for *what*?

"Good." Gabe leaned back in the booth and smiled at him. "Because if you run Lexi off, all the women in town are likely to hunt you down and kill you."

Gavin choked a little on his drink. "Even sweet Jordan?"

Gabe's eyes got soft. Nothing about this huge man was soft except his face when talking about his fiancée. "She'll probably just be the lookout."

Finn chuckled. "Charlie will do it."

Nobody at the table doubted it. Finn's tiny wife was a force to be reckoned with.

"I'm not going to run her off." He studied Lexi as she delivered an order to a table and stopped to talk to them for a moment.

She was quick with a wink and easy smile for them like she was for nearly everyone, but it wasn't quite authentic. It was her way of keeping them from looking at her too closely, of not paying too much attention to her. Her MO—hiding in plain sight.

He'd spent enough time watching her to recognize her signs of fatigue, especially now that he knew to look for them. She'd been going home to rest some in the afternoons, which probably helped.

But exhaustion clouded her eyes now. No bags or purple

underneath—she was way too skilled with makeup to allow her tiredness to be that evident. The fatigue was in those green eyes themselves. She wasn't at breakdown levels yet, but she was heading in that direction if she didn't get some rest.

Another secret she kept from everyone. He only knew about it by sheer accident.

And had she been eating decently? He'd left her the groceries he'd bought that morning two weeks ago, leaving them outside her door. He had no idea if she'd used them or been so pissed she'd thrown them away.

He'd worried about whether she had decent food to eat nearly every day since then. His brain always whirled like a cyclone when it came to her, worrying about if she had food, remembering how she'd said his name in that alley, trying to figure out what she was hiding.

Rinse and repeat. His thoughts all battled constantly.

Finn stood up. "All right, fellas, I got the text to get my ass home before the baby drives Charlie crazy."

"I hear some weather is coming in. You guys make sure you're stocked up," Gabe said.

Anyone who'd lived in this part of Wyoming for any amount of time knew that December weather could be unpredictable. You might be outside in jeans and a sweatshirt without needing a jacket, or you might get caught in three feet of snow. Everyone kept extra supplies in their house just in case.

Gavin looked over at Lexi again. "Yeah, I'm going to make sure Lexi has enough groceries. She may not know how quickly things can turn around here."

All three men shook their heads.

"What?" Gavin rolled his eyes. "You'd rather I leave her unprepared in all this? I know neither of you have lived here long, but you know what things can get like."

Gabe held out his hands in a gesture of surrender. "No. I'm pretty sure we all think it's great. It's just you and Lexi . . ."

"What?" Gavin asked. They thought he was going to let actual harm come to someone because he didn't necessarily trust her? "What about me and Lexi?"

Jesus. Was that anger in his voice? He needed to lock that shit down. What was the matter with him?

Finn shrugged and slapped him on the shoulder. "Nothing, man. It's just that this is the weirdest courtship of all time."

"That." Gabe pointed at Finn. "That, exactly."

Kendrick let out a huge laugh. "Oh my gosh, you're so right."

Gavin crossed his arms over his chest. "What the hell are you talking about? I'm not courting her."

"Oh, but you really are," Finn said. "You're always watching after her to make sure she gets home safely. You're the first one to jump up and help out if things get too busy for her here. You're the one who notices when she's tired or hungry. It may not be a courtship, but you're definitely protective of her."

He couldn't deny that. Especially since he was about to go buy groceries for her. Again.

"Fuck off."

Finn slapped him on the shoulder again, and he and Gabe left. Kendrick was sliding out of the booth too, but stopped.

Gavin raised an eyebrow. "Got more to say about me courting Lexi?"

"No, I need to ask you something." His laughter from a moment ago was gone.

It was strange to see the normally lighthearted and charming man look so serious. "What's up, Blaze?"

Kendrick didn't smile at his appointed codename the way he normally did.

He rubbed at his hair like he was trying to fix it, even though it was so short his hands didn't make any difference. "Listen, I don't want to ruffle any feathers or hurt any feelings, but I need to let you know something."

"Okay."

"That weekend Quinn was kidnapped, and I was doing all the computer searches to help figure out who had her, I did a little digging on Lexi. I was digging into everyone, trying to find any leads I could, so it wasn't just her."

But he'd found something on Lexi. Gavin tensed. "What did you find?"

"To be honest, nothing crazy. It wasn't setting off red flags, maybe . . . pink ones. When I dug into her ID, it came back weird. Like, something more was there but I'd have to dig for it."

"Did you?" Did he really want to know whatever Kendrick had found?

"No. At that point, I had much bigger fish to fry and time was of the essence. I had to eliminate her as a suspect in what was going on with Quinn and left it alone."

"Did you go back and check Lexi out further afterward?"

Kendrick let out a sigh. "It's hard sometimes when you have computer hacking skills to remain on the side of the angels. Information is there, ripe for the picking if you know how."

And Kendrick definitely knew how. "So you did dig into her."

The man looked down at his hands. "No, I left it alone and didn't dig deeper. Just because I can find information doesn't mean I always should."

Gavin glanced over at Lexi. "Yeah, I'm learning that lesson myself."

Kendrick looked up. "But I thought you should know that there is definitely more, at least electronically, to Lexi Johnson than what is immediately available. I'm sure if you want Neo and I to dig, we can provide you more details about her."

Neo was both Kendrick's love interest and greatest computer rival. It made for another interesting courtship.

Gavin looked over at where Lexi was running beers to a table. She was holding her tray low and with both hands. That meant she was getting tired.

How many days had it been since she slept? How many more would it be until she did?

He wanted to help her. Wanted her to trust him. But she was never going to do that if he kept treating her like she was untrustworthy. He'd done it too many times already. Doing it again, now with Kendrick, would cross a line Gavin couldn't get back over. No number of obnoxiously named drinks would make up for it.

She looked over at him right at that moment and caught him staring. She tilted her head to the side and raised an eyebrow at him, straightening her shoulders. She didn't want him to see her feeling weak.

Damn it, he wanted to help. He wanted her *to know* he wanted to help.

When she turned and walked back to the bar, he looked back at Kendrick. "Thanks for the offer, Blaze, but if Lexi has secrets, then she has the right to keep them until she chooses to tell them. I don't want to keep screwing up with her."

Kendrick nodded, his shoulders relaxing. "Sounds good to me. I just wanted to make the offer. Now, speaking of bad weather, I'm going to chat with Neo and make sure she knows it's headed this way."

"You still don't know where she lives?"

Kendrick shrugged. "Ironically . . . she asked me not to search. She takes her privacy very seriously too. I'm tempted to do it anyway because I know she's got that info buried under so many different cyber layers that it would be a true challenge to figure it out, but like I said . . ."

"On the side of the angels," they both said at the same time.

They shook hands and the other man took off. Gavin's eyes were drawn to Lexi once again.

He hoped choosing the side of the angels was the right one.

15

"What are you doing here, missy?"

Lexi looked up from the billing invoices she was working on. Mac had made the decision to close the Eagle's Nest because of the storm scheduled to come in later today. It was already snowing pretty steadily but was supposed to get worse in a few hours.

Hopefully, the storm was what he was talking about, not the fact that she'd dragged all the paperwork out here to the booth Gavin always sat at. Because that somehow made her feel closer to him. And because she was obviously an idiot.

"Just getting caught up on a few things, since the storm means I actually have time to do it."

"You're supposed to be at your apartment before it gets too bad out there."

Good, he did mean the storm. She raised an eyebrow. "Mac, I live two blocks from here. I don't have to drive, so I may as well stay and get stuff done as long as I can."

She picked up the coffee mug she'd been drinking from and walked it over to the sink to rinse it out, studying him. His grimace as he leaned against the bar spoke volumes. "What are you doing here? Driving in this isn't safe."

Mac let out a grunt. "I was driving in this weather before you were born."

"No need to get sassy. I know you wouldn't be here away from your beloved space heater if there wasn't a reason."

He shot her a little sheepish look. "I knocked over my heart pills, and they went down the drain. I thought I might have some here."

"Which ones?"

But she already knew. He wouldn't be here unless it was the important ones.

He nodded at her, confirming her suspicions. "The one Doc said I needed to have with me all the time."

She linked arms with him. "Let's go check your office."

A few minutes later, they were both muttering curses. Mac had extras of all of his pills except for the thrombolytics he'd need in case of a heart attack or stroke. She held up the sticky note he'd written to himself. "Need refill."

He rubbed his eyes, his shoulders hunched. "Yeah. I thought that would remind me to get by the pharmacy but I'm not on that side of town very often."

"That side of town?" She rolled her eyes. "This town is only a couple of miles from one end to the other. You'd never survive in LA, Mac."

"Hmph. Don't know why anyone would want to survive in Los Angeles anyway. Guess I'm going to the drugstore before this gets worse."

"Like hell you will. I'll drive you home, then go get your prescription, way far away on the other side of town. You will immediately go home before this gets any worse and huddle in beside your pretty space heater."

"I ain't dead yet, missy."

She reached over and grabbed the older man's hand, running her thumb along his wrinkled, dark skin. "You took me in and gave me a chance, Mac. You didn't have to, not even as a favor to Markus. So driving a couple of miles for you is no problem."

"Fine," he grumbled. "But you're going to drive my truck. No way you're walking in that ridiculous jacket of yours."

She'd expected more of an argument. He must really not be feeling well. "I know. I know. I'm going into Reddington City right after Christmas to get one, promise. They'll probably have some good sales then."

Mac grumbled the entire time as she helped him into his truck, then drove to his house. He'd moved on to talking about how terrible her car was for Wyoming weather, even with snow tires. Mostly she just listened since he was right, and there wasn't much argument she could make. Her car did suck.

They pulled up in front of his small house on the outskirts of town. Mac's truck was much better suited for the Wyoming environment. It even had heated seats—true luxury.

Oh, how her life had changed if she thought heated seats were true luxury.

"What are you grinning at?" he asked as he got out of the truck.

She winked at him. "Your fancy heated seats keeping my ass warm."

Mac hooted with laughter and climbed the rest of the way out. "You be careful."

The drive to the pharmacy wasn't bad. The snow was starting to stick, and the wind was picking up, but it wasn't a problem in the truck. She was able to find a parking spot at the front and ran quickly inside.

She vaguely recognized the pharmacist. He'd probably

been in the bar a couple times, but didn't know the guy's name. "I'm picking up a refill prescription for Mac Templeton. He accidentally spilled his thrombolytics down the drain, and we weren't sure how long this snowstorm is going to last. His cardiologist said he should have some with him all the time."

"No problem." The pharmacist took the prescription paper. "It's a common issue with some of our elderly patients."

She walked around the store while the pharmacist was in the back. She had no idea how long Wyoming blizzards lasted. Did she need extra supplies? Would the power go out? Thanks to Gavin—nosy pain in the ass that he might be—her cabinets were better stocked than they normally would be. And the money she hadn't had to spend on groceries over the past couple of weeks she could use for emergency supplies now. She grabbed a shopping basket.

The drugstore didn't have a lot of selection in terms of food, but they had some nutrition bars. She grabbed a handful of those. They would be good if the power went out and she couldn't heat anything.

She walked down the next aisle, ignoring the magazines sporting people on the cover she'd worked with and had once called her friends. Not a single one of them had offered to help her out when she'd gotten in trouble.

On one hand, she couldn't blame them. The press had crucified her, and anyone aligning themselves with her would've been committing professional suicide.

But on the other hand, no one had reached out, even privately. No one had been interested in hearing her side of the story—not that her reasons had excused her actions. No one had offered to help out when it became public that she was pretty much penniless.

So looking at them on magazines now didn't really interest her. She'd been shown more kindness from people in this tiny town who'd just met her than people who'd known her for years.

She walked past the rest of the magazines without a glance. Farther down the aisle was makeup she also ignored—the one place she didn't skimp was her makeup. It was too critical to her survival.

She rounded the next aisle and found the feminine products. Didn't need those currently either. Then birth control and sexual protection aisle. She grabbed a pack of condoms, calling herself all sorts of names because she could feel herself blushing.

Why should she blush? She was allowed to buy condoms if she wanted. That didn't mean she was going to invite Sheriff Redwood over to . . . show her his wood.

She swallowed the laugh she couldn't smother, which just caused a coughing fit.

"You okay?" the pharmacist asked, walking out from the back. She shifted the bars in her basket so the condoms weren't so evident.

"Yeah." She smiled at him. "Got a tickle in my throat."

"I have bad news. We don't have Mr. Mac's thrombolytics in stock. I called over to the Sublette County pharmacy. They have it, but they're not doing any more deliveries because of the storm about to come in."

Damn it. "Mac really needs that medicine. If he doesn't have it for multiple days, he could be in trouble."

The man nodded. "I know. You can go out there and get it yourself, it's only about fifteen miles out of town. That would probably be the easiest way if you've got a vehicle for it."

"I've got Mac's F-150 truck. It's pretty new and nice. Would that be okay?"

The man's face lit up, and he pushed his narrow glasses up on his nose. "Oh, absolutely. I've seen that truck around and have been quite envious of it. It will get you there no problem. But I would suggest you hurry in case the storm hits earlier."

"Okay, will do. Thanks for your help."

She rushed her items to the front to pay, and the individual-sized bottles of champagne on display caught her eye. She grabbed one and then a small container of orange juice out of the cooler by the register. It was completely frivolous, and probably wouldn't be that great given the quality of the alcohol and juice, but she would make her own mimosas and sip them while sitting in her apartment during the snowstorm.

And she would only wish a little bit that Gavin was with her. And she would not think about condoms and Sheriff Redwood.

She paid and rushed out the door. The sooner she got Mac's medicine, the sooner she could get back and have her own snowstorm party. She didn't have a cell phone to call Mac and let him know what was going on. She needed to get some sort of cheap phone that didn't require an ID or credit check. Nothing fancy, just something that would allow her to send texts or make a call.

Since she was already in the direction of the Sublette County pharmacy, she wouldn't go back to his house and tell him what she needed to do. He'd just try to talk her out of it anyway.

She was about ten miles out of town when the trouble really started. The snow had been steady, causing her to drive slower than she normally would on State Road 191, but it hadn't been bad enough to make her feel the need to stop or turn around. Then all of a sudden she couldn't see anything in front of her, even with her lights and windshield wipers on.

Everything around her was completely white. Like darkness, but the wrong color.

She gripped the steering wheel, knuckles going white. What the hell was going on? The snowstorm wasn't supposed to be here for another couple of hours. But this snowsquall was like nothing she'd ever seen. It didn't take her longer than a minute to figure out she wasn't going to make it to the pharmacy.

She slowed her speed way down, the whiteness spinning around her making it impossible to see where the road was. Both hands gripped the steering wheel so hard her fingers ached, but she didn't dare loosen them.

She needed to get off this road. There was no way she could head back to Oak Creek because turning around wasn't an option at all.

She stopped driving so she could take a look at the GPS. There wasn't much along the road at this point. The Cactus Motel, which she'd heard was little sketchy, was only another couple of miles away. She didn't care how gross it was if it meant she could get out of this blinding whiteness. But a couple of miles might as well be a hundred. There was also a gas station, but that was even farther away.

Staying here on this road wasn't an option. She needed to keep going forward. She started again moving at barely more than a snail's pace.

Thank God she wasn't going any faster and was able to swerve out of the way when an eighteen wheeler traveling in the opposite direction appeared out of nowhere.

"Fuck."

She wasn't sure the other guy saw her. She jerked the steering wheel to make sure they wouldn't collide, then let out a scream as her truck found the edge of the road and started to slide down the embankment. There was nothing she could do but hang on until the sliding finally stopped.

Her heart thundered in her chest, and all she could hear

was her breathing inside the truck's cab as she took stock of the situation. She was okay. She just needed to get back up on the road.

She put the truck in reverse to try to get some momentum to climb back up from the ditch. The bank wasn't very steep or tall, but the tires wouldn't grip enough to get her back up there. After fifteen minutes of trying, she finally put the truck in park and slammed her hand against the steering wheel.

What did she do now? Nobody knew she was out here. She had no idea how long the storm would last. Hell, at this point she wasn't entirely sure which direction the truck was facing. And once she got out, she wouldn't have a GPS to let her know if she was going in the right direction if she tried to walk to the Cactus Motel. Staying here in the truck and waiting out the storm seemed like the least terrible option.

Although it still seemed pretty damn terrible.

Was it going to keep snowing? Had the temperature dropped outside? Would she freeze to death in the truck?

She would only turn on the truck when it got so cold she couldn't stand it. Then maybe she'd have enough gas to last however long the storm did without freezing to death. And at least she had some nutrition bars and orange juice.

She let out a hysterical laugh. If she was going to die in a Wyoming snowstorm at least she could do it sipping mimosas and clutching condoms she'd never get to use with a man she'd wanted more than anyone else she'd ever known.

She stared out into the canvas of white, trying to ignore the howling wind. And the fact that the cab of this truck suddenly felt like a coffin.

16

Gavin might no longer work for the sheriff's department full-time, but on a day like today, in a situation like this, it didn't matter.

Residents of Wyoming took winters seriously. A big storm in December wasn't uncommon, and they'd been known to happen much earlier than that. But a sudden squall, especially the first one of the season, sometimes caught even the most cautious people off guard.

Gavin and the rest of the Linear Tactical guys had worked all morning helping the sheriff's office in whatever way they could as the storm approached. They'd split up and stopped by multiple homes, making sure the elderly and some of the single moms had the necessary generators and fuel. Power was predicted to go out, and might be out for a while with a storm this size coming in.

Power was already flickering when Gavin got the warning on his phone from the weather service that whiteout conditions had developed outside of Reddington City and would hit Oak Creek.

Shit. That would just make a bad situation worse.

Everyone needed to get off the road. Gavin had lived in Wyoming all his life and knew what all longtime residents did: winter storms were bad enough. Whiteouts were damned scary. He needed to get to his own house, which was only a couple miles out of town.

He was headed that way when a call came through, and he put it on speakerphone inside his SUV. It was Patricia Rosales, who ran the sheriff's office and 911 switchboard.

"What's up, Patricia?" She wouldn't be calling unless she needed him.

"Gavin, have you seen Lexi Johnson?"

"No." He tried to ignore the dread pooling in his gut. "I'm assuming someone has tried her apartment and the Eagle's Nest? Did anyone call Mac?"

"Mac is the one who called it in. Evidently, she went to pick up some of his heart medicine at the pharmacy, but that was more than an hour ago, and she hasn't come back yet. He thought maybe you might know something."

"Maybe she had trouble driving in the snow. I'm still in my vehicle. I'll swing back around and check it out." He was already pulling a U turn in the middle of the road.

"Okay, but be careful. You got the warning about whiteout conditions, right? It's already moved up to Sublette County."

Shit. That meant it was coming this way quicker than anticipated. "Roger that. I'll check out the pharmacy first since that's closest."

He maintained his slower speed as he drove toward the pharmacy. There was no sign of Lexi's car anywhere along the road. He wasn't sure if he should be relieved or worried about that—that thing barely had business driving on a summer day much less in a winter storm. He pulled up as Richard Huffman, the town's pharmacist, was coming out and locking the door behind him.

Richard turned toward Gavin as he jumped out of his SUV. "I'm closing up, Gavin. Are you picking up a prescription for someone? I can run back in."

Gavin shook the man's outstretched hand. "No, I'm wondering if you've seen Lexi Johnson who works over at the Eagle's Nest. Mac said he sent her to pick up a prescription"

Richard nodded. "Sure, she was here about forty-five minutes ago. We were out of Mac's prescription, so she was going to drive to Sublette County pharmacy to get it."

"In the middle of a whiteout warning?"

Richard shook his head. "She left right before the warning came in. I figured she'd get the alert on her phone like all of us and decide not to go. I called the hospital to see if they had enough of the medication for Mac to get through the storm. I talked to Dr. Anne Griffin, and she was going to have Zac run it by."

"But you weren't able to tell Lexi that." The sinking feeling in his gut that had started the moment Patricia mentioned Lexi's name grew worse.

"No. I let Mac know the medicine was coming from the hospital, but I didn't have Lexi's contact information. I'd figured Mac would tell her."

Mac couldn't tell her because she didn't have a phone for him to contact her through.

Gavin turned and ran back to his SUV, yelling his thanks back to Richard as he went. Lexi didn't have a phone. She hadn't gotten the emergency message about the whiteout.

She didn't know about the deadly weather headed their way. She only knew Mac—the only person Gavin had seen her get close to—needed his medicine.

Gavin was driving back through town, about to call Patricia to get the number for the Sublette County pharmacy, when he saw Lexi's car parked in its normal spot. Relief nearly swamped him. He parked next to her and rushed up to knock on her apartment door. He needed to see that she was okay and that she had everything to get through the storm.

Nobody answered.

He knocked louder, cursing when there was no response. She wasn't there. Maybe she was at the bar. She couldn't be far without her car. But if she was, she needed to get back to her apartment before the whiteout hit here. He turned toward the Eagle's Nest and found Mac walking toward him.

"Did you get my message about Lexi?" The older man's face was pinched. "I still ain't seen her."

"She must be over at the bar. Her car is here so she can't be too far."

"She's not driving her car. She took my truck. I got a call from Zac McKay saying he was going to be bringing my pills by, but I still haven't heard anything from Lexi. She's not at the bar, I walked and checked."

Gavin scrubbed a hand down his face. "I think she drove to Sublette County to get your prescription filled."

Mac let out a curse Gavin wouldn't have expected from the older man. "Why would she do that in this weather?"

"She doesn't have a phone," Gavin whispered. "I don't think she knows how bad it is."

And it was already turning worse. The snow was piling up and low-lying clouds of the same color were making it more difficult to see—sure signs of the approaching whiteout. He got Mac into his SUV and drove him back to his house while getting on the phone with the Sublette County pharmacy. They confirmed that Richard had sent the prescription request, but Lexi had never picked it up.

"I never should've sent her," Mac muttered after Gavin disconnected the call. "She doesn't know anything about driving around here."

"She's in your truck, that's better than her crappy car."

But they both knew in a whiteout it didn't matter what type of vehicle you were in.

"I wish we knew how far she got."

Maybe she'd stopped somewhere before it got too bad. Maybe she'd recognized the signs.

"My truck has that onboard GPS. Could you track that?" Mac asked.

"Yes, that's great idea. We don't need a warrant because you're giving us permission."

But by the time Gavin got back to the office and ran it himself, it would be another thirty minutes before he'd be on his way, another couple hours before he actually got to her. If Lexi was in trouble, she might not have that long.

But if he started from here and let someone else at the sheriff's office run the GPS tracker, he could be well on his way to Sublette County by the time they pinpointed her location. Although that also meant that he'd be driving directly into a whiteout, which wasn't much more than a death wish.

"What are you thinking?" Mac asked.

He looked the older man in the eye. "I'm thinking you mean a lot to Lexi and she drove to a farther pharmacy to get you that medicine. I'm thinking she didn't know that this whiteout was coming and she's in trouble. I'm thinking I'm going to get her. I'll start driving, and the sheriff's office can get me the GPS location as soon as they have it."

Mac didn't try to tell him how dangerous this was. They both already knew it. But they both also knew how much trouble Lexi might be in, how easy it was to get disoriented in a snow squall.

If she got out of the truck for any reason . . .

"I'm remembering Billy Bradshaw." Mac shook his head. "That was before your time here."

"It was, but I think everybody in the state of Wyoming knows about Billy Bradshaw."

The guy had walked outside to get a book out of his car in the middle of a whiteout. Maybe thirty feet. He'd gotten the book, but then walking back had gotten disoriented and had missed his house, the place he'd lived his whole life. He had frozen to death ten yards from his house because he couldn't see it and didn't know where he was.

Billy Bradshaw had become the unfortunate poster child for snowstorm safety, the cautionary tale parents told their kids about the dangers of a whiteout.

And Gavin was about to drive into one. Because he damned well wasn't leaving Lexi out there in it alone.

He looked over at Mac. "I'll get her home safely."

The old man nodded. "I know you will."

17

Every minute Gavin drove, the worse the weather got. He'd already called in Mac's truck GPS info, and it was only a matter of time before the sheriff's office got back to him with the location.

He was aware that he could be risking his own life for nothing. If Lexi had found somewhere safe to stop, Gavin might be the one in trouble soon. But he had to take that risk despite every second becoming more perilous. He was moving at barely more than a walking pace, the snow truly blinding now. When his phone rang, he pressed the button to put it through on his SUV speakers without his eyes ever leaving the road.

Not that he could see the road.

"Talk to me."

"Gavin, it's Nelson." The older man, the town's elected sheriff, sounded grave. That wasn't good.

"Hey, Sheriff. Did you find Lexi?"

"The truck isn't moving. It's sitting near the road about ten miles outside of town."

Shit. There wasn't much around that area in terms of shelter. If Lexi had stopped and gotten out of the truck, she could already be dead.

"I've got somebody here who is going to walk you through finding her."

A few seconds later Kendrick's voice came on the line. "Hey, Gavin. Zac found out what was going on and sent me over to help. The GPS company was giving us some pushback, wanting to double-check Mac's identification after he'd given approval, so I hacked them. Forget the side of the angels."

"Damned straight," Gavin muttered.

"And the word *hack* is my cue to leave," Sheriff Nelson said. "Let us know when you find her safely, Gavin. I know you will."

Gavin wasn't quite as sure.

"You're only three miles from her, it looks like," Kendrick said.

"Three miles is going to take a long time in this weather. I'm currently maxing out at about ten miles an hour." And even that felt reckless.

"According to the truck's GPS, she hasn't moved in nearly forty-five minutes."

"Hopefully, that means she stayed inside the truck."

Kendrick stayed on the line with him as Gavin kept plodding through the blizzard. "I appreciate you coming out to the office and doing this, Blaze. Sheriff Nelson has his hands full with everything else."

"This whiteout shit is not to be messed with," Kendrick said. "I thought I had seen pretty bad winter stuff in Boston, but people would fall over and die in something like this."

"Believe me, people fall over and die in it out here too." He prayed Lexi wouldn't be one of them.

It took way too long to make it the three miles, probably more than thirty minutes.

"Okay, you're there," Kendrick told him. "You should see her."

Gavin stopped his vehicle, but couldn't see anything. "Visibility is basically zero. She could literally be right next to me, and I wouldn't be able to see her. I'm going to have to get out and walk around."

"Is that safe? Sheriff Nelson's been talking about how people can lose their bearings out in the white."

"I have a rope. I'll keep it attached to the SUV."

"Be careful."

"I'll call you when I have her."

Gavin disconnected the call and climbed into the back seat to get the rope. He didn't waste any time once he had it. He got on his gloves, pulled up his hood, and fastened his coat as tight as he could.

He felt the biting cold the second he opened the door. It had dropped at least ten degrees since he'd left Oak Creek, and it had been pretty damned cold to begin with.

And he couldn't see his hand in front of his face. He hooked the carabiner at the end of his rock climbing rope around the ski rack on the top of his SUV and tested it for stability. This was the only thing that would allow him to get back to the vehicle. Attaching the other carabiner to a special loop on his coat, he started moving in the direction Kendrick had said Lexi would be.

As soon as he stepped away from his vehicle, he could no longer see it. Coupled with the howling wind, it was truly disorienting. He was literally going to have to run into Mac's truck in order to find her.

He walked until the rope pulled taut, then began walking perpendicularly as far as he could. He stopped, staring straight ahead as something caught his attention. Had he seen some flash of color in the whiteness? Mac's black truck maybe ten feet ahead?

The only way to know would be to let go of the rope.

Gavin would not be like Billy Bradshaw—would not be overconfident in his abilities. He would take every care and precaution.

Gavin unhooked the rope from his jacket and moved very carefully, counting his steps and keeping them as consistent as possible. He would give himself ten steps, and if he hadn't found the truck at that point, he would backtrack the exact number of steps he'd come.

It was a solid plan, but it was still absurdly dangerous.

At five steps, he wasn't any closer to seeing anything and was fairly sure he'd made a mistake.

At step nine, he ran into the corner of the back bumper of Mac's truck with his legs. If he had been another six inches farther to the right, he might've missed the truck completely.

He kept his hand against the vehicle as he moved up toward the front, praying when he got to the door he would find Lexi inside. He couldn't see anything.

"Lexi!" He found the handle and pulled it open.

A shrill shriek greeted him, but it was the most beautiful sound he'd ever heard. Lexi was here. She was alive.

"Lexi, it's Gavin." He climbed inside the cab, pulling the door closed behind him. It was definitely warmer in here out of the wind.

"*Gavin*? What are you doing here?" She scooted over so he had more room, water and snow dripping from him everywhere. He shuddered as his body adjusted to the change in temperature.

"Mac got worried when you didn't come back. Richard at the drugstore told us you went to the Sublette County pharmacy."

She was pale, her hair a mess, more disheveled than he'd ever seen her. "I didn't know it was going to be like this. I thought I had time before the storm came in." She started rocking back and forth. "I wasn't sure what to do. When I ran off the road, I didn't know if I should stay in here or if I should try to find shelter and I—"

Gavin reached over midsentence and yanked her against him, plastering his lips to hers. It was part kiss, part prayer of thanks, part branding—she was his.

All he knew was there was no way he couldn't *not* touch her right now.

If she had gotten out of this truck . . .

"You did the right thing," he finally said when he could force his lips to let hers go. "This is a whiteout—so much worse and sudden than a blizzard. They don't happen very often. Staying in the truck was the right thing to do. You would've been dead long before you made it to any sort of shelter, if you could've found your way at all."

"How did you find me?"

He took off his gloves and trailed his fingers over her hair. "We used the truck's GPS system."

"It had to have been dangerous for you to come out here in this."

He leaned his forehead against hers. "I had to try."

"You risked your life for me. Thank you."

He pulled back. "Don't thank me yet. I've still got to get us back to my SUV and then were going to head for the Cactus Motel, which is about three miles away." Getting there wouldn't be easy. "We'll have to hunker down there until the storm is done."

"I have some supplies. I bought them at the drugstore, although I should warn you that I tried one of the nutrition bars, and they are pretty gross."

He had to chuckle at that. "But they've got what your body needs. They won't taste so bad if that's all we have to eat for a couple of days."

"What my body really needs is the mimosa supplies I bought."

He raised an eyebrow. "You have champagne and orange juice?"

She shrugged. "They had it at the drugstore. It seemed like a good idea at the time."

He winked at her. "By all means, bring that too."

Some of the tension left her face, a little color returning. She'd been scared. He didn't blame her. This truck felt a little like a tomb. Hell, it might have become one if the snow drifts had gotten high enough.

That wasn't going to happen on his watch.

But he knew the most dangerous part of this was still in front of them. It was going to take every bit of training and instinct that had been honed over years of both serving in the Special Forces and teaching classes on wilderness survival at Linear Tactical to get them back to his SUV.

Then they had miles to drive in the blinding snow. Equally as dangerous.

One crisis at a time. They needed to get back to his SUV. There was no way he'd be able to get this truck up the embankment.

She still had that same jacket that wasn't anywhere near suitable for what she was about to walk through. He couldn't give her his own jacket, but he could give her some of his other clothing.

He handed her his gloves and unbuckled his coat. "I'm going to give you one of my shirts and my gloves. It's gotten a lot colder out there, and you need every layer you can get."

"What about you?"

"I've got a lot more mass as well as muscle. It will keep me warmer longer." He pulled his black Henley over his head. She slipped off her own jacket and pulled his shirt over her head.

"Warm." She snuggled into it.

He couldn't begin to unpack how much he liked the sight of her in his clothes. Right now, he had to stay focused on keeping them alive. She slipped her jacket back on, and he helped her into the gloves.

"What's the visibility like out there?"

He wasn't going to lie to her. That wouldn't help either of them. "Basically zero."

"Do you know where your SUV is?"

He gave her a one-shoulder shrug. "Nine steps one and a half feet apart at a seventy-five-degree angle from your truck's back right bumper corner."

"That's very specific."

"Specific is the only way we're going to survive the walk from your vehicle to mine in that whiteout. Staying here is not an option."

"Gavin, I'm so sorry. You have to think that I'm a complete idiot—"

He put a finger over her lips. "You were trying to get Mac the medicine he needs. That's anything but stupid. By the way, the hospital had enough to get him through a couple of days, so he's going to be fine. Annie had Zac deliver it."

"Thank God." She bit her lip. "I was afraid I had driven myself out here to die in a Wyoming ditch and Mac was going to be in danger anyway."

"You're not going to die in a Wyoming ditch." He grinned at her. "You might die trying to get *out* of a Wyoming ditch, but it's not the same."

They loaded the stuff they'd be carrying—hell yeah, he'd

be bringing the mimosa ingredients—into their pockets. "When we get outside, you can't let go of me for any reason. I'm going to need both hands to get us to the truck. It'll be loud, so we won't be able to talk. Your one job is to hold on to me and not let go."

She nodded. "I'll never let go, Jack, I'll never let go."

He rolled his eyes. She was quoting *Titanic* to him at a time like this? But at least she was keeping her sense of humor. "If memory serves, Jack ended up dead because of an iceberg. Maybe that's not entirely appropriate."

He made sure both of them were wrapped up as warmly as they could get, then grabbed the lapels of her jacket and pulled her until their faces were only a couple inches apart. "Thank you for trusting me."

She leaned her forehead against his. "Thank you for coming to get me when almost nobody else on the planet would have known I was gone, much less searched for me."

There was still so much he wanted to know about this woman.

But instead he said, "Let's go. Ready?"

She nodded, and he opened the door. The sound of the wind was immediately deafening, and the tidal wave of white was as disorienting as it had been the first time. He got out of the truck then reached back to help her. He closed the door then tucked her hand around his jacket at the back. He had to trust her to hold on, because he couldn't make sure she had him and get them back to his SUV. She was trusting him; he would have to trust her.

He kept a careful hand along the truck and slid until they were at the back corner of the bumper where he'd first arrived. This was where things would really get tricky. If he messed up the angle, messed up the length of his steps, messed up nearly anything, they might be pulling a Billy Bradshaw.

Breathing in the bitterly cold air, Gavin took a step away from the relative safety of the truck.

He focused on keeping his body at the exact angle it needed to be for all nine steps, not allowing the wind or his inability to see to move him off course. He didn't reach behind himself to make sure Lexi was still there. That would make it harder to know if he was still going straight. She was there. He trusted her.

Step eight . . . Step nine . . . He reached down his hand, praying his fingers would touch the rope.

They did.

Using the rope he pulled them rest of the way to the SUV. He'd left the engine running, not willing to take a chance on anything freezing up. He scooped Lexi inside, then climbed in behind her. They were both shuddering and breathing heavily. Gavin held his hands out to the heater vent, wincing at the pain the lukewarm air brought to his fingers.

It was cold even inside the vehicle. They needed to get into a building.

He hit the call button to get Kendrick back on speakerphone.

"Gavin, shit, man. Thank God. Are you okay? Did you find Lexi?"

"Yeah," he managed to get out. "I got her. We're okay, but we need to get inside somewhere that's better shelter."

Making it the three miles to the Cactus Motel seemed nearly impossible.

"I found a small warehouse on State Road 191 only half a mile from where you are. I got up the building specs for it, and it's got an office. I contacted the owner, and he said there's an emergency key behind the mailbox. It lifts off. Said to help yourself to anything."

This was why Gavin loved Wyoming. Everyone was willing to work together in a situation like this. "Thank you, Kendrick. You've been busy."

"Let's get you guys somewhere safe. Then you can buy me all the drinks I want to make up for it."

"It's on the house," Lexi said. "As long as you don't tell Mac."

18

Gavin was unflappable driving the short distance to the warehouse. The way he had been getting them back to his SUV. Focused. Controlled. Steady.

If this was how he'd operated under pressure while he was in the military, no wonder they'd given him the codename Redwood. He was solid. He faced down the problem, then handled it.

Just being next to him calmed her. She hadn't told him, but she'd been pretty damned close to panicking inside that truck when he'd arrived. She wasn't prone to claustrophobia, but sitting there listening to the wind had been eating away at her sanity moment by moment.

She'd never been so glad to be scared to death by someone.

Having him next to her now, she was glad to give over control to someone else. He obviously had way more experience dealing with this sort of situation, and she was more than happy to give up the reins.

And snuggle down into his shirt.

With condoms burning a hole in her jacket pocket.

They'd been in the same bag as the nutrition bars, so it'd been easier to grab them both. Yeah, she'd just keep telling herself that.

Kendrick stayed on the line with them until they found the small warehouse. Gavin drove the car so close to the building he could actually touch it when he opened his driver's side door.

"You wait here while I find the door and the key."

He was gone before she could respond, not that she would've argued much anyway. It hadn't taken them more than ten minutes to get from Mac's truck to his SUV, but she had no desire to go back out into that biting wind for a single second longer than she had to. This had definitely convinced her about the need for a proper coat.

But the moment he was gone, the all-encompassing white surrounded her again. She had to fight back panic, despite knowing Gavin was only a few feet away. Today was the first time she'd actively wished for some of the pills Nicholas and Cheryl had given her. At least the benzodiazepines—usually Xanax or Valium, she'd found out later as she'd gone through withdrawal—they'd encouraged her to take had caused her not to feel *anything*. That was better than the crippling fear that she'd trapped herself inside a vehicle-shaped tomb.

"You're okay now." She said it out loud in the hope that would make it true. But still she counted the seconds until Gavin reappeared.

Gavin was back 367 of them later. He jumped in and slammed the door behind him, shuddering. "Got the key. We're all set."

She nodded, throat a little tight. She was being ridiculous.

"You okay?" he asked.

She nodded, then shrugged. "The white, the wind . . . they're starting to get to me."

"Believe me, that's a real thing. It can make you a little crazy. Being inside where you can't see or hear it will help restore your equilibrium and settle your nerves."

She nodded, having to blink back tears and resist the urge to cover her ears with her hands. She had already been enough of a burden to Gavin; she wasn't going to be a complete nincompoop.

He grabbed the two blankets he had in the back of his SUV. "We need to take anything we may want with us. This may be over in three or four hours, but it could be three or four days. If the latter is the case, the snowdrifts will make it impossible to get back to the vehicle for a while."

The cold was just as biting this time as they got out in it. Gavin set her hand against the building and pressed on it, obviously signifying that she wasn't to let go. He didn't need to worry, she wasn't planning on it. She was well aware that if she lost touch with this wall it was all over.

They moved together, hand on the wall, until Gavin stopped them. They must be at the door. He opened it, scooped an arm around her, and pushed them both inside, closing it behind them.

It was impossible to see anything for the first few seconds, the contrast between the blinding white of the snow and the darkness in here quite jarring. Eventually, their eyes adjusted to the dim light.

"Okay."

The relief in his voice was apparent. He might have been stoic out there under the worst of circumstances, but he hadn't been unaffected. He just hadn't let stress or fear get in the way of completing his mission.

"I'll bet you were one hell of a soldier," she mumbled.

"I didn't fight in many blizzards." He chuckled. "But I'll

always be thankful for my training in the army. It's saved my life multiple times over."

"Including today."

"Definitely including today." He shot off a message to Kendrick letting him know they were safely inside, then turned to her. "Let's find the office and set up camp. I could definitely use one of those nutrition bars you bought. I don't care how bad they taste."

"You spent a lot of energy getting us to this point. You can have all the nasty bars you want as a reward."

The office was in the back corner of the small warehouse. It wasn't much—two desks, a sofa, and a small fridge in the corner. There was a tiny electric space heater over by one of the desks.

"Go ahead and turn that on." He set the blankets down on the couch. "We want to get it as warm as possible in here in case we lose power, which is likely. I'm a little surprised it hasn't already happened."

She did as he asked while he pulled a small rug from under one of the desk chairs and pressed it in front of the door to help keep the heat inside.

For a long while, they just sat in front of the heater. He ate one of the bars, but she shook her head when he offered her one. There was no way she could stomach any food right now, especially something as dense and tasteless as that.

Eventually, it became warm enough for her to feel her fingers again and to take off their jackets and shoes. Everything was dripping all over the floor as the ice on it thawed.

Gavin shrugged as he hung the coats over the chairs to help dry them and put their shoes near the door. "We'll have to pay the owners for the electricity and any damages."

She would worry about the money for that later. "Plus

anything they have in their minibar." She pointed to the fridge.

"My dad travels all the time for business but won't ever touch anything in a hotel fridge. He'd rather walk two miles to get something from a grocery store than pay minibar prices."

She smiled at that thought. At one time, it would've never occurred to her to worry about how much something cost. Not anymore. "What does your dad do?"

Gavin shrugged and walked over to the fridge. "Um, sales. Development. He wears a lot of different hats." He opened the fridge. "Looks like our minibar options include three cans of Dr Pepper, a Snickers, and half a bottle of ranch dressing."

"I'll definitely take the soda and Snickers if you're the one paying the minibar charges."

"Deal." He tossed her both.

They sat for a long time in comfortable silence. It got warm enough in the small room that Gavin slipped off his long-sleeved shirt and now wore only his T-shirt. She made a tremendous effort not to stare at the well-defined muscles of his arms and chest under the fitted shirt.

She was probably warm enough to take off his Henley but had no plans to do that anytime soon. The fact that she found his essence surrounding her soothing said all sorts of things she was not going to think about.

She concentrated on her candy bar instead, couldn't help but close her eyes in bliss as she took a bite.

"Wow. That's quite a face you're making over a Snickers bar."

How exactly was she supposed to tell him about her love/hate relationship with the sweet treat? How every time she'd eaten a bite of one for ten years, her aunt or uncle—or whatever member of her posse they'd paid to keep an eye on her that day—had immediately started hounding her about her image and weight and whether chocolate was really a good idea.

She took another bite and let the chocolate melt in her mouth. "I think anything tastes good after being trapped in a blizzard."

"Oh, I think it's more than that."

"Okay, I'll admit it. I love chocolate. I once went on a chocolate factory tour in this one tiny town in Germany, and they gave out free samples at the end." She laughed at the memory. That truly had been a great time. "I ate so much, I thought they were going to ask me to leave."

He laughed at that too. "I could see some security guard trying to decide whether to risk a scene by asking you to leave in front of everyone. He probably just wanted to ask you out."

It felt good to laugh. To really laugh. "He was in his seventies, so I doubt he wanted to ask me out. And it was a private tour, so he didn't have to get through throngs of people. He sat there watching me stuff my face piece after piece, probably wondering if the factory would be bankrupt before I finally stopped."

Gavin's laughter changed, and she realized immediately that she'd said too much.

"Private tour?"

Shit. "Um, no, not so much private, as empty, I mean." Empty because if anyone had known she was there, the place would've gotten mobbed. "Like I said, it was a really small town."

"In Germany."

She nodded. "Just outside of a city called Stuttgart." She needed to change this subject immediately. "Have you ever been to Germany?"

"Yes, actually, I was stationed out of Ramstein Air Base for a couple years in the army. I've been to Stuttgart a number of times also. Enough to know you're probably talking about the Ritter Sport factory."

She twisted on the couch to face him, eyes big. "I was! Have you been there?"

"Yep. I love that square chocolate."

"Me too. I used to have it shipped over from Germany." Of course, eating it had usually caused more arguments than it was worth, but just having the shipment arrive each month had made her happy.

"Not anymore?"

She took another bite of her Snickers. "No. I prefer the American classics now." All lies. Better to change the subject. "Did you like being in the army?"

He nodded and stretched his long legs out in front of him on the couch. "Yeah. I joined right after college, mostly to get away from my dad and the plans he felt best suited my life."

"Like what?"

Gavin shrugged. "The family business."

She tucked her legs under her. "And what sort of business is that?"

He turned and raised an eyebrow at her. "I'll answer some of your hard questions if you'll answer some of mine."

That was entirely too dangerous. "Touché. Let's stick to easy ones."

He leaned his head back against the couch. "Okay, easy answer: yes, I did like the army. I had skills that Uncle Sam wanted to put to use and was teamed up with a lot of the other guys that now form Linear Tactical. Those guys are my brothers in every way but blood. So even if I hadn't liked being in the military, I'd still be thankful for the time because it led me to them."

"Fair enough. Do you have any actual biological siblings?"

Damn it, why did she keep asking him questions? It was just inviting him to do the same with her.

But she wanted to know about him. Which might be way more dangerous.

"Yeah. I'm the oldest. Then I have my two brothers, Tristan and Andrew, twins. And then my sister, Lyn, is the baby. She's actually married to one of the Linear guys, Heath Kavanaugh. They live in Egypt."

"*Egypt?*"

"Yeah, she's a wiz in linguistics—particularly dead languages—does different jobs all over the world now that she's finished her Ph.D. Heath kind of works as her bodyguard part-time. He does work for Linear every once in a while. Also does some for another company we're close with, Zodiac Security and Tactical."

She laid her cheek against the back of the sofa. This was all so fascinating to her, hearing him talk about his family. "So your teammate married your little sister." Lexi couldn't help but smile at that thought. "You're obviously protective of her, so I'll bet that stirred the pot a little."

Gavin gave her a mock glare. "I'll admit, there might have been a couple of sparring matches between Heath and me. No brother wants to think about his friend with his sister." He leaned his head back against the sofa too. "Plus, our mom died when Lyn was little from the same heart condition Lyn has. So I'm allowed to be a little protective."

"Fair enough."

"How about I ask you a couple of questions but keep them vague enough that you don't go running into the snowstorm to avoid them?"

That sounded like a terrible plan, but she didn't want to lose this easiness between them. "Okay," she all but growled.

He chuckled. "I'll try not to be overwhelmed by your enthusiasm."

"Just ask your damn questions."

"Let's start with hard ones. Do you have any siblings?"

"No, it's just me."

"Okay, easy one. Parents?"

That was actually harder. "They died in a small plane crash when I was fifteen."

Right after she'd had her first breakout success in television. They'd gone home to clear some stuff out of their old house so they could live near her in LA. If it hadn't been for her, they never would've been on that charter plane.

"That's really hard, I'm sorry. What happened to you then?"

"My aunt and uncle took over guardianship of me."

And her money. All of it.

She'd been so overwhelmed with grief and her newfound fame, had been so young and so freaking naïve, that it had never occurred to her that Nicholas and Cheryl might not have her best interests at heart.

She'd done whatever they told her to. Signed whatever they'd told her to. Taken the pills they'd told her would help with her different issues. Talked to the psychiatrist she'd later found out was on their payroll.

They'd kept her so isolated, and had seemed so genuinely concerned for her well-being, that she'd had no idea they were trapping her in a very beautiful prison, meanwhile making sure all access to her money went through them.

It was how she'd gone from billionaire to penniless virtually overnight. How she'd ended up with a lawyer who had barely passed the bar exam for her trial—because that had been all she'd been able to afford.

"I'm going to guess that you're not in touch with them much now, if at all."

"Why do you say that?"

"Because I think if you'd had any other options that night you took my wallet in Reddington City, you would've gone with those options."

He was right. "I really am sorry about that, you know."

He shrugged. "And I'm sorry about the dumbass stuff I've done since. Let's call it even."

"Deal." They reached over and shook on it. She was completely unaware of how nice his large, capable hand felt around hers. Totally oblivious. And she totally didn't notice when they didn't quite let go of each other afterward, letting their connected hands drop between them on the couch, still touching.

"And you're right. I'm no longer in contact with my aunt and uncle."

The power decided to go out that very second.

"Yup, that's about the sum of our relationship."

Gavin chuckled, then turned on the flashlight he'd found in the desk. "Let's get situated. Then we'll turn the flashlight off so we're sure to have it if we need it later."

She snuggled under the blanket, knowing it would get chilly in here without power. Gavin slipped his arms into his long-sleeve shirt, covering those muscles. Sadly.

They both went to use the connecting bathroom, then got settled on the couch, keeping the food and drinks within arm's reach.

"Okay, now we hunker down and literally wait for the storm to blow over," he said, settling in next to her. "It's like a camping trip."

He switched off the flashlight, and their eyes adjusted to the dimness, the only light from a clock running on battery.

She couldn't see him well, but she could feel him. He was close enough that his leg rested against hers. Shoulder too.

Maybe it was the near-death experience or the chocolate or the talking, but she wanted him closer. She wanted him as close as he could possibly be, and was tired of pretending like she didn't.

"Unfortunately for you, we can still talk without any light." She could hear the smile in his voice. "I mean, honestly, our only options are talking or sleeping. So we might as well—"

"I have condoms."

19

Gavin swallowed and forced himself to breathe normally.

She had condoms.

They were trapped in a building together, possibly for days, snuggled together on a couch, and she felt comfortable enough to announce she had condoms.

Nearly every single piece of him wanted to act on that information. Hell, he'd been around long enough to know that an announcement like that probably meant *she* wanted him to act on that information. He was getting hard just thinking about it.

But he wasn't going to act on it. Because right now, he'd rather continue talking to her than utilize those condoms.

Maybe he'd sustained a head injury in the snow.

"Condoms are good," he finally said. "Healthy."

"In case I was unclear, I made that announcement in hopes that maybe you and I could put them to use."

He closed his eyes, trying to draw on that steadfastness he was known for. It was not easy. He was impossibly aware that all he needed to do was move a few inches and they'd be kissing. A few inches more and he could have her tucked underneath him, not having to worry about a blanket keeping her warm—he'd do it himself.

"I'd be lying if I said I wasn't very interested in that proposal."

"Then why are we still talking?"

He gritted his teeth. He was an idiot. "Well, that's just it. This offer feels a little bit like an attempt to get out of talking."

"Really, Sheriff? You're saying you'd rather listen to stories about my childhood than fuck me right here on this couch?"

He winced at her words for multiple reasons. He didn't need to see her face to know its exact expression. Half smiling, coolly mocking, completely secure.

But he also knew this was how she kept people at bay. How she ensured nobody got too close. He'd seen her give a version of it to him and the guys at the bar multiple times.

It was her mask, but it wasn't who she truly was.

"To be perfectly honest, and at risk of having to surrender my man card if this gets around, yes. I would rather get to know you right now on this couch than do anything else. Including something I really, *really* want to do."

She was silent. A few seconds later, he was calling himself every sort of dumbass there was. Had he actually told her he didn't want to have sex when he'd been thinking about that very thing almost nonstop since the moment he'd spotted her across that bar?

Jesus, this was not his first day as an adult man. She'd bluntly told him she wanted to have sex, and he'd said he'd rather talk. Yeah, his man card was disintegrating by the second.

"Lexi—" He turned, his hands reaching for her. Fuck talking. If she was offering to get physically close with him, he wasn't going to pass that—

"What do you want to know?"

He froze. Jesus, he might be about to give himself sexual whiplash, but if she was going to talk about anything personal, he was damned well going to listen.

"Tell me more about your insomnia."

She let out a sigh. "I struggle with sleeping. What do you need to know?"

"You said it was because of drugs? Tell me more about that. Was it recreational use? Addiction?" He was pressing his luck. But he wanted to help her if that's what she needed. Maybe this would lead to discussing the man she'd met at that alley.

"I know this is going to sound almost impossible to believe, but I didn't know I was on drugs at the time. Well, I did, but not what I was on."

"How?"

She shifted under the blanket, and he thought she might stop talking altogether, but finally she spoke. "It's a complicated story, and I don't want to tell the whole thing, but basically, some medication I thought I was taking for health reasons ended up being harmful to my body."

"I don't understand." But he wanted to.

"Never mind. I told you it was impossible to believe."

No, he wasn't going to let her withdraw. He reached an arm around her and pulled her against his chest. "I didn't say I don't believe you. All I'm saying is I don't understand. Try. Give me a little more information."

"When I was younger, after my parents died, Cheryl and Nicholas came to live with me as my guardians. I was fifteen. I had a hard time sleeping. I saw a specialist, and she gave me a prescription for some sleeping pills."

"Okay, that doesn't seem abnormal for a teenager who'd just lost her parents."

He could feel her breathing against his shirt. "At first they worked fine, but then they started having the opposite effect. It ended up someone was trading out my sleeping pills a little bit at a time, replacing them with stimulants. Mostly Adderall or Ritalin."

He was struggling to wrap his brain around what she was saying. "What the hell?"

"So yeah, too many years of my body associating trying to sleep with the spike of adrenaline the pills caused, it kind of messed me up in the head. Basically my mind doesn't know how to sleep."

He could feel his own adrenaline spiking like there was an enemy to fight right here in this room. Who would do that to a grieving child? "How long did this go on for?"

"About ten years."

Ten years? Holy shit. That meant— "Your aunt and uncle did this to you."

That was the only thing that made sense. The only people she would've trusted for that long—who would've had access to her for so many years.

"Yes," she whispered. "At first they were my guardians, but even after I turned eighteen, they were still in my daily life because of . . . business reasons."

He wanted to press—this *business*, whatever it was, was a key part to understanding her past. But he knew she wouldn't give him the specifics. She'd shut down completely if he insisted.

She'd have to share that when she was ready. He couldn't force it.

"So you finally realized what was going on about two years ago?"

She nodded against his chest. "Yes. How did you know that?"

"Your age came up when I ran you through the system. Twenty-eight." He hoped the reminder wouldn't cause her to withdraw.

"Yeah. Two years ago. And even then, I wasn't actually smart enough to figure it out. I only did because Cheryl and Nicholas left, and my body freaked out and went into complete withdrawal. Doctors had to explain to me what was going on because I had no idea. I was an idiot."

He trailed his fingers up and down her arm. "For trusting someone who was supposed to have your back? No, that's on them."

"You sound like you have personal experience."

He didn't like to talk about how stupid he'd been with Janeen, but she'd opened up, so he could too. "Nothing like what you went through. But I was married back when I was in the army."

She stiffened. "You were? I didn't know."

He shrugged. "Janeen and I divorced five years ago, so I don't talk about it much. We were married three years."

"What happened?"

He wasn't sure exactly how to explain this without getting into details about who his father was. He didn't want to do that. Mentioning the governor would only muddy the waters. He wasn't sure how to phrase the story of his divorce.

"You don't have to talk about it if you don't want to. I know it's super hypocritical of me to butt into your business."

He squeezed her closer against him. "No, I don't feel that way at all. I just . . . I was an idiot, that's all."

"Seems like you're in good company."

The smile in her voice made it easier to talk about. "Janeen and my father are . . . in business together, have been for a while. They're sort of partners. When I got out of the army and made it clear I had no intention of going into the family business, that I was going to be part of Linear Tactical instead, that was basically the end of our marriage."

"Oh. That stinks."

"Worst part was that I decided I wanted to try to fight for our relationship. That I'd taken vows, and I wanted to honor those. I told Zac and Finn I wouldn't be a part of Linear, and I was reconsidering going into the business like she and my dad wanted. I took some leave and came home so we could work something out."

He stopped and bent his neck to the side to crack it and try to release the tension at the base of his skull. He hadn't said these words out loud like this to anyone ever. Including the Linear guys. They hadn't needed details, they'd just gotten drunk with him when he'd told them he was getting a divorce.

"I found Janeen in bed with someone else."

"Ouch."

He shrugged. "I guess. She's married to him now, and he's probably a much better fit for her and her career goals. Ends up she had only married me for my . . . business contacts. Specifically, Dad."

"And he's still working with her despite what she did?" Her indignation on his behalf was heartwarming.

"He doesn't know the details, all he knows is that she and I were too different to make the marriage work. She's good for his career and vice versa, so I just let it go."

"You're a bigger person than I would've been."

"Once I realized it was my pride that had been wounded much more than my actual heart, it was a little easier to come to terms with."

She rested more heavily against him. He liked it. Liked feeling her relaxed against him.

"So." He shifted so they were settled down further into the couch. "We were both betrayed by people we should've been able to trust. But we survived and came out of it the other side."

"The difference being that you made good choices afterward. Some of the ones I made . . . I was more wrong than Nicholas and Cheryl ever were."

"I find that hard to believe."

"Trust me, you wouldn't find it so hard to believe if you'd been there. I don't want to talk anymore."

He knew not to push. "Then don't. I think you've done your due diligence for today."

But hand to God, if she brought up condoms again, there was no way he was going to have the willpower to resist.

"I want to hear you talk some more."

He hadn't really been expecting that. "You do?"

"I like the sound of your voice. It makes me feel safe."

She was tired, he realized, the pauses in her sentences lengthening. After what she'd been through today, he wasn't surprised her body wanted sleep, but she didn't seem to recognize it.

He made her feel safe? Hell, he'd take that any day. Even over putting the condoms to use.

"Okay then, Green Eyes. What do you want me to talk about?"

"Tell me more about being in the army. I'll bet that was interesting."

She leaned more heavily against him. He didn't want to do anything to draw her conscious attention to the fact that her brain was shutting off and her body was following.

"How about I tell you about the time I almost got us killed rappelling down a building in just my skivvies?"

"Oh, I'm going to have so many questions about this. I want every single detail. Just your underwear?"

"Well, really it's Zac Mackay's fault. He was the one who got captured by an East African warlord and—"

She was asleep before he finished his sentence.

20

Lexi blinked her eyes open, trying to remember exactly where she was. This wasn't her apartment. It was too dark and—

"Good morning. Well, actually evening."

Gavin. And her face was buried in his ribs. She sat straight up, still trying to get her bearings. "I fell asleep."

"You did."

She couldn't remember the last time she'd fallen asleep like a normal person. Usually, she was either battling with her mind, trying to convince it to let her rest, or had worked until her body could no longer stay conscious.

"How long have I been asleep?"

"About seven hours. You conked right after the power went out."

"No I didn't." Had she? "We were talking about your time in the army. Something about rappelling in your underwear."

He let out a chuckle. "Yes we were. And how much of that story do you actually remember?"

None of it. She couldn't remember a single thing he'd said. "I—"

His lips moved gently against her forehead. "That's because you fell asleep."

She felt so much different than she normally did. Usually after she woke up, she'd only been asleep an hour and it hadn't been enough rest, or she'd fallen into one of her exhaustion comas, slept fifteen hours, and felt like a zombie. Right now, she just felt . . . *good.*

Except for the fact that she'd evidently fallen asleep in the middle of talking to him. "I'm sorry if I was rude. I promise it wasn't because you were boring me."

"You can fall asleep on me anytime, for any reason. Besides, I probably shouldn't have told the whole skivvy story anyway."

She sat up straighter and smacked him gently on the chest. "You know you'll have to tell me now. Don't be a tease."

"It will cost you a little something if you want to hear the whole thing."

"Let me guess, more information about myself?"

If only she could see his face, but she didn't have to. She knew what his expression would be. Solving problems was in his nature. He liked having all the details about everything. But she didn't have any more facts she could give him. She'd said too much when they were talking earlier.

This was probably going to be the end of the easy peace between them. Something in her grieved at the thought of him pulling away because she couldn't—*wouldn't*—give him any more details about herself.

It's better this way.

The thought didn't comfort her like it should have.

"I had an epiphany while serving as your full-body pillow."

She pulled a little farther away and tucked her legs underneath her. Did she really want to hear this epiphany? None of hers had ever been in time to help her. "Well, you make an excellent pillow. I can provide recommendations if you decide to leave your law enforcement and Linear Tactical days behind you."

"I'll remember that." He paused for a moment. She could feel his eyes on her. Was his night vision better than hers? Because it felt like he was taking in all the details of her face. "Don't you want to hear my epiphany?"

"Honestly, I'm not sure that I do."

"It involves you."

"Then I'm really not sure I want to hear it."

His fingers trailed up and down her back. The front of her was so warm under the blanket and next to him, but her back was colder from sitting up straight, away from the warmth.

The soothing circles of his fingers eased, urging her to relax, but she couldn't quite seem to do it.

"I'm still going to tell you." He spoke slowly, his deep voice resonating inside her. "I realized that if I want to be with you in any sort of way, I'm going to have to allow you your secrets. And that I'm okay with that. You don't owe me anything, Lexi."

"Except for two hundred and eleven dollars."

He chuckled and his fingers kept moving on her back in those sexy little circles. When had circles become sexy? "Not even two hundred and eleven dollars. You've served me that much in obnoxiously named drinks over the past two months."

She gasped as his arms folded around her, picked her up, and draped her across his lap, blanket and all.

His lips fell to her ear. "You're allowed your secrets, Lexi Johnson," he whispered. "It goes against my nature to not try and figure them out, but I'm going to stop."

A shudder ran through her whole body as his teeth bit gently on her earlobe. "I'm here any time anything gets too much for you to handle on your own. If you decide your secrets are too much for you to sustain, I'm here to help share that burden too. I've got wide shoulders. I can carry a lot. Whatever it is you've been through in the past, I'll help if you need me."

She closed her eyes against the tears welling in them. He thought she was a victim. Of course he did. He was a protector. And maybe she was partially a victim, but she was also the villain. She could never forget that.

It was the part he'd never be able to accept, and she couldn't blame him.

"Gavin, my secrets aren't what you think—"

His teeth nipped at her ear again. "It doesn't matter. It doesn't matter what your secrets are, doesn't matter what happened in the past. My epiphany was that I want to be with the Lexi Johnson who is here and now. So, if you want to hear the underwear rappelling story again, the price is not some of your secrets."

"What is the price?"

"A kiss."

That deep voice low in her ear was doing things to her insides she would've sworn were not possible without a physical touch. She didn't want to talk anymore—not even a story about this man traversing down the outside of a building with most of his sexy body on display.

"I'll kiss you on one condition."

"What's that?"

She let out a tiny moan as his lips began to work their way down her jaw. "That you tell me the story much later, not now."

She didn't wait for his response. She sat up and hitched her legs on either side of his, straddling him. Both of them let out a groan as his fingers gripped her hips and pulled her firmly down onto his lap. She threaded her fingers in his thick hair at the back of his head, fisting it, holding him where she wanted him.

And brought their lips together—a melding of mouths, hot and honest and raw.

Surrounded by darkness, in the snowstorm raging outside, there was nowhere else to go and nothing else to do but enjoy each other. *Devour* each other.

She would've kissed him like that in the darkness for hours and not gotten tired of it. The way his tongue teased and dueled with hers? The way he nipped at her bottom lip, then soothed the gentle pain with his tongue? She wanted to stay in his embrace forever.

But her body had other plans. It remembered how it felt when he'd pressed her up against that wall outside the Eagle's Nest and the orgasm that had ripped through her. She wanted that again. Wanted him inside her when it happened.

The blanket slipped off her shoulders but she didn't feel any cold. She let go of his hair to pull his shirt over her head, slipping hers underneath it off also.

She hadn't worn a bra. Hadn't planned to be doing anything today but hanging out as the storm passed.

She sucked in her breath as his fingers trailed up over the naked skin of her back and shoulders and moved around to cup her breasts. His own breath came out in a hiss as his palms, then fingers trailed across her hardening nipples. Teasing them, toying with them.

He wrapped one arm behind her back, his fingers cupping her shoulder and leaning her back, holding her weight as his lips moved down to tease her breasts the way his fingers had.

Her fingers grabbed his hair at the back of his head again, keeping him clutched to her.

"Gavin," she whispered. There was no need for him to

force her to say it this time. She definitely knew where she was and who she was with.

But soon, his talented mouth wasn't enough. She wanted more. She wrapped her arms around his neck, then pulled them both back up until she could reach his shirt.

"Off," she demanded as she tugged at it. She wanted to feel his naked chest against hers.

"Yes ma'am." His arms moved away from her as he shrugged off his long-sleeve shirt and the T-shirt beneath it. Both of them hissed out a breath at the feel of skin on skin.

His fingers were once again trailing up and down her back as his lips moved to her throat and his hips thrust up against hers. His voice was gritty. "I wanted to take this slowly, but you're making it damned hard to do that."

His open-mouthed kisses along her throat were making it difficult for her to breathe, much less form coherent sentences. "I don't want slow. I want to feel you inside me right now."

She let out a moan as his arms yanked her up, so her weight was on her knees, his lips finding her breast again. He bit at her nipple, hard enough to make her squirm and moan against him.

"Yes. Harder."

"You're going to be the death of me, woman. Where are those condoms that brought on this whole brouhaha?" He nipped at her again, sending lightning straight to her core.

"In the pocket of my jacket. I'll find them. You get undressed."

He helped set her on her feet, then stood himself. She should be feeling the cold, but she wasn't. All she could feel was the need to get close to him once more. It only took a few seconds to find the condoms, especially when the flashlight flipped on to help.

"Found them." She spun around holding the condoms package.

She swallowed as she got a good look at a fully naked Gavin Zimmerman in the dim light. He was every bit the specimen she'd known he would be from the moment she'd seen him across that bar in Reddington City. Strong, fit, and capable. And so very, very sexy.

And, God. *Redwood* indeed.

She wanted to say something, something flirty and fun, but all thoughts slid away as her gaze moved back up to his face.

He was looking at her like he was a starving man and she was the last meal in the world.

"You have too many clothes on." His voice was so deep as he grabbed her, it was almost unrecognizable.

She reached for the button of her jeans, but he moved her hands out of the way.

"Let me."

She nodded but wasn't expecting him to drop down on his knees right in front of her, kissing along her abdomen as he unbuckled and unzipped her jeans.

"Beautiful."

His lips trailed the same path the clothing took as he peeled her jeans and underwear down her legs. Teasing her just enough to suck all the breath from her body, but not enough to give her what she really wanted.

He kissed down her thighs and her knees before pulling her jeans and lace panties the rest of the way off. He kissed back up her thigh to her outer hip while tapping her socked foot. "We'll leave these on so those toes don't get too cold."

She let out a small laugh. "That's not very sexy." Then she gasped as his lips trailed back across her stomach and down her navel once again.

"Your well-being is more important. Besides, there's plenty of sexy here."

Her hands tunneled into his hair. Oh God, wasn't this how she'd gotten into this whole mess to begin with? Because she'd wanted someone who'd wanted to take care of her and look out for her well-being?

She'd wanted someone who wanted to know *Lexi*, who was not the same as Alexandra.

But then, every thought in her head fled as his lips stopped messing around and decided to really drive her crazy. All she could hear was the sound of her own cries as he drove her body relentlessly higher with his lips. His tongue torturing her.

"Gavin, I want you inside me. Please."

Without a word he kissed back up her body, taking the condom she'd all but crushed in her fist out of her hand. She couldn't stop watching as he rolled it over his length, then sat back on the blanket on the couch.

He held a hand out. Immediately she straddled his legs once again and lowered herself onto him. His deep groan echoed with the same sort of desperate need she felt as he filled her completely. His hands threaded into her hair and pulled her in for a kiss as her body adjusted to the feel of him.

It wasn't long before she needed more. Needed more of Gavin. More of them together.

Her lips left his as she raised and lowered herself on him, her hands clutching at his shoulders. His hands found her hips and increased the pace, sending streaks of heat spiraling through her.

"Lexi."

She loved the sound of her name on his lips, and their rhythm became wilder. Her fingers gripped his shoulders as she ground down against him, the friction pushing her over the edge, pleasure washing over her in waves.

The moment she fell apart, he snapped, gripping her hips, thrusting deeper from underneath her. She threw her head back and allowed herself to drown in pleasure as he called out her name in his own release.

She collapsed against him, feeling their heartbeats thundering in tandem, as they both attempted to regain their equilibrium.

She should wake up this way every day.

21

By dawn, the storm had blown itself out. Their first sign was that the power had come back on.

Despite the use of two more condoms, and her once again falling asleep in his arms—or maybe because of those things—Lexi looked decidedly uncomfortable once they got word from Sheriff Nelson that the roads had been cleared enough for them to make their way back to town. Baby Bollinger would get a tow truck out to rescue Mac's truck.

There wasn't much talk between them as they packed up all their stuff and cleaned the small office as best they could. He would definitely be sending a cleaning service to the office. Because as much as the thought of him having Lexi bent over that desk still turned him on, the respectful thing to do was to have the place thoroughly cleaned before the gracious owners got back in there.

He hated that he was so unsure how to handle Lexi. What was going on in that mind of hers as they finished in the office and walked out to his SUV?

But what else was new? He never knew exactly what she was thinking.

They made mundane small talk about the recovery process after a blizzard. Wyoming certainly knew how to get things up and running again as soon as possible or else they'd never be able to function during the winter.

Lexi kept touching her face. She'd opened the visor from her perch on the passenger side and looked at herself twice in the ten minutes since they'd left the warehouse.

Yes, her makeup was smudged, and her hair was a mess. They both needed showers. But Lexi obviously wasn't thinking about the amazing sex they'd had. Or if she was, her reaction was very different than his.

He finally reached over and grabbed her hand where it was balled into a little fist in her lap. He had to at least try and see if she would talk about whatever she was thinking. "Hey. You okay? Wished that you'd chosen to talk about yourself rather than use those condoms?"

The thought that she might regret what had happened, when it had been one of the most amazing nights of his existence for multiple reasons, twisted his guts into knots.

But she smiled at him. "No, I'll choose condoms with you any day."

She squeezed his hand. Okay. That was a start. "You sure you're all right?"

She nodded but then brought her other hand up to touch her face again. "I need to get home. Get to my stuff. Take a shower."

"Are you sure you don't want to come hang out at my house? You won't be able to open the Eagle's Nest today anyway. And believe it or not, I have relatively decent shampoo and conditioner if you want to use it."

She looked out the window. "Rain check? I need a minute to regroup. I'm not sorry about last night, I promise. It was amazing and everything I wanted and needed."

Don't push. You promised to give her what she needed. If that's space, so be it. He brought her hand up to his lips and kissed the back of her palm. "Ditto."

"Thank you for understanding." A shadow fell across her face, a look that bordered on despair.

"Hey." He kissed her hand again. "You'd tell me if something was wrong, right?"

As soon as the words came out of his mouth, he wondered why he'd said it. Of course she wouldn't tell him if something was wrong.

Don't push.

But his instincts screamed the opposite. Told him to make a stand right here and demand every piece of information from her. That it was the best way for them to move forward— maybe the only way.

But he'd given his word. He'd let her keep her secrets unless she wanted to share them.

"Sure, I'd tell you if something was wrong," she whispered.

They both knew she was lying.

OVER THE NEXT WEEK, Gavin found out that a person could see you every single day, have sex with you a couple of those days, and still avoid you. Lexi had it down to an art.

Twice in the past week, she'd come over to his house after her shift at the Eagle's Nest. And though their lovemaking had been as mind-blowing as it had in the warehouse office, he hadn't been able to talk her into spending the night with him afterward.

She was struggling with sleep again. He told her he didn't mind if she stayed awake—she could eat anything in his fridge, wander around any room, or his personal favorite, keep him awake for more sex.

She'd smiled, but she'd still left. And he'd let her go. He'd wanted to help—especially now that he knew more about the history of her insomnia and how it was tied to her guardians' twisted use of medication. She'd been conditioned not to sleep, to be dependent on others. He wanted to help recondition her brain to feel safe enough to sleep.

But that was going to take trust, and trust took time.

So all he could do was let her know he had a place for her in his life and hope she would slowly learn to fit herself into it.

But here he was on Christmas morning about to pressure her yet again. He wanted her to come with him to Dad's house. To spend the holiday with his family—his brothers and sister and two little nieces.

He didn't want her to be alone. But more than that, he didn't want to be without her. Insisting she join him was as much for him as it was for her.

He'd invited her last night when he'd seen her, but she'd said she had plans.

So here he was, back to his old ways, sitting outside of her apartment waiting to see if her "plans" were what he thought they were: going over and hanging out at the Eagle's Nest by herself. He hadn't seen her so far, so maybe she'd been telling the truth.

Maybe Mac had invited her to spend the holiday with him and his family. Or maybe Wavy had invited her over for the Bollinger family festivities—they pretty much invited everyone who wanted to come. Wavy was the only person he'd ever seen Lexi talk to outside of the bar. Lexi's friend—to the degree Lexi had friends.

But if his hunch was right, even if Mac or Wavy had

invited Lexi, she had turned them down, not wanting to intrude on a family holiday.

Not wanting to get too close.

Sure enough, not a minute later, she came bounding out of her apartment and turned toward the Eagle's Nest.

He shook his head. That little liar. She was so good at telling people what she thought they wanted to hear. At pretending and playing a role.

He sighed and gripped the steering wheel. He should leave her alone. He'd told her he wasn't going to press and would let her keep her secrets.

But damn it, nobody should be alone at Christmas unless that was what they really wanted.

He got out of his SUV and followed along behind her, telling himself if she really wanted to be alone, he would let her with no pressure. But she was going to have to convince him of that first.

At least she was wearing the matching hat, scarf, and gloves set he'd gotten her for Christmas. He'd wanted to get her something more—something beautiful and much less practical, or *more* practical, like a high-end coat suitable for Wyoming winters—but knew she wouldn't accept any of those things. So he'd start with what she would accept and move from there.

He was learning that lesson with damned near everything about her.

He reached her before she got inside the bar only because she walked all the way across the parking lot to get the bar's mail from the mailbox. She was staring at a letter in her hand as he approached from behind.

"I never believed you for a second, you know."

She spun around, obviously in a panic. There wasn't a bit of color on her face. "Wh-what?"

"Jesus, Lexi, I'm sorry. I didn't mean to startle you." He took a step toward her to steady her, but she moved back so quickly she almost stumbled. Her eyes were huge in her face, her movements jerky.

"Wh-what did you say?"

He wanted to grab her, pull her into his arms, and tell her he'd been kidding, but instead he forced himself to stand absolutely still. Moving toward her right now was the wrong thing to do. "I was making a joke. A really bad one. I was saying I didn't believe it yesterday when you said you had other plans. I'm sorry."

"I . . . Other plans?"

"You know, Christmas? I invited you for Christmas brunch with my family?" A little bit of the color was coming to her face now, thank God. He took a step toward her, profoundly relieved when she didn't back away.

"Right. You didn't believe I had other plans. That's what you meant." The words were as stiff as her shoulders.

He was such a dumbass. "Lex, I'm so sorry. I shouldn't have snuck up on you. I wasn't trying to, but that's no excuse."

She looked down at the letter she had clutched in her hand. "No. I overreacted. I . . ." She held up the mail. "I got startled by the mail."

"The mail? Not the dumbass sneaking up on you?"

She laughed weakly. "Maybe that too."

"Merry Christmas, Green Eyes." Slowly, very careful not to make this situation any worse, he pulled her into his arms. "I like seeing you wear the stuff I got you."

She wrapped her arms around him, and he could finally breathe. "I like being nice and warm in them. Merry Christmas. What are you doing here?"

"As I not so gently stated, I knew you were fibbing yesterday about having other Christmas plans. Catching you in the act and dragging you off for the holiday seemed like a good idea right up to the point when I scared you to death."

She stiffened again. "I promise I wasn't trying to lie. I—"

"You've been emotionally avoiding me since we made love at the warehouse, and having Christmas with my family would be a step in the wrong direction if you're attempting to put distance between us."

She shot him a surprised look.

"Am I right?" he asked.

"You're not wrong."

"I know I said I would give you space, and I will if that's what you really want. If you want to spend the day alone in peace and quiet, and not be around my family—which is very definitely neither quiet nor peaceful—then that's totally fine. But I want you to do that because that's what you *really* want."

"Gavin . . ."

He kissed the tip of her nose. "There's plenty of time to put more distance between us tomorrow. It's Christmas today, come be with me."

She looked back down at the mail again like it was going to give her answers, then finally looked back up and nodded.

"Okay. I'll come with you."

22

She'd made a huge mistake. She knew it as soon as they pulled up in front of the house in a gated community in the outskirts of Reddington City a little over an hour later. *House* wasn't the word for it, more like *stately manor*.

She probably wouldn't have said yes at all if that letter hadn't thrown her into a panic, coupled with Gavin's innocent, yet untimely words about not believing her.

No one had believed her last time she'd gotten a letter from the stalker right before he'd found her and almost killed her. For a brief moment, she'd been thrown back in the middle of that. Discombobulated enough to say yes to his invitation.

That, plus the fact that she'd been keeping her distance for the past week and he had ever so gently called her out on it. She hadn't expected him to realize she was holding herself apart. He was getting sex, so he shouldn't have noticed if she kept her emotional distance.

But he had. And she had to admit she was impressed. So she'd said yes.

When Gavin had walked her back from the Eagle's Nest

and explained that his family dressed up for brunch, that had actually made sense to her. Every place she'd traveled on Christmas Day had a more formal dress code.

He'd assured her that the dress she'd been wearing the night they met, the one she'd found at a thrift shop and repaired herself, would be fine. He looked so ridiculously handsome himself in his dark pressed pants, white collared shirt, and blazer.

For just a little while, driving here had felt so normal, like from her old life. Granted, her old life hadn't included much Wyoming. But dressing up to go out to a nice holiday brunch? No work or money or stalker problems hanging over her head? That was a part of the old life she'd gladly visit again. A nice meal with good company at a restaurant that would serve delicious food.

They weren't at a restaurant or a country club. They were at his father's house, which was large enough to tell her she wasn't the only one who'd been keeping secrets.

"Actually, this isn't Dad's main house," Gavin said as they drove past the front of the house to turn down the driveaway.

"This isn't his main house?" The size of this house shouldn't affect her at all. She'd owned a house bigger than this in Los Angeles, although she'd only actually gone to visit it half a dozen times.

And at the end, she hadn't really owned it at all—it had been in Nicholas's and Cheryl's names.

"No." Gavin turned into the long driveway. "Dad's . . . business is more in Cheyenne than here."

"Evidently, business is booming." She turned to him with eyes narrowed. "You haven't told me everything, Sheriff Redwood."

He shot her a sheepish look. "The important thing is, you're going to like my family. My baby sister, Lyn, is here, and she's possibly the kindest person on the planet. My brothers, Trouble Twins Part One, are going to flirt with you, not only because you're super sexy, but also to drive me insane. Andrew's daughters are too adorable to survive in this world. And you'll love Dad, because, well, *everybody* loves Dad."

He was talking faster than she'd ever heard him. He was *nervous*. She'd seen him drive through a freaking whiteout with more aplomb than he was showing now.

She reached over and wrapped her fingers around his wrist where he gripped the steering wheel. "Gavin. Are you sure you want me here?"

"What? Yes, I promise *you're* not the problem. We're going to have a great time. You'll see."

Was he trying to convince her or himself?

"Shit," he muttered. "It looks like Dad also invited my ex-wife and her husband for the festivities."

He pulled up in front of one of the six garage spots and punched a code in on his phone. The door opened, and they pulled inside.

"Are you . . . okay with that?"

He shrugged as he turned off the SUV. "It's not like I want to spend time with her, but I've accepted that she's attached to Dad because of their . . . business."

Lexi shook her head and studied him. There was something he wasn't telling her. "You know I don't understand, right? Whatever it is you're not telling me—I'm not able to put the pieces together on my own."

He raised an eyebrow that fairly screamed *touché*. She chuckled at that. She had to admit, being kept in the dark was frustrating. She had a new respect for his restraint in not demanding answers from her.

He picked up her hand and brought it to his lips. "I'm glad

you're here with me and that we get to spend this time together."

She smiled, ignoring the warmth spreading through her chest at his words. "Me too."

They got out of the car and walked into the house through a side door. That told her a lot—not entering through the formal front door like they were guests. Gavin took her coat and hung hers beside his on hooks by the door.

Lexi wasn't exactly sure what she'd been expecting inside the *stately manor*, but Alvin and the Chipmunks blaring a Christmas song was not it. Neither was the sound of children laughing hysterically.

"My nieces, Trouble Twins Part Two, Caroline and Olivia. Two and a half years old."

"Oh, I didn't realize either of your brothers was married."

Gavin shook his head. "They're not. Andrew is a single dad."

"Uncle Gabbin! Uncle Gabbin!"

Two curly-headed waifs, one dressed in red and the other in green, barreled toward Gavin, obviously ecstatic to see him.

Something in Lexi's heart clenched at the sight of him picking up those two little girls and letting them kiss him all over his face.

"There's my chipmunks. I missed you so much. This pretty lady is Miss Lexi." He bounced the red-dress girl. "This is Olivia." Green dress. "This is Caroline."

They waved but weren't nearly as interested in her as they were their Uncle Gabbin.

Caroline patted him on his face with her tiny hands. "Come see my new dolly."

"I got a football, Uncle Gabbin," Olivia chimed in.

He set them down. "I want to see! Let's go."

Lexi grinned at him as they followed the girls into the

huge, high-ceilinged living room that opened to a dining area set with a giant buffet of food across the table.

"Gavin!" a huge male voice boomed. "I didn't think you were going to make it, but I'm glad you did. And you brought a friend. Thank God, now maybe you won't be so cranky."

"You didn't tell them I was coming," she murmured, elbowing him in the stomach.

"Does it look like there's not enough food?" he whispered back.

That was definitely true. The spread on the table in the dining room could feed most of Oak Creek.

The girls had run to their huge pile of toys over in the corner, Gavin forgotten as they revisited their treasures.

Gavin led her further in with a hand on her back. "Merry Christmas, Dad. Everybody, this is Lexi."

Lexi looked around the room, smiling and giving a little wave. "Merry Christmas. Thanks for having me."

There wasn't time for an awkward pause before one of the twins—the *adult* male, just-as-sexy-as-Gavin twins, she wasn't sure which one—winked at her.

"Now that Sheriff Pain-in-the-Ass is here, can we please eat?" winking twin said. "I call the seat by Lexi. She's obviously more interesting than anybody else here."

There was a bout of laughter.

"Yes, let's eat, then we'll talk more with Lexi about her questionable life choices, like hanging out with my son," Mr. Zimmerman said with a good-natured grin. He looked around the room. "I'm thankful to have all of you here, thankful all of you are safe." The big man reached over and wrapped his arm around a woman who looked like a miniature version of Gavin. That had to be Gavin's sister, Lyn. "I'm thankful all of you are healthy."

A member of the house staff—Lexi wasn't at all surprised

to see them here, this food had obviously come from some-where—brought around a tray of champagne flutes and everyone took one.

Gavin's dad held his up. "To family. To old friends. To new friends. All are welcome in this house. Merry Christmas."

"Merry Christmas," they all responded.

They all clinked their glasses, then Gavin's brothers made a rush for the table. Lyn hugged her dad, then walked across the room to kiss a man who'd been standing near the window, silent but smiling. That must be her husband, Heath. He had that same aware gaze as Gavin, the one all the Linear guys had.

"Hungry?" Gavin whispered in her ear.

"Always." He winced at her words, and she realized that probably wasn't the right thing to say given his feelings about her empty pantry. "I mean . . ."

He wrapped an arm around her and kissed her temple. "I know what you mean. And you're welcome to eat everyone under the table here. Although good luck beating my brothers."

He winked at her, his face so soft and playful, she couldn't help but reach up and touch that strong jaw. He was relaxed here with his family. He might not agree with all the choices his dad had made, but he didn't need to be on guard here. That was what family was supposed to mean.

When they finally looked away from each other, every-body in the room was staring at them.

Gavin ignored it and took her hand, pulling her toward the buffet table. His dad was filling a plate. "Dad, this is my friend Lexi. She lives in Oak Creek."

"It's nice to meet you, Mr. Zimmerman."

"Please, call me Ronald. So happy for you to be here with us today. So tell me, are you a registered voter in Wyoming?"

"Dad . . ." Gavin warned.

"Just trying to figure out if I'm courting a voter or being myself today."

Gavin rolled his eyes. "Aren't they the same?"

She took the plate Gavin handed her. "No, I'm not registered to vote in Wyoming."

Ronald winked at her. "Good. Then I can be myself."

"You're in politics?"

Ronald glanced at Gavin, then back at her. "I dabble."

A woman dressed impeccably in a pleated vintage Halston dress walked up to the other side of the table, taking some fruit from a bowl. "Your toast was beautiful and eloquent as always, Governor."

Governor?

23

Governor Ronald Zimmerman smiled. "Thank you, Janeen."

Lexi looked around between Gavin, who had suddenly become very interested in piling some bacon on his plate, Janeen—of course Gavin's ex-wife would be dressed in designer wear—and Ronald, who merely smiled.

"Dabble?" she asked Ronald.

He patted her on the arm. "I'm trying to keep my son out of trouble. Evidently, he had the good sense not to mention my profession, since I'm sure you wouldn't have come here today if you'd known."

It all made so much sense now. The *family business* was politics.

And she definitely wouldn't have come here if she'd known.

Lexi glanced at Gavin, who shot her a sheepish smile, and offered her a piece of bacon.

She raised an eyebrow. "I don't think bacon is going to get you off the hook here, buddy."

"But it's really good bacon."

Ronald chuckled as Lexi put the offered bacon on her plate. Across the table, Janeen's smile was a little smug.

She'd done this on purpose, stirring the pot. Trying to cause tension between her and Gavin.

Well, this woman didn't know who she was dealing with. Lexi had rubbed shoulders with people a lot richer and more powerful than the governor of Wyoming. It wasn't a life Lexi was part of anymore, but that didn't mean she couldn't hold her own against a social piranha or two. She shot Janeen a not-quite-genuine smile of her own.

"Gavin is obviously as smart as his father." She looked back at the governor. "But no, I probably wouldn't have crashed your Christmas morning if I'd known."

"Nonsense!" Ronald smiled at her. "We've had half the Linear Tactical crew here at Christmas one year or another. And you're much prettier than them, so welcome."

She could see why Gavin was sure everyone would like his dad. Ronald was infinitely likable.

That remained true for the rest of the morning. Lexi had been prepared to play her role of charmed, and charming, guest, but the first half wasn't necessary.

She was charmed. No acting required.

The family patriarch enjoyed having his family here surrounding him. He got down and played with Olivia and Caroline every time they requested. Lexi had caught him glancing at pictures of his deceased wife more than once.

"He never did remarry." Lyn came over to stand next to Lexi as she looked at the wall of photos by the huge bay window. Gavin was over playing with the girls and talking to his brothers. "Mom has been gone now for nearly twenty years, and Dad has never found anyone else he looked at the same way."

Lexi stepped a little closer to the images. "I'd like to think that's how my parents felt about each other too. They died when I was a teenager, so I can't really remember. I wish I could go back and see the way they looked at each other. I don't even have any pictures."

Lexi had no idea why she'd said that. Yeah, she wished she had pictures of her parents, but that was just one more thing of hers that her aunt and uncle had taken. Had undoubtedly destroyed. Cheryl and Nicholas had never been ones for sentimental mementos.

Lexi had thought she'd made peace with that, but looking at these photos now, she really hadn't. She took a sip of her champagne, hoping to wash down the bitterness clogging her throat.

Lyn reached over and squeezed her arm. "Not having any pictures is really hard, I'm sure. But I'm glad you at least remember that's how they felt about each other. That's the important thing. That they loved each other to distraction."

Lexi forced a smile. "That's how you look at your husband too."

Lyn's cheeks turned the prettiest shade of pink. "He is my own personal superhero. I don't know how I would live without Heath."

Lexi winked at her. "Good thing you married him then."

Lyn was flushing even deeper when her nieces called her over to help paint their nails. She wasn't gone very long before Janeen took Lyn's place at Lexi's side.

Lexi wasn't surprised. She'd known Janeen was going to make some sort of power move since her earlier attempt at the buffet table.

"Your dress is Carolina Herrera?"

Lexi glanced over at her with a short smile before returning her gaze to the pictures. "It is. Good eye. And yours is vintage Halston if I'm not mistaken."

Janeen nodded. "Yes. I can't resist them, despite their exorbitant prices."

What would Janeen say if she knew Lexi had bought her dress at a thrift store for less than fifty dollars?

"So, how do you know our Gavin?"

Our Gavin. Another attempt to stir the pot. Janeen really had no idea who she was messing with right now. Certainly, Lexi wasn't going to lose her cool that easily. Lexi took a sip of her champagne. "Oh, the usual. I picked him up in a bar and stole his wallet."

They both laughed, but Janeen's was a little forced. "Honestly, I was surprised to see he'd brought someone. At least not one of his Linear Tactical friends." Janeen's words were tinged with disdain. "I know for a while Ronald was a little bit in hopes that Gavin and I might reconcile. I'm running for state senator right now, but I have my eyes on a U.S. Senate seat. Ronald is my mentor. We have plans."

Lexi tilted her head. "Yes, Ronald strikes me as someone who can spot a good politician."

"We all thought Gavin would go into politics when he got out of the army, but that didn't happen."

Lexi didn't glance away from the photos. "Maybe coming home and finding his wife in bed with another man made him decide certain politicians weren't quite as trustworthy as he'd hoped."

"What happened between him and me is none of your business."

Now she did glance over. "Oh honey, believe me, I have no interest in digging up what Gavin has completely buried."

Behind Janeen, Gavin was walking toward them. He was worried about her, Lexi realized, knew his ex-wife had a sharp tongue and thought Lexi might need a rescue. She shot him a wink while Janeen wasn't looking. Gavin stopped, close enough to hear, but he didn't intervene.

Lexi put a hand on Janeen's arm. She didn't need to be rescued. She already knew how to beat Janeen at her own game. "Janeen, I'm not trying to make an enemy out of you. Actually, I should thank you. Gavin's been talking a lot about getting back into politics. I think it was just the wrong time before. Now is the right time. Can't you see it? Zimmerman and Zimmerman, father and son, running for office together. And I want to be right by Gavin's side for the whole thing."

"I thought you didn't know Ronald was the governor." Color leaked out of Janeen's face and she drank down the rest of her champagne in one gulp. She was really making this too easy.

Lexi leaned in. "No, that was planned. You know, to help me get on Ronald's good side," she whispered conspiratorially. "I think it worked. I think Ronald really likes me. I've obviously got a knack for politics myself. I think I'll ride it as far as it will take me."

Janeen's eyes narrowed. "You're making all this up. Gavin has no interest in politics."

"Maybe." Lexi moved in closer. "But don't doubt that I could talk him into it if I wanted to. I think I'd look good on a senator's arm, don't you?"

Janeen's grip on the champagne flute tightened. She obviously realized how much she'd underestimated Lexi. Lexi just smiled. She'd been working rooms filled with power-hungry sharks for years. Janeen was a guppy in comparison.

"Ladies, can I refill your glasses?" Gavin stepped smoothly in between them, bottle of champagne in his hand. His eyes twinkled as he smiled down at Lexi. He'd heard everything.

Janeen wasn't ready to give up the battle so easily. "Gavin, shame on you. Lexi here was telling me that you guys have been talking about you going into politics and how she has what it takes to stand by your side as you do it."

Janeen shot Lexi a triumphant smile that Gavin couldn't see. Obviously, she thought she was exposing Lexi in a lie. Which of course she was.

Gavin didn't miss a beat.

"Naughty Lexi. Don't go around telling all my secrets." He slipped an arm around her waist and tugged her against him, then poured champagne into her glass. "But you would definitely look good on a senator's arm, as long as that senator was me."

He kissed her on the nose, then let her go to fill Janeen's glass. The woman's mouth opened and closed like she couldn't figure out what to say—a vague imitation of a fish caught out of water.

"Excuse me," she finally murmured. "I see Fletcher is trying to get my attention."

As soon as she was out of earshot, Gavin started laughing softly. "That was the sexiest thing I've ever seen. I've never known anyone to figure out Janeen so quickly and handle her so deftly."

Lexi hooked her arm with his. "She wasn't terribly difficult to figure out. I've handled a lot worse than her when it comes to the power hungry."

Gavin raised an eyebrow but didn't press for details. God. She had to be more careful.

He stayed close the rest of the morning. The family didn't exchange gifts, instead choosing to make donations to local charities in each other's names. The baby twins, however, had been showered with gifts.

Lexi enjoyed being there, enjoyed seeing Gavin interact with his family and nieces. She especially enjoyed when Janeen realized Lexi had fooled her and Gavin had no interest in entering the political arena. She handled it with more humor than Lexi would've expected. Lexi understood why Ronald saw such political potential in Janeen. She was young, personable, and smart.

Of course, she was dumbass stupid for having cheated on someone like Gavin, but Lexi had been known to do a couple of dumbass stupid things herself, so she wouldn't judge too harshly.

Lexi was glad she'd come. Andrew and Tristan were outrageous in their flirtations, but both genuinely likable. Heath and Lyn were mostly inseparable—Heath constantly pulling the curvy woman onto his lap and kissing her, despite the hilarious faces her brothers made. Even Janeen and Fletcher were enjoyable now that Janeen wasn't making everything a power struggle.

Lexi sat on the sofa, Gavin next to her with a sleeping Olivia resting in the crook of his arm. Lyn was down on the floor with Caroline. Heath and Tristan argued about some hockey teams. Everyone was so lazy. It was all so peaceful, Lexi could feel her eyes start to close of their own accord, the heat from Gavin's big body lulling her.

She must have dozed off, at least for a little while, because she woke to Ronald's voice in the doorway behind her.

"Okay, everybody, it's time." Ronald clapped his hands twice. "They say it's too cloudy outside, so we're going to do the shot by the fireplace."

Tristan took the sleeping Olivia from Gavin and began gently waking her with soft kisses. Lyn smoothed back Caroline's hair and put it in a barrette. Lexi stood up as everyone else did, all of them straightening their clothing.

"What's going on?" Lexi asked. "Time for what?"

Gavin walked over to grab his blazer from the chair he'd thrown it over. Andrew gave Lexi a smile and grabbed Caroline from Lyn, kissing her little fingers to stop her from grabbing the barrette Lyn had just fastened in her hair.

"A thing the *Wyoming Gazette* has been doing for decades with the governor on Christmas Day. Sort of a peek inside the life of Wyoming's first family. It used to be a bigger deal, but now it's mostly used for social media. They do a formal shot and some candids."

Lexi felt like the air had been sucked out of the room.

Lyn helped Heath adjust his tie. "People love it because there are pictures of us when we were young when Dad was first governor. Now that he's governor again, everyone is gaga over the then-and-now pics. You know how it is."

Lexi did know how it was. She also knew she couldn't be anywhere in this room while the press was here. The family wouldn't want her in the formal shot, but she couldn't take a chance on the candids either. She needed to get out before they got into the room.

"Good to see you, Gianna, you look lovely. Thanks for coming out on your Christmas." Ronald greeted the press members at the door. "Simeon. How are you and your camera? How's the wife?"

Fuck. She was too late.

Lexi stood there, planted, unable to figure out what she should do. Ronald chatted with the man and woman, obviously in his element. Simeon had already snapped a couple of pictures of Tristan and Caroline from the doorway.

Lexi would have to walk right by them to get out of here, and there was no way Ronald wouldn't introduce her. It simply wasn't in his nature. And if she demanded to not be in the photos, that was going to draw unwanted attention to her.

One thing she knew about the press was to not present them with anything that seemed like a mystery. That only gave them something to hound.

What was she going to do?

She reached up and pulled her hair more sharply along her face, covering as much of her features as possible. She kept her eyes pinned on the ground, trying to disappear in plain sight.

Think, Lexi. Figure out a plan.

She had nothing.

"Lexi, tell me what's wrong." Gavin wrapped his arm around her waist, and she turned toward him, putting her back to the press members.

"Gavin..."

He wasn't going to understand this. He was going to ask questions. She didn't have time; she didn't have an escape. Once the press noticed her or Ronald introduced her, there'd be no way of getting out of this without a scene. She stared at the front of his shirt, her heart thundering in her chest. Sweat pooled at the small of her back.

Gavin cupped her face in his hands. "Lexi. Look at me."

She did what he asked. She had no other choice.

"Tell me what you need. Let me help."

"I have to get out of here," she whispered.

"Why? Did Janeen say something to upset you?"

"No." She didn't have time to explain. She waved a hand toward the press who were now fully inside the living room. "I can't do this. I can't be here for this."

"Okay, we'll leave together." He ran his thumbs across her cheeks, but that made her panic worse. What if he'd smudged some of her makeup? What if the reporter or photographer recognized her? They'd have much more reason to.

They couldn't leave together, that would be too conspicuous. "No, you have to stay."

"But—"

"Gavin." She gripped his wrists. "I'm asking you for help. But I need you to give me the help *my* way, not yours."

He was taken aback by that, maybe even offended, but she had to give him credit, he recovered fast. "You're right. Okay, tell me what you need."

"I need to get out of here without those members of the press paying attention to me at all."

He didn't understand. She could tell he was resisting the urge to ask for clarification. But he nodded.

He kept himself between her and the photographers and walked her over to the table. He threw a folded white napkin over her shoulder.

"Grab a tray of food from the table and walk it out. If they look at you at all, they'll assume you're part of Dad's house staff. I'll distract them."

She wanted to say thank you, but he turned and walked away, grabbing little Caroline from Tristan and twirling her around so she laughed with glee. Immediately, the photographer recognized the money shot and began snapping pictures.

Lexi grabbed the tray, lowered her head, and walked out.

24

"If I'm not mistaken, your date stole your car. If that's not the Christmas spirit, I don't know what is."

Gavin sat at the dining room table, which had been cleared off by the staff—the actual staff, not including the pretend member—while the press had gotten the photos they wanted.

Andrew sat down on one side, handing him a tumbler of scotch, and Tristan sat down on the other. Dad and Janeen were doing a short interview about upcoming campaign stuff with the reporter and photographer in the formal living room. The twins were napping, and Heath and Lyn were with Fletcher on the far side of the living room watching *Die Hard*, an annual Christmas tradition Gavin had been looking forward to sharing.

Sharing with Lexi. Who was gone. Freaked out to the point that she'd taken his SUV and bolted a little over an hour ago.

"Don't get me wrong," Tristan said. "We like her better because she left you stranded here. And we already liked her a lot before."

They'd finished the pictures for the newspaper. Dad, to his

credit, hadn't lost any composure when he'd asked if Lexi wanted to be in the pictures and Gavin had told him she'd had to leave. Dad had immediately refocused the conversation, not bringing any further attention to her absence. Ever the politician.

"If you're looking for answers, I don't have them." He took a healthy sip of the scotch. "Something about the press being here freaked her out."

Andrew shrugged. "Maybe she values her privacy."

"The skid marks from the tires peeling out in the driveway would argue it's a tad more than that." It was an exaggeration, but not by much. "But with Lexi, you never know."

When he'd heard the truck in the driveway, he hadn't known what the fuck to think. Evidently, when she said she needed to *leave*, she'd been serious.

Tristan got up and poured himself his own drink from the wet bar. "Did you guys fight? You say something stupid?"

"No. She was fine." She'd been sleeping, for Christ's sake. Relaxed enough to turn off her mind for a few minutes, sitting up against him on the couch.

He'd had little Olivia sleeping in his other arm, and he'd been happy. His family surrounding him, he'd even been happy Janeen was here. She and Fletch had shared a smile and Gavin had known the two of them would be way happier than he and she had ever been. She and Fletcher didn't have any other family, which was why Dad kept inviting them to Zimmerman family stuff, not just because of political reasons. They'd been part of each other's lives for a long time. And probably would be for a long time to come.

Gavin was ready to make peace with that. Because Lexi gently snoozing next to him and Olivia lying in his arm had given him a glimpse of what his future could look like: holding a miniature version of Lexi while she slept instead.

And damned if the thought hadn't seemed so *right*. Like everything in his life was finally falling into place.

Five minutes later, Lexi had stolen his vehicle to bolt off the premises.

He scrubbed a hand down his face. "She wasn't upset at all. Not until the reporter and photographer got here."

Tristan sat back down beside him, drink in hand. "Look, you obviously like Lexi. Nobody is happier than us to see that. It's great that you brought her..."

"But that woman has secrets," Andrew finished for him.

Gavin was used to the two of them finishing each other's sentences. They'd been doing it since they were old enough to talk.

"I know that. She knows that. I had to accept that if I wanted to be with her, I was not going to have all the answers."

"Did you run her?" Andrew asked, the charming side of him gone.

Both his brothers had enough of Dad's personality to be able to dazzle damned near anyone when they wanted to. And they used that to their advantage all the time to get people to underestimate them.

But their alluring charm was just the surface. His brothers were both trained in weapons, close-quarters combat, and hostage rescue—civilian versions of what Gavin had done in the Special Forces. Zac Mackay had tried to recruit them into Linear multiple times, but they weren't interested.

Andrew and Tristan worked for Zodiac, a world-renowned tactical training and security business. They faced down danger every bit as much as Gavin did. They knew what they were talking about.

"Yes. Both name and prints. Everything came back clean."

Tristan and Andrew exchanged a look. Gavin knew they

were thinking what he'd first thought . . . that clean was sometimes more suspicious than dirty.

"Do you want us to look into her further for you, off the books?" Andrew asked. "Whatever it is, we'll get to the bottom of it, and unless it's something you need to know, then you never need to know."

Tristan shrugged and slapped him on the back. "And whatever skeletons we find in her closet, as long as they aren't a danger to anyone, we'll forget they exist, and you never need to know a thing."

Gavin thought about the man she'd met in that alley. How she'd given him money. He wanted to know what that was all about. But more, he wanted Lexi to trust him enough to tell him herself. Her secrets were important to her, and he'd told her he'd respect her need to keep them.

Although his brothers' plan was probably smarter in the long run.

He took another sip of his drink. "Thanks you guys, I appreciate it, but no. I told her I wouldn't push. Promised I would be there to help her in whatever way she needed."

Tristan chuckled. "Evidently her needs involved stealing your SUV today."

Gavin forced a smile but couldn't get Lexi's panicked face out of his mind.

"What was it exactly that set her off?" Andrew asked. "I was paying more attention to the girls than to Lexi. Did someone say something to her? Did she know the press people?"

"No." Gavin shook his head. "It was after Lyn told her about the yearly photo shoot."

"She had to know that none of us would expect her to be in the family photos if she didn't want to be," Tristan said.

"I don't think it was just the family photos. I think she didn't want to be in *any* photos at all." Gavin rubbed his eyes.

"Some sort of weird picture-taking phobia?" Andrew asked.

"Probably more like she didn't want her face to end up anywhere online," Gavin responded. She'd done the same sort of thing during that girls' night out. Quinn had tried to talk Lexi into being in the photo with them, but Lexi had refused. Made up a reason not to be.

Andrew let out a low curse. "Not wanting to have her picture online—to the point where she would steal a vehicle to get out of it—usually isn't good news, big brother."

Gavin rubbed his face again. "No it's not."

The twins had both done their fair share of private investigative work for Zodiac. Mostly they did close cover or special kidnap and ransom assignments, but they knew the signs of a guilty party.

Tristan sat up straighter. "Could she be married? A criminal on the run?"

"Her prints would've shown up if she had a record or any APB out on her. But married? Fuck. That had never occurred to me." But it should've.

"Hey." Andrew put his hand on Gavin's shoulder. "Let's not assume the worst. If there is anything that Noah and Marilyn's relationship has taught us, it's that someone can be married according to some piece of paper, but that marriage might be nothing but a living hell."

Gavin nodded. Their cousin Noah had fallen in love with a sweet, young woman whose life had been threatened by her abusive, estranged husband. She might have been legally married to him, but nobody in their right mind would've called the "marriage" anything less than a sham.

"Lexi and Marilyn are completely different." Gavin

gripped his glass. "I can't imagine Lexi putting up with any of the shit Marilyn did."

"Her nose has been broken," Andrew said. "I noticed that when she turned from the window. I think she wears makeup to keep it from being obvious."

Was that why she always had a ton of makeup on? To hide previous trauma to her face? "She does wear a lot of makeup."

Andrew shrugged. "Her and most of the female gender, so that's not unusual. And I agree that she doesn't show any of the classic signs of an abuse survivor like Marilyn."

"And if she was married, that would've come up when you ran her, right?" Tristan asked.

"It should've. But the system isn't perfect."

"Have there been any other men around?" Tristan pressed. "Has she made any suspicious calls? Texts?"

Gavin shook his head. "No. She doesn't own a phone."

Neither brother said anything. They didn't have to. Gavin had always thought it was strange she didn't have a phone.

Married? Jesus. Given how everything had gone down with Janeen, Lexi had to know he would've never slept with her if he'd known she was married. Could she be on the run from an abusive husband?

They sat in silence for a long minute. His brothers were probably trying as hard as he was to come up with something to make him feel better.

"I'll tell you one thing," Andrew finally said. "A couple times today when Lexi was laughing I could've sworn I knew her from somewhere."

"Yes! Damn it, I felt the exact same way." Tristan tapped the table with his palm multiple times. "But not when she was laughing. It was when she was giving Janeen a sly look. This little smirk. I swear I thought I'd met her before. I almost brought it up, but I was afraid you'd take me out and kick my ass for using that as a pickup line."

Gavin had to chuckle. "I might have. I don't know what to tell you guys about her looking familiar—I don't think you guys have ever run in the same circles. And you both need to stop looking at her so hard, or I will take you out and kick your asses."

But the fact was, Gavin didn't really know what circles Lexi had run in, did he? He didn't think Tristan or Andrew had met her before—they would've definitely remembered.

There was only one thing he knew for sure. He couldn't stay here any longer. He needed to find Lexi.

"Can one of you guys give me a ride back to my house before Dad and Janeen get finished? I don't want to go into all of this with them."

Especially since once again with Lexi, he had more questions than he did answers.

25

W as there any way she could've screwed this up worse? Lexi thumped her forehead against the steering wheel of Gavin's SUV where she'd parked it outside his house.

The SUV she'd *stolen*. She hadn't been a hundred percent certain she wouldn't get pulled over by a cop on her way home and arrested for grand theft auto. And could she really have blamed Gavin if he'd put out some sort of APB on her?

She'd acted like a complete ass and put him in an impossible situation. She'd gone out to the SUV to hide, but when she'd seen the remote starter sitting there, she hadn't let herself think about it. She'd just climbed over to the driver's side and left.

She didn't have a way of getting in touch with him to apologize. She thumped her head against the steering wheel again. Maybe the arresting officer would deliver a message for her before dragging her off to prison.

At least she was leaving the SUV at his house, although that was like slapping a Band-Aid over a gaping wound. Maybe the three-mile walk back to her apartment in town would give her a chance to think about what she'd done. Not just the running off in the middle of a Christmas family get-together, but the fact that she'd been there to begin with.

The fact that she couldn't seem to force herself to stay out of Gavin's life.

He made her happy. That was the long and short of it. There was nothing she liked more than hearing his gruff voice. He was so growly on the outside but so protective and considerate on the inside.

He'd bought her groceries. He'd watched over her during one of her insomnia comas, caring enough to call a doctor. He'd gotten her matching scarf and gloves and hat for Christmas. A green he'd said matched her eyes.

And what had she gotten him? Some condoms in a little box with bow on it. He'd laughed, then they'd used a couple last night.

She'd chickened out before giving him the other gift she'd found for him when Mac had sent her to pick up an order of locally made wine at the county market last week. She'd been walking around looking at the other vendors while they'd boxed up the order.

She'd found some wooden keychains with trees carved into them. Most of the carvings were Fraser firs, probably popular at Christmas. Some were round maple tree carvings. But one was very definitely a redwood.

Redwoods didn't make for the most interesting carving pattern. They were too tall and their trunks were too barren up until the top. But the second she'd run her fingers across it, she'd known she had to buy it for Gavin.

It was everything he was: strong, solid, steady.

Everything she wasn't.

She took it out of her small purse now, still wrapped in the plain tissue paper. She set it on the dash next to the SUV's remote starter key. She had no idea what Gavin would do with it when he found it. Maybe toss it in the trash. She couldn't blame him for that.

She got out, closing the door carefully behind her, and started her hike of shame back into town. She wrapped her jacket more firmly around her. Her hat, gloves, and scarf helped, but she still needed a real winter coat.

But every time she'd been about to buy one, she'd stopped. A proper Wyoming-winter coat was a couple hundred dollars —money she would need if she was going to run again anytime soon.

Invest in a coat if she was going to stick it out here as long as possible. Save the money if she was going to bolt soon.

But for God's sake, make a decision.

She was deep in thought when a car pulled up beside her. "Lexi?"

It was Dr. Anne.

"Hi." She gave the other woman a small, awkward wave. Jesus, there was no good excuse for her to be walking out here.

"Did your car break down? Are you okay?"

"Yeah, car problems." Something like that.

"I'm heading into town for my shift at the hospital. Please, let me give you a ride. That jacket doesn't look like it's meant for hikes."

"Sure. Okay."

Lexi got into Anne's car partly because she wasn't stupid enough to walk in the cold when there was another option and partly because by now Gavin would probably be on his way. The situation was bad enough without him tracking her down walking in the cold.

"Merry Christmas to you." Anne pulled back onto the road once Lexi was inside with her seatbelt on.

"Thanks. Same to you. Sorry you have to work."

The doctor smiled and gave a little shrug. "Occupational hazard. I got most of the morning off, so that's fine."

They drove in silence for a minute or two.

"Look, Lexi, I wasn't going to ask, because it's none of my business, but I want to make sure you're okay. The only thing out in the direction you could be coming from is the Linear Tactical property or Gavin's house. I know you weren't coming from the Linear property, so . . . did you and Gavin have a fight or something?"

Lexi stared out the window, unsure of exactly what to say. "No. It's really a long story and just know that Gavin's not at fault. He's a good man."

"Believe me, I know that. As a matter fact, I cannot ascertain under what circumstances Gavin Zimmerman would be allowing you to *walk* from his house back into town."

Lexi had to smile at that. Because she couldn't imagine circumstances in which he'd allow that either. "He doesn't know I was walking. I was returning his SUV."

"I see," Anne said in a way that obviously meant she didn't understand at all. Lexi couldn't blame her for being confused. "Does Gavin know you borrowed his SUV?" she asked after a beat.

Lexi shrugged. "I'm sure he does by now."

Anne let out a low chuckle, and Lexi turned to look at her. "You keep him on his toes, that's for sure. That man hasn't known what to do with himself since the moment you arrived in town. You've had him discombobulated from the first day."

"He didn't trust me." He had good instincts.

Anne glanced over at her. "Gavin doesn't trust anyone easily. None of the Special Forces guys do. But regardless, he was enamored with you."

Lexi let out a low laugh. "That's not the word I would've

used for it. He was watching me like I was some convicted criminal."

Again, good instincts.

Anne shook her head. "Gavin could've had any number of people from either the sheriff's office or from Linear helping him keep an eye on you. He was concerned you were taking advantage of Mac, and there's not a single person in this town who wouldn't have volunteered to take a shift or two to make sure that didn't happen."

"I'm really not trying to take advantage of Mac."

"Oh, I know. That became obvious to everyone about a week after you got here. If you had wanted to run off with the contents of the cash register, you had multiple opportunities to do that." Anne slowed down as they took one of the winding curves. "My point is, Gavin used that as an excuse to get close to you whenever possible. And yes, I'm sure he wanted you close to keep an eye on you. But he also just wanted you close."

"Gavin is a good man. One of the best I know."

"Amen to that," Anne said. "Stubborn. Gruff. Honest to a fault."

"That's why I have to stay away from him." The words were out of Lexi's mouth before she could stop them. "I don't deserve Gavin. I don't deserve any happiness."

Anne didn't say anything for a long minute. What could she say? Lexi huddled in on herself and stared out the window some more.

"I don't know you, Lexi," Anne finally said. "So I'm not going to pretend I understand what a statement like that means coming from you. But I know this. We believe in second chances around here. If it wasn't for second chances, Zac and I wouldn't be getting married in a month and a half."

"Not everybody deserves a second chance. At least I don't."

"If you think you don't, that probably proves you actually do."

Lexi started to argue but Anne held out a hand. "Listen, I had breakfast this morning with some of the Linear Tactical team. Aiden Teague and his fiancée, Violet."

"She owns Fancy Pants Bakery. Those treats are addictive."

"She does. I'm no dummy, and therefore she'll be invited to every holiday at my house until the end of time. But we also invited her brother Gabe and his fiancée, Jordan."

"Yeah, I've seen them around. She's quiet. He's got huge muscles."

"Yeah. Former Navy SEAL. And yes, Jordan is very quiet. I'm thankful she came to our house. And I was thankful to see her and Zac hug. Because for a lot of years Jordan believed she didn't deserve a second chance."

"What did she do?"

"She fell asleep behind the wheel eight years ago, ran a red light, and T-boned the car Zac's wife and toddler son were in. Killed them both. Becky was my best friend, and it was a tragic loss in every possible way."

"I'm sorry."

"Thank you, it's a complicated mix of emotions because I would give anything to have Becky and Micah back, but I'm also head over heels in love with Zac, so I won't deny that the past is what shaped my future."

"But what Jordan did was an accident."

"Yes it was. And I don't know what your circumstances are, so I can't speak to that. All I can say to you is this. The past shapes who we are, there's no denying that. But at some point, you have to let it go to create your future. Otherwise you're in a loop you can't ever get out of."

They drove in silence the rest of the short distance to town. Anne stopped in front of Lexi's apartment. "Thanks for the ride." She reached for the door handle, unsure of what else to say.

"Lexi." Anne reached out and touched her arm. "I hope I didn't say too much. Believe me, I know what it is to want to fly under the radar, and you have to do what's right for you. But give Gavin a chance. Whatever it is in your past, maybe he'd be able to look past it."

"Yeah, maybe." Asking that was too much even for him. "Thanks again."

"Listen, you should come out to the house for dinner or something. Zac is a master of cooking on the grill. He has it set up so he can cook out on the deck even in winter."

"Yeah, that sounds really nice. Thanks."

And it did sound really nice. Lexi got out and waved as Anne drove away. She stood there, cold. It really was time to choose: invest in the coat or leave.

26

Lexi studied the empty streets of Oak Creek after Anne drove off. The holiday lights stretching from one side of Main Street to the other would turn on later this afternoon as the sun went down. Right now, the majestic Tetons made a beautiful backdrop to the rather plain buildings of the town itself.

Oak Creek was a good place with good people. She never would've been interested in coming here in her old life, would've argued that a tiny town in the middle of Wyoming would have nothing useful to offer her. And honestly, maybe given who she'd been in her old life, that would've been true.

But never coming here, never experiencing this town where the main street was actually named Main Street, the mayor was an older lady who personally directed the placement of the Christmas lights each year, and where people grew up and left, but then came back because this place had somehow gotten into their blood . . . that would've been her loss.

Having never met these people would've been her loss.

She walked inside her apartment and took off her dress,

wanting to let it drop to the floor but knowing nobody would come and pick it up later, so she might as well clean it up herself now.

She hung her dress and slipped on leggings and a sweatshirt. And then she saw it. That blank envelope that had been sitting in the Eagle's Nest mailbox. It had spooked her this morning, doubled by Gavin walking up just as she'd seen it.

I never believed you for a second, you know.

He'd meant the words innocently, but she'd taken them as someone with a guilty conscience would—as an attack. Then he'd felt so bad about it, she'd forgotten the blank envelope that had started the panic in the first place.

Looking at it now sitting there so innocently on the counter, she could feel her breathing shallow out.

This was how it had started before when the stalker had found her. A blank envelope with a typed letter inside telling her she deserved to have a stalker for real. She deserved to be hurt for real. She deserved to understand how it really felt to have everything taken from her.

Sweat trickled down her back as she stared at the envelope. She needed to open it, but her body refused to cooperate. Her hands shook down by her side, not willing to move toward the envelope no matter how much her brain demanded it.

"Get yourself under control. It's just an envelope. Open it."

She stared at it way too long before finally grabbing it and ripping it open.

She opened the folded paper, her eyes falling to the first words.

You deserve . . .

She didn't read any further. She didn't have to. She deserved to be hurt. She deserved to lose everything.

The worst part was that it was true. She did deserve those

things. The paper fell from her numb fingers as she ran over to the sink and vomited.

The stalker had found her. She'd been so careful, but he'd still found her. She needed to leave—had to get out of here. Right now. It might already be too late.

She wanted to rip it up and throw it into the trash can, but she couldn't stand the thought of it still being in her house.

Her heart thundered in her chest as she looked around. She didn't know where she would go, but she couldn't stay here.

She ran for her clothes and her suitcase, but stopped.

Would Gavin believe her if she showed him the letter? If she drove back over to his house and waited for him and explained... everything, would he at least believe her about this?

She walked back over and picked up the letter. If he read this, would he take the threat seriously?

She forced herself to open the paper again and look at it. Steeled herself to get through it.

You deserve...

She swallowed and kept reading.

...the chance to ring in the New Year right. As a valued customer of Cowboy State Liquor, we'd liked to offer the Eagle's Nest our priority delivery service . . .

What?

She sank down on the edge of her bed. Not a letter from the stalker at all. But she was still shaken. Still spooked.

Still reminded that there was someone out there who wanted to hurt her, *destroy* her. It didn't matter how innocent the letter was, she couldn't keep it here. She didn't even want it in her trash can.

She would take it outside and throw it in the big trash. It wouldn't be able to hurt her there.

She was still shaky as she rushed toward her stairs, tripping and barely catching herself on the way down. She grabbed for the door handle, her breath sawing in and out of her chest as she ran outside.

She was in her socks, didn't have any shoes on, didn't have on a jacket. The cold bit at her as she stared at the piece of paper in her hand.

You deserve...

You deserve...

You deserve...

She did deserve everything that stalker had promised to do to her. Throwing away this letter wasn't going to change that.

She couldn't seem to force her body to go forward, and she couldn't figure out how to go back inside. She was frozen in place.

Couldn't move forward. Couldn't go back.

She closed her eyes, trying to suck air back into her lungs.

"*Lexi.*"

Was that really Gavin's voice, or had her mind actually cracked? She shook her head.

"Lexi, tell me how I can help you."

The same words he'd said during panic attack number one today. She still wasn't sure if he was really here or if she was hallucinating. At this moment, either seemed possible.

She held up the fisted letter without opening her eyes. "It has to go in the big trash. It can't be inside my house. I can't have it in there."

The paper left her hand. She opened her eyes.

Gavin was here. Strong, solid, steady.

"You go inside. I'll throw this in the big trash."

She nodded and turned back around. Gavin would take care of it.

She sat on the stairs, waiting for him. But every second she got herself back under control was more time to realize how ridiculous this all had to seem to him. He'd found her outside in her stockinged feet, no coat, panicked over the need to throw away a letter from an alcohol vendor.

She looked up at him as he came through the door. "You have to think I'm crazy."

She'd basically given him a checklist of reasons today: freaked out at his dad's house, stolen his vehicle, now this. He could take his pick.

He sat down on the stairs beside her. "I think you were having a panic attack outside, the way you were earlier today."

"Did you look at the letter?"

He nodded. "It didn't seem...problematic in any way. Was there something I missed?"

"Only that I'm crazy."

"Having a panic attack doesn't make you crazy."

"I left you and ran off with your car. You're not mad about that?"

He slid his hat off his head and dropped it on the stair beside him. "I'm not nearly as mad at that as I am that you left the damned SUV at my house rather than bringing it here. Did you walk from my house?"

"I was going to. But Anne saw me and gave me a ride."

"Good."

They sat in silence for a long moment. "I suppose I owe you an explanation." He had to have so many questions.

"No." He turned toward her. "I asked you to tell me what you needed so I could help you. Earlier today you needed to get out of that house so your picture wasn't taken. I'm not going to pretend like I understand why, but I don't have to understand. Like now. I don't understand what's happening with that letter, but I know it's something that has you terri-fied, so I want to help if there's any way that I can."

"Even if I don't tell you why?" Because she couldn't bear to see the disappointment in his eyes if she told him the truth.

"I do hope someday you'll tell me. But yes, I want to help regardless of whether you tell me or not." He looked away, pulling slightly at the collar of his jacket. "There's really only one question that, for me, needs to be answered now. And before I ask it, I want you to know that your response doesn't mean I can't be with you if you say yes."

"Okay." She would try to answer as honestly as she possibly could. She owed him that much.

Those brown eyes pinned hers. "Are you married?"

That was so far from what she'd expected him to say, it ate away the rest of her residual panic from the letter. "Married? *What*?"

"My cousin Noah's girlfriend was married, and her husband was abusive. She was trying to stay out of his clutches when she met Noah. And I was wondering if perhaps your situation was similar. If so, I'd like to help. It doesn't matter if you're still married to him, I want to help."

She closed her eyes briefly before opening them again. Gavin was such a good man. A protector. A hero. "No, I'm not married. I've never been married. But thank you."

"But there's something going on. Something that makes you afraid. Earlier at Dad's house. And right now with that letter."

She had to tell him something. "I got into a little trouble a couple of years ago. I'm away from it now, but sometimes it seems like the past is just waiting for me to screw up."

That was completely true without giving him any usable details at all.

And he knew it.

He let out a sigh. "I want to protect you, Lexi."

"I know you do."

"Let me. You don't have to tell me anything else. Just let me be here with you."

Could she do that? Could she take the next few months, save up the money she needed while enjoying having someone like Gavin care so much about her.

Buy the coat. Stay awhile.

Yes. Maybe it made her weak and selfish—again—but she wanted this time with him looking at her like she was someone worthwhile.

Maybe it would keep her warm in the future, in all the years when she would be alone.

27

She woke up in Gavin's arms the next morning and every morning after that for the next month.

She didn't try to hold herself distant from him. Didn't keep one foot out the door. Yeah, she had to rush into the bathroom to touch up her industrial-grade makeup each morning. And she might not have told him anything more about herself— and he was careful not to ask—but she gave herself over to just being with him.

It was like nothing she'd ever felt before in her whole life.

She was smiling all the time. Laughing all the time. Stealing kisses behind the Eagle's Nest. Having breakfast with him at the Frontier Diner. He'd taken her for dinner more than once at New Brothers Pizza—and the taste was as good as the scents that wafted into her apartment all the time.

And she slept.

Nearly every single night for at least a few hours, she actually slept. Part of it was knowing he was there and would keep her safe. He might not feel the same way about protecting her once he found out who she really was, but she knew without a doubt that right now, her Redwood would stand firm against anything that threatened her.

His deep voice lulled her to sleep every night. Her personal, nonmusical lullaby.

She tried to stay awake, to listen to whatever story he was telling. It wasn't that she didn't find his tales interesting—she truly loved getting to know him. But something about lying against his chest in his bed, her body replete and relaxed from their lovemaking, listening to that voice . . . her brain gave up the fight of forcing her to stay awake.

Of course, Gavin teased her about it constantly during the day, accused her of giving him an inferiority complex. But he always said it with a smile. And she knew he would give himself a complex a dozen times over if it meant she got the rest she needed.

God, how she loved this new pattern they were in.

She smiled over at him where he sat in his booth for lunch. Since Quinn had started teaching college again full-time, Lexi was back to being the only lunch waitstaff, but she didn't mind. They'd hired a new cook, so Mac was helping at the front of the house. And winter meant things were generally slower.

Gavin was there to talk to her nearly every day, to the point where Zac kept threatening to fire him from Linear Tactical. Or at least he had when she and Gavin had gone over to Zac and Anne's for dinner last week.

A date. A normal couple thing. The only one Lexi could ever remember being on that hadn't involved the press in some way.

Yet another way her aunt and uncle had pulled her puppet strings. The dates Lexi had gone on over the years that they'd carefully orchestrated. The nights she'd gone home with a man and wondered how the press had found her the next morning. Looking back at it now, it was probably because Cheryl and Nicholas had tipped them off.

The more press Lexi got, the more popular she became, the more money she made. That they stole.

But that wasn't a factor anymore.

The look of pleasant surprise on Gavin's face when she'd agreed to have dinner with him at Zac and Anne's had made the evening sweeter. He wanted to do this sort of stuff with her but was afraid to ask, she realized. Afraid to tip this delicate balance between them.

But she wanted to do this stuff with him also.

Her smile slipped a little. Wasn't this the same selfish behavior that had gotten her in trouble in her old life? She carried her tray to the back.

Two years ago, a sexy security expert had started working on the set of *Day's End*. Lexi had found him attractive, but he'd only had eyes for the show's producer, Chloe Jeffries.

Instead of accepting that with any sort of dignity or grace, Lexi had sabotaged her own trailer, made it look like a stalker was after her, and insisted Shane guard her since *she* was the one in danger.

And then Chloe and Chloe's best friend, Nadine, had nearly been killed because of Lexi's selfishness when the real stalker went after them. Poor Nadine had scars—physical and undoubtedly emotional ones too—because of the selfish choices Lexi had made.

Lexi set her tray on the counter next to the dishwasher to be loaded, then leaned on it, shoulders hunched.

At the time she'd thought she wanted Shane for herself, but she realized now that hadn't been it at all. She'd just wanted someone of her own. Someone who looked at her with that protective gaze—the way Shane had with Chloe.

The way Gavin did with her.

Someone who showed up at the end of every shift to make sure she made it home safely. Someone who made sure her cupboards were full. Who held her while she slept. Who cleared out a drawer for her to keep her stuff in his bathroom.

Someone who made her laugh, and made her sleep. Someone who had nothing to gain by knowing her, but showed up anyway.

The irony of her whole existence was that she'd never truly been happy as an actress. It had come easily to her, and she'd made a lot of money doing it, but she would've given the fame and wealth up in a heartbeat to have what she had here in Oak Creek: a job she enjoyed, a community that cared so much about each other.

Gavin.

She curled around herself more. He wouldn't recognize the person she'd been two years ago, and not just because of all the differences her makeup and broken nose made. He wouldn't recognize the selfish shrew who'd nearly gotten two other people killed. He wouldn't tolerate that person for an instant.

But that was who Lexi was. Had been. And no amount of screaming *I've changed! I've changed!* actually changed anything in the past.

She placed a stack of dishes in the dishwasher cart and grabbed the faucet hose to spray them off.

She was so familiar with his touch that she didn't startle when Gavin's hands gripped her hips from behind and his lips nuzzled her neck. "What would it take for me to talk you into a quickie in Mac's bathroom?"

She closed her eyes and breathed in. Breathed *him* in. She'd given up all rights to happiness with her choices two years ago, but she would steal as many moments of it as she could anyway. Still selfish, but she couldn't resist.

"Mac will definitely fire me. But I guess if you get fired and I get fired, we can both be in the unemployment line together." She shifted her hips back to feel his hardness against her. She was rewarded by the sound of him sucking in his breath, then nipping at her ear.

"I promise I'll be so fast Mac won't notice you're gone."

"You're not supposed to be back here, you know. What would the good citizens of Oak Creek say if they could hear you now, Sheriff Redwood? Propositioning me." She poked her ass back against him again.

"It's a cold Tuesday, and you've got barely any customers. The good citizens of Oak Creek are at home or at work where they belong."

She loved this playful side of him. It had been coming out more and more over the past month.

"Lexi, you've got a two-top that just came in."

At Mac's words from the swinging door leading out to the bar, Gavin let her go. He might talk a good dirty game, and would probably act on it, but he was a gentleman first and would never do anything that might harm her reputation.

She was in love with this man.

"Whoa, careful there!" Gavin laughed and grabbed the wild hose out of her hand, stopping the spray of water ricocheting off the wall in front of them. "Better stick with your day job and not apply for a firefighter position."

She *loved* him.

Was she really that surprised? She'd been half in love with him since she'd seen him in that bar in Reddington City.

He shut off the water and turned her in his arms. "Hey, you okay?"

She wanted to say the words but swallowed them. Telling him that would be the height of selfishness on a level she couldn't justify. So she kissed him. And was tempted to drag him back to Mac's bathroom and make good on his dirty threat.

"Lexi," Mac called from the front. "Do I need to put a lock on this door to keep Zimmerman out? I'm trying to run a business here."

They broke apart laughing, and Lexi rushed to the front, grabbing her tray, Gavin right behind her.

"Sorry, Mac, I had to make a change in my order." Gavin grinned at the old man as he rushed by.

Mac rolled his eyes. "You two are like a couple of teenagers, I swear."

Gavin's laughter rang out, and nearly everyone in the place turned to look at him, Lexi included. What a beautiful sound.

Gavin didn't seem to notice, just kissed her on the nose, then went back to his seat at his booth.

Lexi took orders and brought everybody's food out. She flirted with Gavin a little bit more before he announced he had to get back to Linear before he really did get fired. Everyone there was getting ready for Zac and Anne's destination wedding next week on San Amado, part of the Channel Islands off the coast of California. Gavin had asked Lexi multiple times to come with him as his guest, but she'd said no.

She wanted to say yes. There was so much about it she wanted to say yes to. Seeing her friends get married, warm weather on a tropical island, a chance to snorkel—one of her favorite pastimes, one she hadn't so much as thought about for the past two years much less done.

And to do it all with Gavin? She couldn't think of a single thing in the world she'd like more. But that would be pushing it too far, so she'd said no.

She kissed him on the cheek, and he told her he would see her tonight. She grabbed another tray and headed back to the kitchen. She'd barely set it down before someone squawked up front.

"No, I need to see her myself! Where is she?"

Was that *Wavy*?

Lexi left the tray on the counter and rushed back out front. "What's going on?"

Gavin and Mac flanked Wavy. She stood there, face ashen, lips trembling between them.

"See?" Mac said. "She's fine. Right here."

"Wavy, what the hell is wrong?" Gavin asked.

Wavy ignored them both. She pressed a hand to her stomach and let out a huge breath. "Oh thank God."

Lexi rushed forward, grabbed Wavy by the arms. "What? What happened?"

Wavy held up her phone. "I— You—" She let the phone drop back to her side as she trailed off.

"What in tarnation is going on here?" Mac threw up his hands. "If you kids drive my blood pressure back up, I'm going to make you all come to my cardiologist appointment and explain."

"Wavy, I don't understand." Lexi squeezed her arms. "Is someone hurt? What happened?"

Wavy still looked shaken. "No. I got your . . . text about us not being able to have dinner and . . . I was concerned."

Lexi had no idea what text Wavy was talking about. But it was something that was making the normally calm and competent woman act completely erratic.

"You got a text from Lexi?" Gavin asked.

Everybody knew Lexi didn't have a cell phone.

"I, uh, I meant a message." Wavy stepped closer to Lexi. "Can I talk to you in the back?"

Mac shook his head and walked off muttering, but Gavin

was still looking back and forth between Lexi and Wavy, trying to figure out what was going on.

"Do you want me to stay?" he finally asked.

"No," Wavy answered for her, voice tight. Then she turned to him with an obviously forced smile. "Girl stuff."

Not girl stuff, Lexi realized. *Alexandra Adams stuff.*

Gavin looked ready to argue, protective as ever. Lexi touched his arm. "It's no big deal. Get back to work before you get fired. I'll see you tonight."

He obviously didn't want to go, but he didn't have an option when Wavy grabbed Lexi's arm and pulled her to the back. She didn't stop until they were in Mac's office, and Wavy turned and shut the door.

"What?" Lexi asked. "What happened?"

"You're dead," Wavy said.

Wavy held up her phone and spun it around so that Lexi could read the news report.

Disgraced former television star Alexandra Adams dies in fire.

Lexi took the phone and read the rest of the article from an entertainment news site. According to the report, she'd died in a meth lab explosion along with two other people.

Great. Not only a fake death, but a drug-related one also.

"The article said they couldn't identify the bodies yet, but they had a witness who said she saw you go in." Wavy was pacing back and forth. "I completely freaked out, in spite of it being a gossip rag rather than a legit news source. I thought maybe they'd gotten hold of the story early."

Lexi reached up to rub the back of her neck where tension had settled. "I can attest I didn't die in some drug house explosion in . . . where did they say it happened? I didn't read far enough. LA? New York?"

Wavy took the phone Lexi held out to her. "That's what

really freaked me out. They said it happened in Reddington City."

Lexi grabbed the phone again. *Reddington City?*

"What?" Wavy asked.

Oh God. "It's too close."

"Too close for what?"

"Just . . . Reddington City is so close. I didn't expect that."

The stalker was hunting her again and wanted her to know he'd picked up her trail. He knew she'd been in Reddington City recently. Otherwise orchestrating a fake death there wouldn't make any sense.

"Since it's so close, are you going to go and set the record straight? You don't have to let them know you're living in Oak Creek."

That was exactly what the stalker wanted, for Lexi to go out in the open. "No. Law enforcement will figure it out. I'm just going to stay here and keep my head down."

And pray the stalker didn't find her.

28

That haunted look was back in Lexi's eyes. It had been so absent for the past month that Gavin had almost forgotten how difficult it was to see her features pinched and guarded. To see her withdraw in on herself.

She wasn't sleeping again.

He hadn't taken for granted one single hour that she'd slept in his arms since Christmas. He'd known her trust was a precious gift and had treated it as such.

And found it highly amusing that it was his stories about being in the army, arguably the most interesting parts of his life, that were quickest to lull her. He was never offended—the exact opposite. He loved that the sound of his voice helped her feel safe enough to rest. Loved that he could in some way help her brain shut off and stop fighting all its demons.

He would tell every story he had, then start making some up like he was a fucking Grimm brother, if it meant she could sleep.

But for the past six days—since Wavy had run into the Eagle's Nest in a panic—sleep had been nearly nonexistent for Lexi.

At first, he'd thought the two women had gotten into some sort of fight, but he'd seen them both since, and there hadn't been any ill feelings toward one another. They'd chatted, smiled, even hugged.

But something had triggered both women that day. Wavy had seemed convinced Lexi was . . . what? Hurt? Dead? And she'd refused to accept his or Mac's word that she was fine, insisting on seeing Lexi herself.

Why?

As always, it came back to Lexi's secrets.

He was done with them. Her secrets were costing too high a price, and Lexi was paying it with her physical and emotional health. This couldn't continue.

It wasn't about him needing to know all the details for his own curiosity. This was about him being able to protect the woman he was falling in love with.

He could barely admit these feelings to himself, much less share them with her, until he knew she was safe from whatever haunted her.

But right now, his hands were tied for a few days. He was on his way out of town for Zac and Anne's wedding. The whole Linear crew was on their way to Reddington City to take a plane to the island off the coast of California, courtesy of country music superstar—and friend—Cade Conner.

But Gavin had a separate stop to make first. He pulled into the same garage he'd used on Christmas Day with Lexi. Tristan's truck was already here at Dad's house, although nobody else was.

As expected, Gavin found his brother in the kitchen making himself a sandwich. The guy was thirty, but he and Andrew both still ate like they were on the high school football team.

Gavin slapped him on the shoulder as he walked by. "You are nothing if not predictable, Tits."

Tristan took another bite and rolled his eyes at the nickname that had stemmed from their mother's love of the musical *A Chorus Line*. The song "Dance: Ten; Looks: Three" with its iconic chorus about "tits and ass" had immediately become Gavin's nickname for his brothers, since their names began with T and A.

"Ian says he's going to bill you by the hour, that I'm one of his best men, and you're going to cause his company to go under."

"Right. Tell DeRose I'll come bail him out of the poor-house when that happens."

Which wouldn't be anytime soon. Ian DeRose was a billionaire. He might choose to work on the frontline for Zodiac Tactical, his security company, but it wasn't because he needed the paycheck.

Tristan took a bite of his sandwich. "What's up, Uncle Gabbin?"

"I'm heading out this afternoon to the Channel Islands for Zac and Anne's wedding. I'll be gone for four days."

"Okay, good for them. I assume I'm not invited because Zac's still butt-hurt over the fact that Andrew and I won't join Linear."

"Probably. But I need you here anyway." Gavin grabbed himself a water bottle out of the fridge and sat down on one of the kitchen island stools. "I'd like to take you up on the offer you and Andrew made at Christmas."

Tristan set down his sandwich. "Lexi."

"Did you already look into her?"

"No, but only out of deepest respect for you, believe me. We were both beyond tempted."

"I appreciate it. But it's time. Past time. I don't want to wait until after this weekend. I'm hoping that by the time I'm back, you'll have actionable intel."

"No problem, I'm on it. What made you change your mind? Trouble with her?"

"I can't protect her if I don't know what I'm up against. Something definitely has a chokehold on her, and it's time to eliminate that." He slid his phone over to Tristan and tapped the screen. "I'll send you the picture. But start with this guy."

"Who's he?"

"He's the guy she pays in cash once a month." Gavin had followed her again two days ago. This time, he'd made sure to get good photos of the man she met with.

"Does he give her anything for the cash?"

Gavin shook his head. "No. It's not a sale. I don't know what it is."

"Blackmail?" Tristan studied the picture.

"That's what I'm thinking." And if that was the case, it was going to stop.

"All right, I'm on it."

"Also, I know this is below your pay grade, but I need you to dig up any events that happened six days ago."

Tristan raised an eyebrow. "*Any* event? Can you be a little more specific?"

Gavin told him about Wavy's panic at the Eagle's Nest last week. "Everything was fine until that point, then Lexi's emotional stability went to shit. It's not something between the two of them, I checked. I don't know what it is, but it's something."

"That's still pretty vague."

"I thought maybe if you IDed the guy in the picture, that might lead to something more specific."

"Maybe." Tristan took another bite of his sandwich. "Anything else you can give me?"

Gavin scrubbed a hand down his face. He didn't want to cross this line, but he was willing to if it meant making sure Lexi was safe.

"Yeah. Three days ago, at oh nine thirty, if you run the phone records on the Eagle's Nest, I think you might get some info."

"Now that's *very* specific."

"I stopped by the bar, and Lexi was on the phone in Mac's office. She saw me and shut the door."

"That might not mean anything. She could've been ordering more booze or something."

Gavin nodded. "Maybe. Just check it. Between IDing that guy and the phone call, I think you'll be able to piece something together."

Tristan let out a sigh. "Are you sure this is what you want to do, Gavin? There's no coming back from this."

No. "Yes. I have to keep her safe."

"And you want me to keep an eye on her while you're at the wedding, don't you? That's why we didn't handle all this over the phone."

Gavin shot him a grin. "You always were the smartest of my siblings."

They both laughed at that. Lyn was off-the-charts smart when it came to languages, and Andrew could do complex math equations in his head. Tristan and Gavin were both smart, but not like either of them.

But Tristan's past was what made him perfect to help right now. Both of them knew it, though they didn't say it.

"I'll keep your woman safe, big brother. And hopefully, find some clues as to what the hell is going on."

Gavin slapped him on the shoulder. "Meanwhile, I'll be partying my ass off on a tropical island with my buddies."

Wishing the entire time he was back in Oak Creek.

"Lexi, why don't you come have a sit-down here with me."

"I'm working here, Mac."

"You trying to convince me that bar needs wiping down again? Or that floor needs to be swept again? Or those glasses rearranged? We haven't had a customer in here damn near all day. Come sit down."

She didn't want to sit down. At least doing all that other stuff, she could forget about the five-hundred-pound rock currently residing in her chest.

She glanced over at Gavin's empty booth again, for the millionth time since he'd left this morning.

"He's not there."

Lexi side-eyed Mac. "I'm aware, thanks." She turned to go back behind the bar.

"Why are you here, Lexi?"

She shook her head with a sigh. "Because this is my job."

"Come sit down with me."

"Mac, come on. I don't want—"

"Sit with me, Alexandra."

It took a second for the name to register. Then the bottom fell out of the pit of her stomach.

Mac *knew*.

In all the weeks she'd been here, he'd never given any indication he knew her actual identity. Nothing more than knowing she was associated with Hollywood somehow.

She froze, then walked over and locked the front door so no one else could come in. Wiping her hands on her apron, she took a seat across from Mac at one of the booths.

He slid a magazine toward her, open to a page near the back. "That's not a very flattering picture of you."

She glanced down. It was an older picture of her on her

way to the courthouse for her trial. "No, the worse the picture is, the more the press likes to run it. How long have you known who I really am?"

"Believe it or not, I just figured it out this week."

"Markus didn't tell you when he asked you to give me a job?"

Mac shook his head. "Nope. All he said was he had a former friend who needed a job, no questions asked. I didn't know if you'd be male or female, black or white, old or young until you showed up."

She leaned back against the booth with a thump. "Why? Why would you do that?"

Mac shrugged. "Because that's what you do when family asks you for something. It doesn't matter that I haven't seen Markus in probably twenty years, he's still family."

"I suppose you want more information about me now. You have questions."

He folded up the magazine and slid it to the side. "No."

"No? That's it? Just... no?"

"One thing I've learned running this bar over the years, especially since those Linear Tactical people moved into town... sometimes you don't ask questions."

Mac ran a hand over his dark, bald head. "Hell, somebody was kidnapped out of our parking lot a couple months ago, and the boys had to go all the way to Egypt to get her back. I didn't ask any questions. Almost a year ago, a girl came in and shot the fuse box with an arrow. An *arrow*. Now that was a little tricky explaining to the insurance company, but I did it, and I didn't ask any questions."

"So you don't have questions about me?"

Mac leaned back in the booth and studied her for a long minute. "I watched your show a few times. I liked you as Tia Day. I liked you because you stood up for those who couldn't stand up for themselves. You fought evil when other people quit."

"That was a role, Mac. I was just the actress."

"Maybe. But I think there was a lot of you in that role."

Lexi reached over and tapped the magazine on the side of the table. "And what about this? You know why I was going to the courthouse that day? Do you know why I went to prison?"

"I think you made a shitty decision. You aren't the first person in the world to do that, and you won't be the last. I think you did your time, you learned from it"—he tapped the magazine—"and that's not who you are anymore, literally or figuratively."

"You're a lot quicker to forgive than most people." She grabbed the magazine and opened it up to the pages about her again. It was about her "death" last week. As usual, the article was slanted. Carefully selected "facts" strung together to make her look as bad as possible. They'd made it sound like it was her fault. That she'd deliberately faked her own death, once again trying to get attention.

Mac slid the paper from her. "It's those people's job to keep as much drama floating around as possible. Their opinion doesn't matter."

That they could agree on. She nodded. "Their opinion doesn't matter to me, not anymore. But they're not the only people who have a low opinion of me. Or would if they knew the truth."

"Is that what you think? That people around here won't give you a second chance?"

She shrugged. "Not wanting to have anything to do with me wouldn't be a sign of intolerance on their part, it would be good judgment."

"Don't you think you ought to let them make that decision? Gavin especially?"

Definitely. "Maybe."

"But there's more, isn't there? You being here in Oak Creek isn't just about making a stupid choice two years ago, is it? I always knew you were running from something."

"Not the law. I'm not running from cops."

"I know you're not running from the law because you've been making a call to a parole officer once a month from my office since you've been here."

"How did you know?" She'd always tried to schedule them when Mac wouldn't be around.

"My phone still lists the calls that are made each month on the bill. Very old school."

She stared down at her hands. "I should've told you. I'm sorry. But I'm not on the run."

"Oh, I think you very much are on the run. Just not from the law."

"Maybe." She looked up into that weathered face. Steady, brown eyes stared her down.

"Why are you here rather than on that island with all your friends, Lexi? That's my question when I ask *why are you here*."

"I—" She swallowed, hardly able to form a sentence. "I needed to be here to help you. To work."

"I was running this bar a long time before you got here, and I'll be running it again if you decide it's not what you want. I don't need you here every single weekend. If I get tired, I'll just close."

"Mac—"

"It's time to tell him. Not just the part about you being in jail, the part that's got that look of fear in your eyes. Whatever it is."

"If I tell him about my past, he won't look at me the same."

"Is that better than not looking at you at all? If you have to run and be alone?" Mac reached his wrinkled, dark hand across the table and grabbed hers. "Who you were then is not who you are now. Gavin will come around. But the other, the *bad*, you've got to deal with that before it deals with you."

"I—"

"For a month, right after Christmas, I watched you blossom, young lady. Your eyes twinkled. You laughed and looked full and rested. You still worked hard. But you didn't work like the hounds of hell were going to catch you if you didn't."

He let go of her hand and touched the magazine. "That changed last week. You got that scared look back in your eye. It's because of this, isn't it? Them reporting you died spooked you in some way."

"I have a stalker." She blurted the words out before she could stop herself. "A real one this time. I'm not making it up. That's who I'm running from. I think he had something to do with that report, trying to get me to go public and set the record straight."

She waited for him to roll his eyes, to tell her all the reasons why it was unlikely that she had a stalker. That she was imagining things, or crying wolf again.

But he didn't. "You need to tell Gavin."

"The person stalking me is dangerous, Mac. For real."

"People around here can handle danger."

"People around here don't know who I am. They won't care about me once they do."

"People around here don't know Alexandra Adams, and you're right, they probably don't care about her at all. But they do know Lexi Johnson, and *her* they will want to help."

"I don't know, Mac. That's a lot to ask of anyone."

"Give them a chance."

She shrugged. "I want to. I . . . I don't want to lose everything I've built here."

"Why don't you go out to the wedding? There's not going to be much business here all weekend with that crew gone."

"I missed the flight."

"Let's see if we can't get you on another flight. It's on me. God knows I've got the money to splurge a little."

"I don't know, Mac. I don't even know if Gavin will want to see me. The past week, he's been kind of distant. Cold."

"I reckon that's because he's watched the same thing I have: you getting scared out of your mind again. He can't stand to see you go back to that. Can't stand to see you retreat back into that shell. That boy loves you."

"What?"

"Enough that he's got his brother out sitting in the parking lot, making sure you're all right."

"*What*?" She ran over to the window. There was only one vehicle in the parking lot, and sure enough someone was sitting in it. "I've got to go talk to him."

"First, here." Mac walked over, holding out a cell phone. "I know it's not a new or fancy one, but it works. And it's in my name, so no one will be looking for you with it."

Tears welled to her eyes. "Mac, I—"

"Take it." He took her hand and placed the phone in it. "We can take the fees for it out of your paycheck every month if you want. But it's about time you have a way to call one of us if you need us. More than that, you need to believe we'll come for you if you do."

She threw her arms around the old man. "Thank you, Mac."

He patted her back awkwardly. "Okay, okay. Let's not get carried away. Now go out there and talk to your beau's brother. And then let's get you to that island so you can give your man your phone number."

She put on her coat then ran out outside. Sure enough, there was Tristan, sitting in a truck, working on a computer.

She tapped on the window, raising an eyebrow. "What are you doing out here?"

He looked surprised to see her. "Gavin asked me to keep an eye on you. Make sure you were okay. I was going to come inside, but I thought it might be too obvious since he just left today."

A thought occurred to her. "Did he have you watching me to make sure I was okay or to make sure I didn't run?"

Tristan shrugged. "Probably a little of both, honestly."

"Well, I'm officially giving you the weekend off."

"Lexi . . ." Tristan cleared his throat. "I can't do that. He's counting on me. If something were to happen to you while—"

"I'm giving you the weekend off because I'm going to the Channel Islands. I'm going to Gavin. If I can get a flight."

"You are?"

She nodded. "He and I need to talk."

"Hell, if a flight is all you need, I can get you to him no problem. But he'll owe me one."

"So will I."

"Then let's do this."

29

"I want to thank all of you for leaving the cold mountains of Wyoming to come celebrate our nuptials on a beautiful, exotic island." Zac held his glass to the room full of family and friends who loved him and Anne both.

"You know your true friends are the people who are willing to suffer like this for you!" Finn called out, his arm wrapped around Charlie as always.

The night was winding down, and they were all enjoying being together.

No missions, no danger, just each other. It didn't happen often enough.

There were a few of their group missing: Lyn and Heath were over in Egypt checking out a potential job for her. Wyatt had received a cryptic message from an informant he worked with every once in a while and had gone to Las Vegas. Dorian and Ray . . . well, no one had actually expected them to come.

And Lexi was missing. Gavin was amazed at how much he wanted her here to experience this with him. He should've kidnapped the damn woman.

Everywhere around Gavin were couples. The amount of

love in this room was humbling for a group of soldiers who'd been a lot better at fighting than they had been at interpersonal relationships. Each warrior knew he'd been blessed beyond measure by the woman now standing so proudly next to him. There wasn't anything in the world these men wouldn't do for the women they loved, no hell they wouldn't walk through to protect them.

Although Gavin had always appreciated their love in theory, it was only now, looking at the empty seat beside him, that he could recognize his feelings for what they were. He loved Lexi. And he wasn't going to let her keep her distance anymore.

"Truly, you are our family." Anne stood up next to Zac, and everyone quieted down to listen to the soft-spoken doctor. "A family I thought I would never have. You took care of this man when I wasn't around and have been doing it ever since. You guys are all trouble, but you're our trouble, and we love you. Thank you for being here." She raised her glass. "To friends who are family and family who are friends."

"Hear, hear!" Everybody clinked their glasses and hugged each other, laughing and talking.

"Can we talk about the real news?" Baby finally called out. "The fact that Noah has a hickey on his neck? Forget the wedding stuff!"

Gavin chuckled at the sight of his normally stoic cousin, who suffered from PTSD, grinning hugely with his arm around sweet, quiet Marilyn. Whose face looked like it was on fire.

"You're all going to have to keep your jealousy in check," Noah said.

Marilyn slapped at his chest, but it was easy to see the love radiating in her eyes. Nobody let the cat out of the bag that Noah had a big proposal planned for tomorrow. He'd already enlisted all the guys for help, so evidently they'd be spending the morning helping him spell out *will you marry me* on the beach.

As all former Special Forces soldiers did at least once in their life.

His phone buzzing in his pocket drew Gavin's attention away from the reverie. A text from Tristan.

I have a present for you.

Gavin let out a breath and responded. *Did you find something on Lexi?*

Better.

He couldn't think of anything that would be better than knowing what danger Lexi faced. But he'd give his brother the benefit of the doubt.

OK. Hit me.

You really owe Ian one for this.

Gavin wasn't sure why Tristan had gotten Ian involved at this point, but there was no doubt that DeRose had contacts in all sorts of places—legal and illegal—that Linear and Gavin would never have. So bringing him in now probably wasn't a bad idea.

You know how I love being in DeRose's debt.

I think this will be worth it.

Gavin waited for Tristan to provide whatever data would be so worth it. Would it come as a file, an email, or another text? But nothing came.

Are you sending it? I'm not getting anything. File too large?

Actually I sent it about 6 hours ago. You should be getting it any moment according to my reports.

Six hours ago? What sort of file took six hours to arrive?

I'm not getting it. Just give me the basics and I'll read the file later.

You're welcome, big brother.

Gavin rolled his eyes. *I'm welcome for what?*

You'll know it when you see it.

Tristan's brain was wired to play games. They'd all accepted that in the family as part of what had happened to him. But Gavin really didn't feel like playing them right now.

And then he saw her.

Lexi was standing at the edge of the party room, looking inside like she wasn't sure if she should come in or not.

Oh hell no, she belonged in here, with him, with this family.

He stood up. She saw him and gave him a tentative wave, signaling for him to come out to the portico. Gavin set down his glass and walked straight to her.

"Hi." She gave him that awkward little wave again as the door shut behind him, leaving them alone. "The front desk has my bag because it occurred to me that maybe I needed to ask you before I moved my stuff into y—"

He kissed her.

He reached down, wrapped his arms around her hips, hoisted her up against him, and kissed her.

"You and I need to talk," she said against his lips.

"Later." She was here. That was all that mattered.

"It's bad."

"Are you in danger?"

"No."

"Then it can wait." He started carrying her toward the door.

"What about your friends?"

"They won't miss us." And if they did, he didn't care. He didn't care about anything except getting Lexi back to his room. To the bed. He wasn't sure he was going to make it that far.

Without putting her down, he headed for the door. He

didn't care what everyone thought. Whatever it was, it was nothing but the truth—he couldn't keep his hands off this woman, and he didn't care who knew.

He swung her up in his arms, not breaking the kiss. It was grandiose, but he still didn't care.

She didn't weigh enough to slow him down for a second as he made his way back to his oceanside room. He set her down so he could get his key card out at the door, but he didn't let her go.

"Gavin, I want this, I really do, but maybe we should talk—"

He pushed her through the door, then pressed her up against it with his body, his lips finding hers.

"Talk later." Jesus, he could barely get coherent sentences out. "I missed you."

He could feel her smile. "You just saw me a few hours ago."

"Yeah, but I missed you," he growled. "I want to bury myself inside of you until we can't tell where you end and I begin."

"I think we need fewer clothes then." She pushed against his chest with a finger, walking him backward. They unbuttoned their clothes as they went, leaving them scattered all over the floor.

The need to bury himself inside her wet heat clawed at him, but he pushed it down. They could do fast and hard later. Right now he wanted to worship her. Celebrate that she was here with him—the whys and hows didn't matter.

He sat on the bed and pulled her down to straddle him, diving in for another kiss before flipping her until she was in the middle of the bed, head resting on the pillow, and he was in between her widespread legs.

He rose up onto his knees and clamped his hands on her hips, pulling her to him. He slid inside her slowly, so slowly, just the slightest bit, wringing a moan from both of them, then stopped.

Lexi's eyelashes fluttered as he eased in and out of her and then repeated the action, an achingly slow series of shallow penetrations. He wasn't sure who he was driving crazy more, him or her. He watched where their bodies joined as he slid in and out, in and out, her moisture coating his skin until they gleamed together.

Just like he'd promised, neither of them could tell where one stopped and the other began.

"Gavin." Her hips moved, trying to meet his thrusts. "What are you... I need..." Her head arched back on the pillow as she tried to push up against him, to get him to go deeper.

No. Not yet. He had a good grip on her, holding her steady, continuing the torturous pace. "I want this to last, Green Eyes."

She let out a shuddery breath. "But . . ."

"Just enjoy." He leaned over, keeping their bodies joined at the shallow angle, and flicked his tongue over her nipple before pulling it into his mouth and sucking then biting.

They both moaned as he couldn't avoid slipping a little farther inside her, but he stayed still, simply stretching her, listening to the sounds she was making—a mix of frustration and yearning.

He sat back up and resumed the slow, shallow thrusts, ignoring his body's nearly overwhelming urge for more. Her moans grew louder, her hips struggled to lift, and her legs wrapped around his hips to pull him toward her. But he was bigger and stronger and had leverage, so the pulling got her nowhere. Neither did her plucking at his hands on her hips to get them off. The slow, constant friction sensitized both of them, driving them crazy, but he kept going when her limbs moved restlessly as she tried to thrust, the motion instinctive.

"Gavin." Her back arched again, her heels driving into the mattress. "More. Please more."

He reached down and grabbed one of her feet and brought it up to his shoulder, kissing at the tender arch. He looked down to see the whole long, glorious line of her body spread out in front of him, her head tossing, tangled hair crackling around her, while her hands grasped at him, her voice pleading.

"Please, Gavin, please. More. I want all of you."

He let go.

He leaned forward, catching himself on his hands, and thrust deep, her leg still up on his shoulder, opening her fully to him. She arched with a choked cry, her hands clutching at his back, fingernails burning into his skin. He gasped for air at the primal sensation, pumping harder.

Hearing her chant his name over and over like a prayer, threw him over the edge, and he shouted her name, spilling endlessly, buried deep inside her.

This woman. She completed him.

And she was here where she belonged.

30

Lexi stretched out in the bed the next morning, staring out at the Pacific from the sliding glass door of Gavin's hotel room. The sun was spraying its light down on the water, an uncommonly calm day out on the waves. Perfect for snorkeling.

Gavin had left a few minutes ago to meet the guys. They were hanging out together, then planning to help Gavin's cousin Noah propose to his girlfriend. Lexi wasn't quite sure why Noah needed help, but Gavin had seemed excited about it.

He'd seemed quite excited to see her too. Multiple times.

She had tried more than once to tell him who she really was, the whole situation, but finally she had let herself be persuaded to wait until they got back to Oak Creek. That was better anyway—no chance of ruining the wedding of one of his best friends.

Plus, who was she kidding? She would take every reprieve she could get. This might be her last weekend with him. The last time they were ever in bed together. She rolled over to look up at the ceiling. Gavin might be willing to help keep her safe but still not want to have anything to do with her personally.

Things were going to change after this weekend, so she might as well enjoy every minute she could.

She reached over and saw the note from him.

Girls are having a spa day. Wavy says to stop kissing me and join them. Terrible plan, in my opinion, but I hope you have fun.

She clutched the note against her chest, breathing deeply. She couldn't let herself think past today, past this weekend. Couldn't let herself think of all she was probably still going to lose.

She needed the water. Alone. No need to talk. No need to think. The spa with the girls would have to wait for another day, if that day ever came.

It didn't take her long to find the snorkel hut out near the beach, and she was soon outfitted with a wetsuit, snorkel gear, and a tiny boat that would allow her to get to the south side of the island more easily. She felt bad about assuring the resort worker that she wouldn't be out alone, since that was an outright lie. But she'd be following the other safety protocols and was experienced enough not to get in trouble.

Plus, there was no way her makeup was going to stay on in the water with the mask and snorkel, so going alone was her only option. She'd take it.

She couldn't stop her grin as the little raft putzed her along the island's edge. It wasn't very fast, and the motor seemed persnickety at best, but she loved the feel of the wind in her face, the sun beaming down. She easily found the place the snorkel shop had suggested, thanks to an odd rock formation on the south side of San Amado that formed a cave close to the shore.

She anchored her raft in about fifteen feet of water maybe fifty yards offshore. She already had her full-body wetsuit on over the bottom half of her bathing suit, so she slipped her arms into the sleeves and zipped it up. The suit would provide enough buoyancy to keep her on the surface. She attached the tiny air tank to a hook on the wetsuit to be used if she wanted to dive a little farther down. She placed the mask over her face and let herself tip backward out of the boat and into the water.

The water was cold, but her wetsuit made it bearable. She let herself float in the water face up for a minute before putting the snorkel into her mouth and turning over. Now, it was just her and the sea life and the quiet. No one to hurt her, no one to judge her. Floating here, weightless, she could almost forget she was the villain in her own story.

She could just *breathe*. Even if it was through a plastic tube.

She loved the schools of fish swarming around and darting off. There wasn't much to see in terms of coral—not like some of the other places she'd snorkeled—but it was interesting enough. At one point, she glanced up and saw two women walking along the rocky shore. They went into the cave the snorkel guy had warned her about. He'd told her not to go in there—the tide could come in fast and trap someone there. Evidently, some kid had drowned there a few years ago.

She kept an eye out in between dives, but she didn't see them come back out. After thirty minutes, the women hadn't come out. The water had risen significantly, enough that her original location wasn't a great place for her to snorkel anymore. Maybe they didn't know about the dangers. She should swim in and make sure they were okay.

She got the raft up as close as she could before dropping her anchor again. The waves were rushing into the cave at too fast a rate for her to take it inside. She jumped back into the water and swam the rest of the way.

Once inside, she realized the cave wasn't truly a cave at all.

The entire top was open to the sky, but the cliff walls ran verti-
cally for about thirty feet.

Lexi spotted the two women immediately over near one of
the rocky edges. Something was wrong. She spit the snorkel
out of her mouth. "Hey, are you guys all right?"

"Lexi?" one of the women called back to her.

Anne?

She was suspended at a strange angle, her foot stuck up
between some rocks, but her body was hanging down. The
other woman was propping her up as best she could.

Lexi swam the rest of the way over to them. "What
happened?"

Anne's voice shook. "My foot is jammed, and the tide is
coming in."

The other woman nodded frantically. "The rock trapping
her leg is too big for us to move. Can you get back to your raft
and go get help?"

Lexi looked from Anne to the other woman to the water
coming into the cave at an alarming rate. Her eyes grew wide.

Anne was going to drown if they didn't get help.

"Yeah, absolutely, yeah. And here." She handed the other
woman the mini scuba tank still attached to the strap on her
wetsuit. Thank God she hadn't used any of it. It would give
them a little more time once the water got higher. "This will
buy you ten, maybe fifteen minutes."

"We're going to need every one of them," the other woman
said. "Hurry. This isn't good."

"I can hear you two, you know, Marilyn," Annie said.

Marilyn. Gavin had talked about her. His cousin's girlfriend who had survived the abusive ex.

Lexi didn't waste time introducing herself. She swam as
hard as she could against the waves back out to her raft. She
kicked off her flippers, then reached back to pull the starter

chain on the engine. She let out a low curse when the motor stalled.

"Come on. You can't do this to me right now." Even with the oxygen tank, Anne wouldn't have enough time if the boat stalled out now. Lexi had to get back and get help.

She yanked on the cord again and let out a little laugh when it started. She put the boat in full throttle and headed back toward the resort.

She wasn't checking out any of the scenery this time, so the trip back was much quicker than it had been on the way out. But when the motor began sputtering again still almost a mile away from the resort, cold dread froze her insides.

"Come on, baby," she muttered. "Just a couple more minutes."

The engine motor stalled.

"No. No, no, no."

She yanked the cord and it started, only to stall out again a few seconds later.

She yanked it again, and when it started, she pointed the boat toward land. She would have to run it ashore, then go the rest of the way on foot.

The tiny boat motor stalled again. She yanked at the cord but when nothing happened, she jumped overboard and swam as hard as she could for the shore. The incoming tide helped her, but once she was on the rocky beach she realized she didn't have any shoes.

She ran anyway. Her feet would heal. Anne being trapped under that rising water would not.

She ignored the pain of the rocks slicing into her feet as best she could, focusing on saving Anne. But it got harder as she went farther—every step agony. She wasn't sure how far she'd gone—halfway?—when she slid on a wet rock, falling hard on her knee, cutting through the neoprene of the wetsuit.

She pushed herself back up, but when her hand came up with blood on it, she realized the rock was wet from her bleeding feet. She forced back a sob. Her feet were cut. So what? She needed to keep going.

She tested her knee. It was fine, just a scrape, so she began running again.

"Come on, Lexi. For once in your life, do something worthwhile."

One foot in front of the other. One foot in front of the other.

She tried to make herself move as fast as possible, but the agony with each step made her slow and bumbling. Way slower than she should be.

She finally reached the edge of the rocks where it started to give way to sand. All the Linear guys were down on the beach. She waved her arms, yelling for them. Yelling for anyone.

"Help! Please, help!" Her voice was hoarse, but she got their attention. She kept moving toward them, much more slowly, as they ran toward her. She tried to get her sobbing breathing under control. *She* wasn't important. *Anne* was important.

She saw Zac first, reached an arm out toward him. "Anne and Marilyn. Trapped in a cave with tide."

She was surrounded by people now—all the Linear guys. Some hotel staff were running over too. Gavin slipped an arm around her. "Your knee is bleeding. Are you okay?"

"Not me, *Anne*. She's trapped." God, her feet hurt so bad, she couldn't stop the sobs from boiling up inside her. "The cave."

"What cave?" Zac demanded. "Anne is supposed to be

getting a massage."

She recognized the guy who'd rented her the snorkel equipment among the hotel staff. She pointed at him. "Two people trapped in the cave you warned me about. Anne's foot is stuck in a rock and the tide—"

The man let out a curse, finally understanding how serious the situation was. Zac turned his attention to him since Lexi wasn't proving very useful with information.

"There is a partial cave at the south side of the island," snorkel guy said. "We tell guests not to go near there because the tide can come in fast. If someone is trapped there—"

"Yes! That's what I'm saying. They have my tiny air tank, but—"

Zac grabbed the man by his collar. "Shortest, fastest way there. Now."

The man nodded frantically, but it was an older man next to him who answered. "The tide is in, so we'll need to go in from the top. The resort trucks have winches—"

Zac and the Linear guys took off in the middle of the man's sentence, dragging him with them. Only Gavin stayed behind. "Are you sure you're okay? Your knee?"

She was about to tell him that it was her feet, and ask him to carry her once again like he had last night, when he reached out to touch her face. "You look totally different."

Oh God. All her makeup was gone. She dropped her head so her hair would hide her face. "You should go with them, in case they need your help."

"Are you sure you're okay?"

"Yeah," she lied. "Anne and Marilyn need your help."

"Shit. Marilyn? That's my cousin's almost-fiancée." He looked at her again, tilting his head to the side. "You don't look like you."

She forced a smile and pushed him. "Go be a hero."

31

Gavin had to force his thoughts away from Lexi as the resort's Jeep flew at a reckless pace along the winding dirt road leading to the south side of the island.

For the first time, he understood what everyone meant when they'd said she seemed familiar to them. But why would that be the case if she'd looked so different than she normally did?

"We need to know everything there is to know about this cave we're headed to," Finn demanded.

He was driving after having literally yanked the snorkel hut employee out of the driver seat. It didn't matter how well the employee knew the terrain. Finn had defensive driving skills the other man was never going to have.

Zac and Noah were in the vehicle ahead of them, Zac at the wheel and driving just as aggressively.

"I-I—"

The guy was obviously terrified. Gavin could hardly blame him. The laid-back, good-natured guests they'd been the past day and a half were gone. Soldiers, very definitely trained to kill, had taken their place.

"What's your name, man?" Gavin asked from the back seat next to Gabe Collingwood. If they were going to get information from this guy, they were going to need him to calm down.

"Alfred."

"Okay, Alfred. My friends and I have some pretty unique skills. Probably skills most of your guests don't have. The women in that cave mean everything to us, and we're going to get them out. We need you to provide as many details as possible so we can do that."

Alfred nodded. "Maybe we should call for the boats. The only way to get to them the way we're going is by using ropes. Climbing down. I don't know how to do that."

"We do," Gavin, Finn, and Gabe all said at the same time.

That seemed to calm Alfred down a little since he wouldn't be the one expected to do the actual rescuing.

Finn's hands clenched on the steering wheel. He wanted to demand more info from Alfred but was holding himself back. One point of contact when you were dealing with a witness or an interrogation was generally best. Gavin had become that point of contact.

"Okay, Alfred, you don't have to worry about the ropes. All you need to worry about is getting us as much information as possible. How long is it going to take us to get there?"

"At this speed?" The man's voice was tight. "About five minutes."

"Then you've got five minutes to give us as much information as you can so that we can help them immediately once we get there. How big is the cave?"

"It's a rock formation where a chunk collapsed a few hundred years ago. Makes it very unique from the top and the bottom."

"Okay, how far from the top to the bottom.?

"Maybe thirty feet?"

Gavin nodded. Thirty feet was very doable. Any of them could rappel that distance in under a minute, even without the correct equipment.

"We stopped telling guests about it when a child drowned there a few years ago. The tide comes in deceptively quickly because of where the cave is located. It only takes a few minutes for the water to fill it."

"Is the tide too strong to swim against?" Gabe asked. As a Navy SEAL, he had more water experience than the rest of them.

Alfred shook his head. "I don't think so. It would be a hard swim, not impossible."

So Marilyn was there to help stay with Anne who was stuck. Not because she couldn't swim out herself.

"It's going to be all about where they're trapped," Finn muttered.

"There are cranks on the back of both these Jeeps," Gabe said. "We're going to have to move fast as soon as we get there."

They all nodded, but they all knew they could already be too late.

Less than a minute later, the Jeeps came to a dusty halt, both parties spun around backward so the cranks and ropes were facing the top of the cave. Evidently, Zac and Noah had gotten the same information from the older hotel employee in their vehicle that they'd gotten from Alfred.

Everyone was out of the Jeeps almost before they stopped.

Noah dashed toward the mouth of the cave, unconcerned for his own safety. "Marilyn!"

The garbled response was barely audible over the sound of the water. But it was a response.

"Fuck. She's going under," Noah yelled.

The rest of them reached the edge. Marilyn's hand was lifting through the water, letting them know where she was.

Gabe and Aiden were already tying foothold knots into the ropes. Ten seconds later, Noah was on his way down one rope, Zac the other. Halfway down, they both jumped into the water. Everyone waited, shoes kicked off, prepared to go down themselves—or to do whatever else was needed—praying to God this was still a rescue mission and not a body recovery for Anne.

A few seconds later, Noah burst through the water, Marilyn in his arms.

Zac didn't resurface.

"We need people down here, stat!" Noah yelled. "And the extra oxygen tanks. It's deep enough. Just clear the rocks."

Gabe launched himself over the edge, oxygen tank in hand, a moment later.

Noah swam Marilyn over to the ropes, getting his foot latched and then holding her against him as he signaled for them to pull him and Marilyn up. Gavin helped haul them up while Finn and Aiden went into the water with a crowbar to get Anne's foot unjammed from the rock.

A couple minutes later, they all breathed a silent sigh of relief when Zac came back through the water with Anne, the scuba oxygen mask pushed over her face. Her coughs were painful to hear, but they meant she was alive. Survival was always the most important thing.

More hotel vehicles showed up. Staff with towels, blankets, hot beverages for the two women who had been in the water for so long. Both of them were chilled, but smiling. The doctor on the scene took a look at Anne's ankle. The good news was the same cold water that had almost killed them had been the best remedy for a sprained ankle, keeping the swelling down. They were going to have it xrayed, but Anne didn't think it was broken and was already insisting the wedding would be held tomorrow as scheduled.

Gavin watched as Zac came over and cupped Marilyn's cheeks in his hands. He whispered something to her no one else could hear but everyone could figure out without knowing the words.

Marilyn had saved Anne's life. Staying in that frigid water, holding the oxygen mask over her face while Anne was unconscious. If Marilyn hadn't done it, Anne would be dead now. It was the absolute height of bravery. Gavin knew Marilyn sometimes thought herself a coward for having stayed with an abusive spouse for so long, but that was complete bullshit.

He hoped Noah would continue the proposal he'd been in the middle of setting up when Lexi had strolled onto the beach to get their attention.

It had been a very close call. Why hadn't she been moving with a little more urgency? Her knee had been scraped up, but Jesus, they'd been only a minute or two away from losing Anne forever.

Nothing about seeing Lexi today was sitting right with him. Now that the crisis was over, he couldn't get her face, and how different her features had looked, out of his mind.

It was more than just water. He'd showered with her a couple of times over the past few weeks, and he'd never felt like he was staring at a stranger. He tried to think back to those exact times and stiffened.

Both times he could think of when they'd showered together, she'd turned the lights down in his bathroom and lit candles. He'd thought it was for ambience. Romance.

But now, he had no idea what the fuck was going on.

He was in a daze all the way back to the resort. Noah and

Marilyn were in the vehicle with him, Marilyn perched in Noah's lap, mostly caught up in each other.

Gavin was still in a daze when they made it back to the same beach they'd been at when Lexi had shown up, this time so Noah could finish the proposal they'd been helping him set up before the day had almost ended in tragedy.

When Marilyn said yes in her soft, gentle way, everyone cheered. Gavin should cheer too. Two people who'd thought they'd never find happiness had found one another against all odds and were going to spend forever together. Gavin should be ecstatic for them.

But instead, his gut was telling him his own life was crumbling. He didn't know why, and more importantly, he didn't know how to stop it.

Almost everyone from the wedding party was out on the beach to congratulate the newly engaged couple and to surround Anne in thankfulness that she was alive and okay.

But not Lexi. She wasn't here. Again, refusing to let herself really get involved with anyone's life.

Because she wasn't who she claimed to be.

His brain was putting it together, although he wasn't sure if his subconscious was trying to hurry that process along or stop it altogether.

His phone buzzed in his pocket. Tristan.

He accepted the call and brought the phone up to his ear but didn't say anything. He didn't have to, Tristan was already talking.

"Gavin, sweet baby Jesus and all his disciple babies, you are not going to believe what I'm about to tell you."

"Lexi isn't who she says she is." His words were emotionless. Numb, like he felt.

"How did you know? Did you figure this out already and not tell me?"

"No." The numbness was taking over his whole body. "I just have my suspicions. Who is she? A criminal?"

It had to be someone he knew, that was why she seemed familiar.

"You were right about it all. The easiest thing to trace was the phone call from Mac's bar. That was a call to a parole officer in North Carolina."

So not a criminal, an ex-criminal. "Why didn't all this show up when I ran her through the system?"

"That ties into the guy whose picture you gave me, the one she's been paying. His name is Justin Romig, and he's irrelevant. But he's tied to Dashawn Cussler, one of the best ID forgers out there. Cussler isn't the type of guy you go to if you're trying to sneak into a club when you're underage. This is the guy you use when you need your ID to withstand a background check."

"So she's not really Lexi Johnson." He'd known that all along. He'd let it go rather than force the issue and then convinced himself it wasn't true, but he'd known from the very beginning that Lexi Johnson wasn't who she really was.

"Nope. But I cross-referenced her parole officer with that date you wanted me to check out to see what had happened in the world—and believe it or not, I got a match."

Gavin scrubbed a hand down his face. "Tell me."

"Alexandra Adams."

It took him a second to place the name. "The actress? The one on the show where Shane Westman took over security?"

"Yep."

Shane had been in the Special Forces with Gavin. He'd planned to join Linear Tactical when he got out of the army a couple years ago, but had taken a security job as a favor for Zac. He'd fallen in love and never made it out of North Carolina.

Alexandra Adams had almost gotten Shane's now-wife killed.

Everything in Gavin's mind shifted. He could see it now, clear as day. "The eyes."

Lexi Johnson's and Alexandra Adams's eyes were the same. Remarkable, unmistakable.

"The eyes," Tristan agreed. "It looks like her nose was broken sometime in the past two years, which changed the fundamental shape of her face, and the rest of her changes are skillfully applied makeup. But yeah, the eyes are the same."

"Send me what you have."

"Are you okay, man?"

"Just send it."

He didn't wait for Tristan to send him the info. All it was going to do was provide proof for what Gavin already knew: Lexi was a liar.

He stormed toward his hotel room, hardly able to fathom his own stupidity at being fooled by a lying woman once again. Evidently he was a complete idiot who let himself get led around by his dick all the time.

The information from Tristan arrived as he got to the door of his hotel room. He didn't stop to read it, but he couldn't keep his eyes from the photo at the start of the file. He enlarged it—Alexandra Adams from three or four years ago. She was coming out of a restaurant or club of some kind, dressed to the nines, smiling at cameras.

She looked nothing like Lexi until he zoomed in on the eyes. The eyes were the same.

He stopped and stared at the picture. Not just the same color . . . the same sadness, the same exhaustion. He tamped that down. What kind of idiot would he have to be to feel sympathy for a woman when he was holding undeniable proof she was a liar? He swiped to the next picture.

Her fucking mugshots.

Still the same eyes.

He resisted the urge to throw his phone against the wall. That wouldn't change any of this.

Nothing would change any of this.

He let himself into the hotel room. Soft noises came from the bathroom. He walked in without knocking and found Lexi sitting on the luxurious padded stool in front of the large mirror, as if it were her throne. Her makeup was spread out in front of her like her subjects. A glass of wine beside them.

He glanced over at the oversize tub. It was filled with nearly every towel in the bathroom.

Evidently while they had been rescuing Anne and Marilyn, Lexi had decided to have a bath and a glass of wine.

Her startled eyes met his in the mirror. Her hands went to her hair, pulling it down to cover most of her face.

How many times had he seen her do that? He'd thought it endearing, a nervous habit. What it really had been was an accomplished actress's tool to make sure she wasn't discovered.

He'd caught her mid-process. She looked different than how she had when he'd seen her down on the beach, but not quite fully Lexi either.

"Marilyn and Anne are fine, in case you were wondering." He leaned against the doorframe. "As a matter fact, Noah just proposed to Marilyn out on the beach."

She nodded, her eyes not meeting his in the mirror. "I'd heard they were okay."

"From who?"

Her eyes darted to the bathtub.

Feeling guilty for taking a bath when somebody might've been dying?

"One of the members of the resort staff told me."

He had no way of knowing whether that was true or not, so he let it go.

"If you give me a minute, I'll be right out," she said, picking up a brush and smoothing it along her hair.

He crossed his arms over his chest. "You know, I've never seen you put on your makeup."

"It's not terribly exciting. Nothing really to see." Now her eyes met his.

He gave her a smile that held no humor whatsoever. "Oh, changing everything about your appearance would definitely be something most people find interesting. I definitely do."

32

H e watched the color drain from her face. She set down the brush in her hand.

"You know. Is it because you recognized me or something else—did someone post about me being here on social media?"

She was concerned about how many likes she got on a photo? Jesus. He raised an eyebrow. "Does it matter?"

She shook her head. "Not to you, I suppose."

He pointed to the makeup. "Take it all off. Surely, since I've seen you naked so many times, I can see what you really look like."

She didn't respond, merely picked up a bottle, poured some of its contents onto a cotton swab, and wiped it across her face.

Gavin wasn't a big television watcher. He'd always been more of a reader. But he'd still heard of Alexandra Adams, of course. Knew who she was, even without the ties Linear had with Shane Westman.

Gavin had applauded when she'd been sent to prison for obstruction of justice and filing a false report by a no-

nonsense judge who didn't care that she was a famous actress. The judge had told her she was lucky she wasn't facing accessory to kidnapping charges with a sentence that would span a decade or more. As far as Gavin was concerned, Alexandra Adams had gotten what she deserved. He hadn't thought of the woman a single day since.

But now that woman sat facing him in the mirror.

She was definitely different without the makeup. Her face a little more full, her cheekbones much less pronounced. Even her nose and forehead looked different.

"I don't understand how it's possible. How you've fooled everyone."

She shrugged with one shoulder. "Most people don't look too closely. It's a mix of regular makeup and special-effects techniques. It tricks the eyes into believing my face is a different shape than it really is."

"You wore this all the time, even when you slept in my bed?"

"My makeup is by far the most expensive thing I own." Her voice was low, calm. "It's long-lasting and mostly waterproof. It's meant to withstand a full day of filming under hot lights or other difficult circumstances."

"But it came off today while you were snorkeling?"

"Today, I made the unfortunate mistake of removing it myself before I went out in the ocean. I didn't think anyone would see me." She took a sip of her wine.

She was relaxed enough to sip her fucking wine, hand loose on the stem. Meanwhile he felt like he was a half second from punching through the wall.

"It's not all just makeup." He'd be damned if he got out his phone and studied the differences between her now and the photos Tristan had sent, but even without any makeup, he could see there was a difference between her face and what it had been a couple of years ago. "Your face is different."

She nodded. "Broken nose and a fractured cheekbone changed the overall shape of my face. Certainly makes the makeup job easier."

"When did you break your nose and cheekbone?"

"Second day of prison. Someone didn't like me." Another sip of wine. "Or, to hear her tell it, she accidentally tripped and fell against me and pushed me into a wall with all her weight. Either story, same result."

Gavin was pissed that he couldn't control his wince at the thought of her face being slammed against a wall with enough force to break bones. "Am I supposed to feel sorry for you?"

Those green eyes fell away from his gaze in the mirror. "No. I don't expect anyone to feel sorry for me."

"Your actions almost got two people killed."

"And I went to prison for it."

She was so icy. So calm. So still. He couldn't believe she was just sitting there. In the months that he'd known her, he'd never known her to be this still.

He had to take a step back. For the first time in his adult life, he wasn't completely sure he was in control of his anger. Jesus, he'd walked in on Janeen fucking another man and hadn't felt one tenth of the fury burning through him now.

And she was sitting there like a queen on her throne.

"So what did you do, Alexandra? Come to Oak Creek to escape the press? That's why you didn't want to be in any photographs? The press would hunt you down and life isn't quite so easy when people won't let you sweep your past sins under the rug?"

She stiffened. "Yes. Exactly. You've got it all figured out, obviously."

He wanted to shake her. Not because he wanted to hurt

her, but because he wanted to knock her out of this cool disdain. She was acting like she was the wronged party. Like she was the one whose world was being ripped piece by piece into nothing.

"You probably should've done better research than coming to the town housing the friends of the people you almost got killed."

Those green eyes got big now. "You know Chloe Jeffries and Nadine MacFarlane?"

"No, but we work with Shane Westman and Wyatt High-field, neither of whom appreciated the danger your stunt put the women they love in."

"They work for Linear Tactical?" Now she seemed a little more rattled.

"Shane took that security job for the studio as a favor to Zac. Wyatt followed to help when the danger skyrocketed—which it did thanks to you. Good thing Wyatt has been away on a mission for the past couple of months. I wonder if he would've recognized you, since you are directly responsible for nearly destroying the life of the woman he loves."

"I-I had no idea either man was part of Linear Tactical."

Gavin shrugged. "Shane never really was. He was about to start when Zac asked him to take the security position, and then he decided to stay with Chloe. Wyatt does a lot of our international work, so he isn't around much."

He had no idea why he was telling her this, as if he should be reassuring her. His hands tightened into fists at his side. "Why didn't you tell me, Lexi? From the very beginning you should've told me who you were."

"I . . ." She stared at her own reflection in the mirror. "It's complicated."

"That doesn't really excuse anything."

"I know." She stood up like she was going to come over to

him, but then sat back down, her face pale. "I just—nobody believes me when I tell them . . ."

"Tell them what?"

Her mouth opened, then closed twice as she swallowed whatever it was she was going to say. "I was going to tell you. That's what I meant last night when I said I wanted to talk. But you said to wait and—"

He let out a snort, his fist pounding low against the door-frame. "Really? You're going to throw this back on me? You should've told me who you were *weeks* ago, Lexi. Not lied to my face every single day."

He left the bathroom. He couldn't stay in there with her. Or he'd say something—or God, *do something*—unforgivable in a moment of anger.

And goddammit, he wanted her to get off that fucking throne of hers and come out here. He wanted them to yell this out. Wanted her to apologize to him for cracking off a huge piece of his fucking heart.

Wanted to be mean enough to her that she would face him eye to eye.

But she didn't come after him. She stayed in the bathroom like the selfish queen she was.

He walked back to the doorway. She was still sitting there. "That's it, huh? We're not worth fighting about?"

If so, then she definitely didn't feel they were worth fighting *for*.

"I can't chase you into the other room, Gavin. I—"

"No need to bother," he cut her off, turning away again. "I get it. You're not going to chase me. That tells me everything I need to know. I'm done with this."

He slammed out of the room before she could say another word.

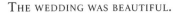

THE WEDDING WAS BEAUTIFUL.

A late-afternoon ceremony with the gorgeous waters of the Pacific as a backdrop would probably make any wedding lovely. But the fact that yesterday could've ended in tragedy made this wedding that much sweeter.

Anne's dress hid the bandage supporting her ankle. Maybe she and Zac did a little less dancing at the reception than they might have if she wasn't dealing with an injury, but it was a fair trade-off.

Zac had an arm clamped around his wife's waist like he was never going to let her go. Of course, that had been true way before yesterday's mishap.

Gavin looked down at the drink napkin in his hand and the cute words embossed on it.

Anne and Zac. Love from A to Z and back again.

Gavin took a sip of his whiskey. Clever. Especially because it was so true.

Lexi hadn't shown up for the wedding. Anne had asked about her, and Gavin had carefully sidestepped the question, mostly telling the gentle doctor he wasn't sure where Lexi was. He definitely wasn't about to tell Anne or Zac that they'd inadvertently invited a notorious actress to their wedding.

Gavin was a little surprised Lexi didn't show. From Anne and Marilyn's telling of the tale, Lexi was as much the hero as Marilyn had been. Again, Gavin didn't set the record straight. Didn't tell anyone how slowly Lexi had been moving when she first arrived to get them.

Maybe her scraped knee had slowed her down, although that hadn't looked like much of an injury. Maybe she was out of shape. In the end, everything had turned out all right.

Jesus, was *he* making excuses for her now too?

Glass in hand, he left the reception on the patio and wandered off toward the beach, where the sun was setting in a glorious blaze of fire on the horizon. Gavin wanted to appreciate it, but he couldn't.

He was foundering. His entire world had been shaken to the core, and it had everything to do with Lexi. Alexandra.

He was in love with the woman, and he wasn't sure what to call her.

His initial wave of fury had subsided. He still had plenty of anger left, but he also had questions. He'd been so angry last night, felt so betrayed, there was no way he would've known what to ask. Not that he would have been willing to listen to any response she would've given anyway.

He'd been up all night. He hadn't gone back to the room at all until he'd been forced to go to get dressed for the wedding today. All her stuff had been gone. The housekeeping staff had been there and all traces of Lexi had been erased.

Like she'd never been here at all.

Was that what he wanted? To erase every trace of Lexi from his life?

No. God, despite the haze of anger and confusion, he knew that wasn't true.

He'd spent most of last night in the resort's small business center at a computer, researching everything he could about Alexandra Adams.

Evidently some of what she'd told him during the blizzard was true. Her parents had died when she was fifteen right as her career skyrocketed, then her aunt and uncle had taken custody of her.

The differences between pictures of fifteen-year-old Alexandra right before her parents had died and the same girl a year later were staggering. The press had blamed grief, but the signs of the drugs her aunt and uncle had been giving her were evident if someone knew to look.

Five years later, at the age of twenty, the height of her career, she was undeniably beautiful.

But her eyes were haunted. Everything about the picture had made him want to reach through the screen and help her.

As her career continued, Alexandra seemed to have everything anyone could ever want: beauty, fame, riches. Multiple relationships, although none of them had lasted long, plenty of travel, and A-list friends.

But in every single picture, those green eyes were the same. Haunted. Sad. Tired.

Always so tired. Not her face—she was gorgeous. But those eyes didn't lie.

And they were the same right up to the point where she'd lied about a stalker and destroyed her own trailer to get attention.

Why had she done it?

That's what he should've asked her last night. Instead of losing his shit over her sitting there sipping wine, he should have lived up to his codename and stayed solid.

So his world had been knocked off its axis yesterday? Hell, his world had been knocked off its axis the moment he'd laid eyes on her in that bar in Reddington City.

Why had she done it?

That had been the only thing he'd been able to think about since he'd shut the computer down and walked along the beach in the middle of the night. He argued with himself that she hadn't offered any explanations, but the truth was he hadn't given her much of a chance to.

He'd done what everyone had done, especially the press: he'd told her she was guilty. Told her she was selfish. A bitch.

And he'd left without ever really trying to get to the bottom of her reasoning.

Why had she done it?

When he stopped looking at it through a lens of betrayal, he realized he already had the answer. Anyone would if they cared enough to look.

She'd made a stupid mistake. She'd been twenty-five years old. She'd been under the influence of drugs she didn't know about. She'd been suffering from exhaustion, and had wanted someone to look out for her.

Had it been selfish? Yes. Had it been reckless for innocent people? Yes, although she probably hadn't intended it that way. Lexi didn't have any ties with the killer. It didn't make it all okay, but her intentions had never been to hurt anyone.

Gavin sat down to watch the sun in its final approach to the horizon. He rubbed his eyes. God, he was tired from just one night without sleep. How did Lexi function feeling this way most of the time?

A couple minutes later, he felt eyes on him, and turned, hoping it was her.

Well, that told him everything he needed to know, didn't it? He wanted to see her. *Needed* to see her.

It wasn't her.

As a matter of fact, it was the last person he was expecting.

"Dorian?"

The big man gave him a smile. "Can I cut in on whatever dance you're having here?"

Gavin smiled back. "It's commonly known as the *I'm a dumbass in more ways than one* tango."

Dorian chuckled and sat down beside him. "Just so happens I am quite familiar with the steps to that dance."

Gavin shook his hand. "I didn't know you were here."

"We're not, at least not on any official roster or registration.

Ray still isn't great with crowds, but neither of us wanted to miss this."

"Do Zac and Annie know you're here?"

"Yeah, we said hello last night after we arrived. Evidently, we missed all the excitement yesterday afternoon."

"Well, you made it for the most important part, that's all that counts."

"My wife spent the past month researching this island, the resort, and ways on and off in case there was an emergency."

"How many exit strategies does she have?"

Dorian smiled, then leaned back in the sand on his elbows. "Four that I know of. Which I assume means she has seven or eight total."

Dorian didn't seem upset at all about the fact that his wife needed to have these stopgaps in place in order to feel safe. He loved her, understood her past, and was willing to give her whatever she needed in order to function.

And Gavin hadn't even been willing to listen to Lexi's full side of the story.

"*Fuck*."

"I'm assuming you finished the dumbass tango and are now moving on to the equally painful *what the hell have I done* mambo?"

Definitely. "Do you remember when Ray almost shot you at the Eagle's Nest?" Gavin could still see it as clearly as the day it happened. The arrow, shot from Ray's crossbow, had landed inches from Dorian's head.

Dorian nodded. "I remember."

"I thought she was trying to kill you."

"If Ray wanted me dead . . ."

"You'd be dead. That's what you told me then too."

"Just as true today as it was with an arrow inches from my skull."

"But you didn't walk away from her."

Dorian looked over at him. "You know Ray wasn't responsible for—"

Gavin held out a hand to stop his friend. "I know. Ray wasn't responsible for any of that stuff. But I think my actual point is . . . it didn't matter to you either way."

Dorian sat back up. "You think I didn't care if my wife was a killer?"

Gavin measured his words carefully. "I think you would've protected her, even if she had been a killer. You sat there looking across that table at me, and you were prepared to do whatever you had to, even if she was the bad guy and it meant you keeping her locked in your basement for the rest of her life."

Dorian considered it. "Yes. I'm glad it didn't turn out that way, but Ray's life and emotional well-being means more to me than anything she could've done in her past. I don't care what it was."

Gavin scrubbed a hand down his face. He'd spent weeks telling Lexi he wanted to give her whatever she needed, then acted like a complete tool when it actually came time to do it. He'd always been steady, dependable—*Redwood*, for God's sake. But not with Lexi when she'd needed it most.

"Cue the *I'm a self-righteous prick* two-step."

Dorian chuckled. "Ray and I had a lot more history than you and your lady friend. I'd lost her once, and that pain wasn't something I could live through again. So you'll have to cut yourself some slack."

"Gavin, you're a self-righteous prick!" Wavy yelled from up the beach.

Dorian raised an eyebrow. "Sounds like Wavy knows this dance too. And I think that's my cue to leave."

"Coward," Gavin muttered.

They both stood up. "What you call cowardice, I call good judgment," Dorian said. Wavy stormed toward them. "That woman is pissed."

"Yeah. Good thing she doesn't have a crossbow."

Dorian slapped him on the shoulder. "Let me tell you the most important thing. After all the dust settles, the only thing that matters is that as long as both of you are still breathing, there's still time. Everything else can be fixed."

Gavin nodded and turned to look at Wavy. When he looked back at Dorian, just like his code name Ghost, he had disappeared.

33

"Did Lexi send you?" Probably not the smartest sentence for him to lead with, given the fire in Wavy's eyes.

"You had no business telling her not to come to the wedding. No matter what her real name is."

"You knew?"

Wavy made a face and rolled her eyes. "It wasn't hard to figure out. Just because most of Oak Creek is blind doesn't mean I have to be."

Gavin had known Wavy for years, but mostly as Finn's and Baby's sister, not so much as her own person. She'd worked at the Frontier Diner for years, and he'd kind of written her off as pleasant but not particularly bright.

Evidently, he'd been wrong. Because she'd spotted what he'd completely missed.

"You should've told me, Wavy."

"Why should I have told you? Lexi wasn't hurting anybody. She was only trying to find some peace. Trying to regain what she'd lost."

"She had a fake ID. That's illegal."

She raised an eyebrow. "Really, Sheriff? That's what you're

mad about here? Are you also going to hunt down half the teenagers in town who have fake IDs like a vigilante, making our streets safe again?"

He crossed his arms over his chest. "Lexi's ID was much more complex than what fucking teenagers have."

But why?

Why would she need one that sophisticated? One that had obviously cost her money she didn't have. Even if he'd run her through the database and found out who she was, it wouldn't have been a big deal.

There was something more.

"What do you know about her?"

"What do *you* know about her?" Wavy countered.

He shook his head. "I have no idea if anything she's told me in the past few months has been the truth. Why is she working as a waitress and pretty much broke?"

"Woeful child-star tale. Her aunt and uncle had guardianship of her when she was younger, then she never took them off her accounts. When she went down, they cleaned her out. After the trial, she had nothing."

He'd known about the drugs they'd had her hooked on, but he hadn't known about them taking all her money. "Jesus. I didn't know."

"You told her that when she was ready to share her secrets you'd be there for her."

"For Christ's sake, Wavy—"

She held out a hand to stop him. "What you meant was you'd be there for her as long as her secrets meant you got to be the hero. The protector. Not if her secrets meant she'd fucked up in the past. Sorry if her secrets didn't fit the narrative you created in your mind, Redwood."

Goddammit. "She almost got two people killed."

"She made a mistake. She wanted attention. She wanted someone to *see* her."

"But it's not just then." As soon as the words were out, he realized that was the bigger part of what had been bothering him. He hadn't realized it until right now. "She's *still* selfish. Still more concerned about herself than she is anybody else. Like yesterday."

"Yesterday Lexi helped save Anne's life. That's not exactly selfish."

"Yesterday Marilyn almost drowned making sure unconscious Anne had the oxygen mask over her face. Meanwhile, yeah, Lexi came to get us for help, but you should've seen her, Wavy. She strolled up onto the beach like she was headed for brunch." The more he thought about it, the angrier he got. "She acted like she was all out of breath, but she couldn't have been at the rate she was moving. She was *acting* to get attention. The way she had two years ago. We were ninety seconds from being too late to save Anne's life. And Lexi didn't give two shits. She went back to the room, had a bath and a glass of wine."

Wavy just stared at him. "Didn't you talk to Lexi afterward?"

He sure fucking had. "She sat there, all of her makeup in front of her, sipping on a glass of wine. Completely cold and shut down. She wouldn't even deign to come after me when I told her I knew who she was and walked out. Said she wouldn't chase me."

And that had bothered him most of all, hadn't it? Not what she'd done in the past, but how she was acting in her *present*.

"You don't know, do you?" Wavy was shaking her head.

"Know what?"

"It hasn't rained. I don't think the tide would be high enough to reach it. Come here, asshole."

She left, not waiting to see if he was behind her. He followed.

The sun was almost completely gone in the sky now as she walked back to the section of beach where Lexi had arrived, yelling for help. Wavy was staring at the ground, searching for something.

She found it. "Here." She pointed at the ground. "This was where she was when she stopped, right?"

He nodded. "Yeah, somewhere around here."

"No, not *somewhere around here*. Right here." She pointed down at the ground. "Why don't you take a look and see if you can figure it out."

Gavin looked down at where Wavy was pointing. There was some sort of stain on the edge of the rocks where the sand smoothed out.

"What is that?"

"You've got all the answers when it comes to Lexi. You tell me."

It didn't take long for him to put it together. "Blood. But I saw Lexi's knee. Her wetsuit was torn but the scrape wasn't bad. Could not have—" It came to him in the middle of his own sentence. "Her feet."

Oh God.

"That's right, Mr. *Lexi-Is-So-Selfish*. The motor on her raft broke, so she ran along these rocks for over a mile in her bare feet. So yes, I'm sure that by the time she arrived here she wasn't quite sprinting."

He felt like he was choking, staring down at the blood-stained rock.

"She didn't tell me." Not that he'd given her any chance.

"I was here when two of the resort staff had to carry her back to her room. She didn't want to go to the infirmary because, goddammit Gavin, she didn't want you to have to pay any extra cost. A medic came back to the room and cleaned out the cuts. A few of them needed stitches. He tried to give her something for pain, but she wouldn't take it because she said she had a bad past history with prescription drugs."

Gavin dragged a hand down his face. She hadn't wanted to take them again because of all the years they'd been used against her.

"So that glass of wine you're so openly scorning was her only buffer against the pain of ripping up her feet while saving the life of someone she's known less than six months."

His jaw clenched as he rubbed the back of his neck. "I handled it badly."

"You think?"

He needed to apologize. He needed to shut his damned mouth and listen to her about the past. He might not condone it, but Lexi wasn't the same person she'd been then.

Wasn't the same person he'd accused her of being now.

"I didn't tell her not to come to the wedding. I haven't seen her since I left my room yesterday afternoon. I assumed she spent the night and today with you."

"I haven't seen her all day."

"I need to apologize. You're right. I never provided her with an atmosphere where she could tell her side of the story. That was my responsibility—one I would give any suspect, and very definitely should've given the woman I love."

"I don't think I actually accused you of that."

Gavin looked down at where blood stained a flat rock. "You should have."

"If she's not staying with you or with me, who would she bunk with? Almost everybody here is a couple."

"I'm not sure. Besides you and Anne, I've never really seen her—"

His phone buzzed in his pocket. He grabbed it, hoping it

could somehow be Lexi even though he knew she didn't have a phone. It was Tristan.

"How are you doing?" his brother asked.

"Honestly, I've been better. And not just because I found out the truth about Lexi. Because of how I handled it."

"Well, I'm not sure if I'm about to make your life easier or harder."

That didn't sound promising. "What?"

"There's more going on here than what I originally thought."

Gavin scrubbed a hand down his face. "How much more? What kind of more?"

"The kind of more that's going to take computer skills I don't possess to get to the bottom of."

"Involving Lexi?"

Tristan's voice was rushed. "She filed two separate police reports, the first a month after she got out of prison and then again six weeks after that."

"Hang on. I'm going to put you on speakerphone. Wavy Bollinger is with me."

"She said someone was following her," Tristan continued. "Stalking her. Given her history, the cops didn't take it seriously."

Shit. "If someone was stalking her, that would explain why she was using a high-end fake ID."

"Here's the thing, I went back to access the police reports today, and they were gone. No longer in the system. Neither of them, from two different precincts."

"What does that mean?" Wavy asked.

"It means somebody's going back and erasing any claims Lexi made about the stalker."

"That sounds kind of ominous," she muttered.

It definitely wasn't good.

"The other not good piece of this puzzle? Dashawn Cussler, the guy who sold her the ID, showed up dead this afternoon. Right about the time the police reports disappeared."

"Somebody's hunting her." Gavin rubbed at his chest. Shit. That was her other secret—her real secret. She had a stalker for real but didn't think anyone would believe her.

"I would say most definitely. You need to get Kendrick on this. I don't think I can help you anymore, big brother."

"Thank you, Tristan."

"I'll be waiting for your call if you need help on this end."

Gavin disconnected the call, already headed back toward the wedding reception. They needed to find Lexi. They needed to get Kendrick on this.

"I knew there was more she wasn't saying," Wavy said next to him. "I knew coming to Oak Creek was about more than hiding out from the press."

"Wavy, can you go look for her? She may not want to talk to me, but we need to make sure she's okay. It's time for the real truth. If she won't trust me enough to give that to me—which at this point I can't blame her for—you've got to talk her into telling it to you."

It ate at him, the thought that he wouldn't be the one she turned to after the months of desperately wanting to be that person. But it was nothing more than he deserved.

He stopped and looked at Wavy. "I was wrong. So damned wrong. She needed me to be the most levelheaded I could be, and I did what everyone else in her life has done. I refused to look any deeper into this. Refused to look into her heart. It's worse because I've spent all my time telling her she could trust me not to do that."

Wavy reached over and squeezed his arm. "I'm sure she'll

be willing to call it square for not giving you all her info up front."

They began walking again. "Just find her. The most important thing right now is keeping her safe. Once we eliminate the threat, then I can practice my groveling skills."

And hope it would be enough.

34

Lexi sat staring straight ahead on the flight from San Amado back to Reddington City. Her arms were clutched around her middle. Maybe if she held herself tight enough, the pieces of her that were shattering inside wouldn't come flying out of her body.

She almost welcomed the pain in her feet. Something she could focus on. Something that would eventually heal and return to normal.

Perhaps the only part of her that would heal.

I'm done with this.

She'd known she would lose Gavin when she told him who she was. She'd always known her past sins would be unforgivable for someone like him who only saw things in black and white.

He always wore the white hat, walked on the side of justice. That was why she'd avoided telling him, right? Because she'd known she would lose him.

But she hadn't known it would be so abrupt. That he wouldn't give her a chance to explain. Wouldn't ask for her side of the story—not that she had a good excuse to give.

I'm done with this.

And then he'd left. She'd so foolishly thought he might actually push forward, want to understand. She'd known ultimately it would probably be too much for him to accept, but somehow she'd thought he would at least hear her out.

But he'd stood there in the bathroom staring at her with such derision. Like everything about her had sickened him. Like she'd done it today rather than two years ago. Like she hadn't changed at all.

If Gavin couldn't see that she wasn't Alexandra Adams anymore, how could she expect anyone else to?

She had to leave Oak Creek. She couldn't stomach the thought of seeing Gavin day after day with him looking at her like that.

Like what, Lexi? Like you're a liar and a criminal? Nothing but the truth.

She wrapped her arms tighter around her middle, forcing herself to breathe. Survive this second. Survive the next one.

This flight had cleaned out most of her cash reserves. She wasn't sure what she was going to do or how long she had. Gavin didn't strike her as the type to report a sighting of her to the media, but she'd been wrong before.

She'd thought that if he couldn't accept what she'd done, he'd still at least help her with the stalker. But he didn't want anything to do with her at all.

Coming up with a plan right now was beyond her. Surviving was all she could do. She'd been in this place before —alone, broke, terrified—but was she strong enough to survive it again?

She had the fistful of pills the resort doctor had given her in case she changed her mind and needed them. If she took them all at once, would it be enough to make all the pain go away? Make it so she wouldn't have to wake up and face it again?

She was too exhausted to berate herself for that thought.

Besides, with her luck, it probably wouldn't be enough to do the job anyway. It would be labeled as one more attempt to get everyone's attention focused on her.

She dug her new phone out of her bag as they landed. She hadn't given Gavin the number—probably would never need to now. She was going to have to call Mac and see if he could come get her at the airport. She didn't have enough money to get to Oak Creek otherwise.

She'd come full circle, hadn't she? Back in Reddington City with no money to get the last few miles to Oak Creek.

Except the town she'd come to love didn't hold much welcome for her anymore. And she was in no shape to find someone's wallet to lift.

She shuffled off the plane, keeping her weight as much as possible on the outside of her feet and away from her heels and arches, which had taken the most abuse from the rocks. Only two cuts had been deep enough to require any stitches, but her feet still felt like big swollen blobs. She'd had to wear her tennis shoes loosened to their maximum points.

She limped down the terminal, past baggage claim since she only had her carry-on bag. Mac would come for her. She didn't need to tell him everything that had happened, just that she and Gavin had fought and things weren't going to work out. She would test the waters and hopefully be able to stay in Oak Creek for a while to build her money back up.

That would make it much easier than having to—

"Is that her?"

"Yes! Alexandra! Alexandra!"

"That's her, right?"

Lexi threw her hand up in front of her face as lights and cameras started flashing around her.

"Alexandra! What are you doing in Wyoming?"

"Alexandra, did you lead authorities to believe it was you who died in the fire?"

"Alexandra, where have you been since you got out of prison?"

They'd found her. The press had found her.

She said nothing, just kept her hand in front of her features, then dashed to the bathroom as quickly as her feet would allow. She didn't stop until she got inside the stall and dropped her small bag to the ground.

They'd found her. God, had she been wrong about Gavin? She hadn't seen him since he'd left their hotel room yesterday, and she'd spent most of today sitting at the small island airport until it was time for her flight. Had he figured out she'd left San Amado and called the press to ambush her here?

Gavin wouldn't do that, right? She couldn't reconcile the thought.

I'm done with this.

Maybe he'd figured out that calling the press would be the fastest way to get her out of Oak Creek. She pressed a fist against her stomach, which was filled with roiling, twisting despair. She didn't know what to believe anymore. She sat down on the toilet. What was she going to do? They had her cornered here in the airport arrivals terminal. The only way out was through them.

She held up her arm against the stall to steady herself as everything spun around her. What was she going to do?

Her phone buzzed in her hand. Mac. She didn't want to drag him into this, but he was all she had right now. Maybe he could help her figure out what to do.

"Mac." She could hardly recognize her own voice. "I need your help."

But it wasn't Mac who responded. "That old man is pretty troublesome for someone his age."

Lexi recognized her aunt's voice immediately. Her fingers tightened around the phone.

"How did you get Mac's phone, Cheryl? I thought you fled the country."

At least focusing on her aunt was bringing her back from the edge of that panic attack.

"Nicholas and I made some arrangements that allowed us to return. You haven't been the easiest person to reach, Alexandra. We've been trying to get in touch with you for weeks now."

"Fuck you."

The anger felt good. It chased away some of that shattering feeling inside. It would undoubtedly be back, but right this minute she didn't have to contend with it.

"That's not very polite, Alexandra."

"I don't give a rat's ass if I'm impolite or if I've made your life inconvenient. The best thing that ever happened to me was getting rid of you and Nicholas."

Her aunt gave a martyr's sigh. "That's a pretty selfish point of view given how we took you in when your parents died."

Lexi's laugh held no humor whatsoever. "Took me in, kept me emotionally and chemically dependent on you, then stole my money."

There was a moment of silence. "Nicholas was right. You've gotten more astute since we saw you last."

"I guess prison will do that to you. I don't know why you have Mac's phone, but put him on. I have nothing else to say to you. Nothing else you can take from me."

"Oh, I think we've found something."

Dread pooled in Lexi's stomach. "What are you doing, Cheryl?" she whispered. "Let me talk to Mac."

"We've been trying to get you to help us out of our predicament since you got out of prison, Lexi. You haven't been very cooperative."

"What are you talking about?"

"We tried to make it as easy for you as possible to go to the police and the press with your stalker story. To get back into the limelight and jumpstart your career."

"*What*?"

"Oh dear. Did you actually think you had a real stalker this time? Oh no. That was Nicholas and me trying to get you back in the game."

"You guys were my stalker?"

"Well, we hired someone to do the actual physical stuff, but tracking you, keeping you running from place to place . . . yes, us."

"I don't understand."

"You don't need to understand right now. What you need to do is go back out to where the press is waiting for you and give a statement."

"No." Hell no. She was done doing what Nicholas and Cheryl told her to do.

"Well, that's up to you, but I'm afraid it's your boss at that ridiculous bar who will pay the price if you resist. He's kind of old."

She ground her teeth. "What are you doing, Cheryl?"

"I'm fixing your screwups, as usual. Now, if you want the old man to be unharmed, you will go back out to the press and give a statement about how you've been hiding here in this godforsaken state."

She listened as Cheryl told her what to say—all of it horrible. But it didn't matter as long as it meant they would let Mac go.

Cheryl and Nicholas were her stalker? She'd never actually been in any real danger at all. It had all been a ploy. She'd cried wolf again without knowing it.

She listened in silence as Cheryl finished. "Say all that, then get in the limousine waiting for you out front."

Lexi disconnected the call and shuffled out of the stall. She didn't know what their end game was, but she wasn't going to allow Mac to be a pawn. Never again was an innocent person going to get hurt because of Lexi's choices.

So she would play Nicholas and Cheryl's game.

She walked over to the sink and pulled out a paper towel. If she was going out there to face the press, she was going out as Alexandra Adams, not Lexi Johnson. She scrubbed her stage makeup off, all contours gone. No shadows, no angles to trick the eye. She reapplied some lipstick and mascara. For her, the makeup was very light, but it least it was obviously Alexandra staring back at her in the mirror.

She forced a smirk on her lips, ignored the pain in her feet, and walked out. She had a role to play, and she would damned well do it.

The press were all still waiting when she came back into the main corridor. There were more of them now.

"Alexandra!" a dozen voices yelled at her at once. She pushed her sunglasses up onto her head and pasted a smile on her lips.

"Have you been in Wyoming all this time?"

"What was prison like?"

"Why are you here?"

The questions fired out at her rapidly, but she just smiled and left them to take her picture.

"Alexandra, why did you run away a few minutes ago?"

That was the question she was waiting for. "You guys bombard me after a three-hour commercial flight and want to know why I rushed into the bathroom to freshen up?"

That got some chuckles and everyone to quiet down a little. It made sense to them that she would run because of vanity. That's what she needed them to think.

"I see you all found me here in my humble home of the past few months."

"Why Wyoming?"

"Well, you might have heard I got into a little bit of trouble a couple of years ago." She smiled as they chuckled. "I decided I needed to do a little soul-searching, and this seemed like a good place for it. I was staying in a little town called Oak Creek trying to get my head on straight."

She turned to look at some of the other reporters. "Ends up, Podunkville with all its backwardness is not for me. There's nothing to like. The people are boring. There was nothing to do but sit around and watch the grass grow. There's nothing for me here in Wyoming. It's definitely time for me to get out of this state."

"Alexandra, are you afraid that you're offending the people of Wyoming with that statement?"

"All seven of them?" She cringed internally, but kept the charming smirk on her face. The people from Oak Creek were going to watch this and think the absolute worst of her. How could they not? "I'm not terribly worried about it. I'm going to take some time, ahem, here, and regroup. Make sure I've got my head on straight with some counseling."

"Did you fake your own death?"

She rolled her eyes, even though she knew Nicholas and Cheryl had to have been the ones to lead the cops into thinking it was her. "I can't take credit for that. Chalk one up to law enforcement incompetency."

"Why have you been hiding?" a male reporter yelled from the back.

"I haven't been hiding." She'd totally been hiding. "I just heard Wyoming was beautiful and thought I should check it out." She made a face. "Evidently not in the middle of winter."

"Are you still broke? Didn't your aunt and uncle spend all your money?"

"I've been in touch with my Aunt Cheryl and Uncle Nicholas." She forced herself not to grimace at their names. "There were a few misunderstandings but we have reconciled, and I'll be staying with them during my time off. They want me to take a year or two to handle my emotional issues too. Although definitely not in Wyoming."

More chuckles.

"Do you think that people are ready to forgive you and welcome you back with open arms?"

"I made a mistake. All I want to do is get my life back on track."

"Acting?"

No. Never. She *never* wanted to set foot in front of the camera ever again. She wanted to go back to Oak Creek, the Eagle's Nest, and stay there with Gavin. Her friends. Mac.

"What else would I do?" She smiled. "I've got to go now, you guys. Quit stalking me or you know I'll call the police and make a security team stay with me twenty-four seven."

More laughs. She turned away, exhausted. She'd done what Cheryl wanted—made it obvious she wouldn't be around for a while. Made sure no one from Oak Creek would come looking for her.

The reporters were yelling over each other again.

"Alexandra, are you ever in touch with any of the cast or crew from *Day's End*?"

"Alexandra, what was prison like? Are you ever going to talk about that?"

"Alexandra, isn't there anything about Wyoming that you like? Will you miss any of it?"

She stopped and looked back over her shoulder. "Redwoods. I'll miss the redwoods."

The reporter who'd asked the questions gave her a weird look. "There are no redwoods in Wyoming."

"There's at least one." She turned away and slipped her sunglasses over her eyes. "That's all the questions I have time for now."

She ignored their further inquiries and walked outside as quickly as she could on her injured feet to get into the waiting limousine.

Both Cheryl and Nicholas were sitting there. Nicholas pressed a button on his phone to make a call as the car pulled away from the curb. "We've got her. Kill the old man. Make sure it looks like a heart attack."

"No!" Lexi lunged for Nicholas and his phone. "No! You said you wouldn't hurt Mac if I cooperated."

Cheryl shook her head. She had a gun and it was pointed at Lexi. "Your chance to cooperate ended the moment you went off the grid to get away from us. Almost cost us everything."

Lexi wasn't going to stay in here with them. She needed to get to Mac. Call someone who could get to his house and stop them from hurting him. She lunged for the car door. She didn't care if she got shot or hurt. She had to try.

Nicholas yanked her back. "I told you," he said to Cheryl. "She's not going to do what we say anymore."

Lexi fought. They weren't going to shoot her. She was no good to them dead. She needed to get out of this car.

She felt a sting in her arm.

"Just because she won't listen to us doesn't mean we can't make her do what we want."

Wooziness settled around her. That same feeling she'd always gotten when they'd given her the pills, but this time it came on much more quickly.

Cheryl grabbed her chin, peering into her eyes. "That ought to calm you down."

"No." She reached for the door again but couldn't seem to find the handle. Heaviness weighted her arms. "No. Don't hurt Mac."

"Since when do you care about other people?" Nicholas asked.

The world grayed around her.

Cheryl pinched her chin. "Like I said, you almost cost us everything, and now you're going to help us get it back."

35

Gavin found Kendrick talking to Baby and his fiancée, Quinn, at one of the bars for the reception as Wavy went off in the other direction. Kendrick and Quinn were deep in a discussion about the nuances of literary analysis, from what Gavin caught.

Considering the two of them had met when Quinn taught at Harvard and Kendrick attended as a student, Gavin wasn't surprised.

Baby didn't seem to have much to contribute to the conversation—the man was a wizard when it came to all things engineering and mechanical, but not so much comparative literature. But he seemed quite content to play with his pretty fiancée's hair and the skin of her shoulder exposed by her strapless dress.

"Gavin." Kendrick slapped him on the shoulder. "Haven't seen you around much. You do know the booze is free for the wedding, right?"

"I need your help."

All three of them recognized the gravity in Gavin's voice.

"What is it?" Kendrick asked. Baby stiffened, slipping a protective arm around Quinn's waist and pulling her closer.

Quinn looked around. "It's Lexi, right? I haven't seen her all day, and she wasn't at the wedding. What's going on?"

Gavin kept his attention focused on Kendrick. "Remember how you told me you were willing to dig deeper into Lexi's past if I needed you to? I need you to."

"Gavin—" Baby said.

Gavin turned to his friend. He couldn't blame Baby for warning Gavin off. Gavin had almost kept Baby and Quinn apart because he hadn't been willing to take Quinn at face value. "This isn't about me being suspicious. Lexi's in trouble. Dangerous trouble, and we need to help her." He turned back to Kendrick. "Do you know a Dashawn Cussler?"

The younger man stiffened. "Are you asking me as an officer of the law?"

"I'm asking because he just showed up dead and has links to Lexi. He provided an ID for her.

Kendrick whistled through his teeth. "When it comes to IDs, especially those that need to actually pass muster, Cussler is the best. *Was* the best. But his prices are pretty exorbitant, and he's definitely not on the side of the angels like we were talking about."

"In what way?"

"He's got a bad reputation for double-crossing and blackmailing. I don't think he himself is actually violent, but he definitely has links to people who are. Why did Lexi need an ID from him? Most people use his work to flee the country or," Kendrick winced, "hide out from the law."

"Lexi's real name is Alexandra Adams."

"The television star?"

That came from Finn. He'd walked up behind them, arm

around his wife Charlie. Gabe and his fiancée, Jordan, were with them.

"Of course!" Charlie slapped Finn's chest with the back of her hand. "I knew there was something familiar about her."

"Look." Gavin glanced around at the gathering circle of his friends. They all knew that lives had almost been lost because of Alexandra's actions two years ago. "I know Linear has a past history with this woman, and it's not particularly pretty. But I think she's in trouble, and she needs our help. If you won't help her for her, help her for *me*."

They all stared at him for a long moment, and he prepared to pull out more arguments. Hopefully Wavy would come back over and help.

"Because you're in love with her, duh," Gabe finally said, the expression humorous on the former Navy SEAL's face. "We've all been aware of that for weeks."

"She deserves a second chance," Jordan said softly. "Whatever mistakes she might've made in the past, she deserves a second chance."

Gabe reached down and wrapped one of his massive arms around the quiet woman and easily lifted her until they were face-to-face. "Thank you for giving me a second chance when I didn't necessarily deserve one."

"I meant—"

He kissed her to stop her words. Everyone around was glad he did. Jordan didn't need to apologize for her past anymore.

Gavin looked back over at Kendrick. "I think Lexi has a stalker, a real one this time, and that's why she ended up in Oak Creek and why she used Dashawn Cussler to get an ID."

"And now Cussler is dead?" Kendrick asked.

"Yes, and two separate police reports Lexi filed have suddenly disappeared."

Kendrick began typing on his phone. "Someone is erasing any sign that she's had trouble."

"Bingo!" Gavin nodded. "I don't know exactly what it means, but it's not good."

"I've already got Neo on it back home," Kendrick said, looking up from his phone for a second. "Silly me, I thought there wouldn't be any international crises while I went away for the weekend, so I didn't bring my system with me."

"You're sure we can trust her?" Gavin asked.

Neo—Neoma LeBarre—had a lot of gray areas herself. She'd helped out the team quite a few times, but she had also made some questionable judgment calls when she'd first come into the picture.

"You want to know about Cussler and the police reports that were erased? Neo will get that for us. And she likes Lexi. Or at least likes that Lexi sent you all those obnoxious drinks." Kendrick grinned down at his phone.

The rest of the team circled around now, including the bride and groom.

Gavin turned toward everyone. "Lexi changed her appearance and spent every dime she had on an ID in an attempt to keep herself safe from the stalker hunting her. We all knew she had a secret, and now we know she actually had two. We can talk to her more about the Alexandra Adams stuff once we know she's safe."

Everyone nodded, faces concerned.

"Where is she?" Anne asked.

Gavin scrubbed a hand down his face. "No one has seen her since yesterday. When I found out who she really was, I didn't handle it well. We need to find her, get the details of exactly what's going on, and help her.

"Oh shit. Neo has already found her. Actually, *everybody* has already found her." Kendrick flipped his phone around.

" 'Alexandra Adams hates Wyoming' is trending all over social media and entertainment news."

Kendrick airdropped his phone screen to the television so they could all see the interview.

"That's at the Reddington City airport," Boy Riley said. "I know that place like the back of my hand. It looks like the press ambushed her coming out of the terminal."

Gavin watched as someone he definitely didn't know, but was similar to the person he'd talked to in the bathroom yesterday, addressed the reporters. She was flippant, cruelly charming in her comments about Oak Creek and its residents. Generally unlikable, yet beautiful.

This was Alexandra Adams, but it was definitely *not* Lexi Johnson.

Jesus, he'd convinced everyone here they needed to help her, and now she'd said all of this. This wasn't real, he knew it, but how could he expect them to?

The whole group went quiet as they watched Alexandra make one obnoxious statement after another.

They were still quiet when it was done. He was going to have to convince them that what she'd said wasn't how she really felt or who she really was.

Of course, he could be wrong. He'd been wrong in a colossal way about Janeen. Lexi could've fooled him and was actually the smirky starlet on the screen right now, talking trash about his home state.

But goddammit, he hadn't given her the benefit of the doubt *once* in the entire time that he'd known her. He'd been accusatory and self-righteous from the beginning, and he wasn't going to make that mistake again.

If she played him for a fool now, then so be it. But he wasn't going to let his suspicious nature cause him to disbelieve her again.

Convincing everyone else to feel the same might not be as easy. "You guys, I know this looks bad. But—"

"She's in trouble," Charlie said, still looking at the TV.

"She definitely needs our help," Zac chimed in.

"Rewind back to the beginning," Anne took the phone out of Kendrick's hand. "They sliced it together, but look . . ."

Lexi had definitely been walking more gingerly—because of her hurt feet—when the press first caught her. She'd hidden her face, so the reporters couldn't see the differences in the makeup that she'd removed in the bathroom.

She'd run from them as Lexi Johnson, but had come back out Alexandra Adams. No hesitancy in her step, ignoring any pain she was in. She was playing a role.

"Something happened while she was in that bathroom," Gabe said.

Quinn, who had worked with Lexi at the Eagle's Nest so probably knew her the best besides him, nodded. "I agree. She never would've said those things. Even if she felt them, she never would've said it if she didn't have to. I think it was a deliberate attempt to make sure we were mad at her."

"To make sure no one comes looking for her if she's gone," Gavin muttered.

Zac, arm still around Anne, caught Gavin's eye. "And she basically announced she'll be gone for a year or two."

Gavin turned to Kendrick. "Can Neo access some other footage to see if there's anyone interesting in the periphery that we can't see from here?"

Kendrick nodded. "You're thinking someone with a weapon?"

"I'm thinking she was definitely coerced into what she said. Someone is forcing her somehow."

"I'll call my pilot and get the jet ready for you guys," Cade said.

He was gone before Gavin could thank him. That was pretty excessive generosity. Cade might have money to spare, but that didn't mean he had to spend it to help Lexi, who was essentially a stranger.

Everyone watched the footage from different sources to see if they could pick up any other clues when Gavin's phone buzzed in his hand.

"Sheriff Nelson?" Crap. He was probably calling about Alexandra's news conference.

"Gavin, I hate to interrupt you while you're at the wedding but we've had an issue here."

"The news statement with Alexandra Adams? I—"

"There was an attempt on Mac Templeton's life."

"What?" Gavin barked into the phone.

"He says a guy came, stole his phone so someone could get in touch with Lexi, then planned to kill him."

"How did Mac stop him?"

The sheriff let out a sigh. "Ethan and Jess saw the guy in town. Thought he was acting suspicious. Saw him following Mac back to his house and came rushing into my office. Those two wouldn't let up until I sent someone over to investigate. You know how little Jess is."

Gavin glanced over at Finn and Charlie, Ethan's parents. Finn was holding the phone so he and Charlie could both hear whatever was being said. Finn's eyes shot to Gavin.

"Is everybody okay?" Gavin asked. "The kids?"

Everyone knew Ethan and Jess could get in more trouble than the rest of the town put together.

"Yeah. Scared Officer Mercer half to death to find someone actually at Mac's house, holding him at gunpoint, but she handled it. Arrested the guy."

Jesus. "Curtis, we're just finding out that Lexi has a stalker."

"Well this guy isn't your stalker. He claims he was hired by some middle-aged white couple. He doesn't have all their details but they called each other Nicholas and Sherri."

Oh fuck. "Cheryl."

"What?"

"Nicholas and *Cheryl*, not Sherri. I know who they are." Lexi's aunt and uncle. "Lexi's in danger. We're on our way back. Keep an eye out around town. I don't know if there will be more trouble headed your way."

He hung up and walked toward Finn and Charlie, who'd finished their call too.

"Evidently Ethan and Jess stumbled into a hot mess." Finn shook his head. "The usual for those two. I just got off the phone with Ethan."

"Looks like they might have saved Mac's life. Someone was trying to kill him to get to Lexi."

Charlie squeezed Finn's arm. "Good thing you've always taught Ethan to follow his instincts."

Gavin got a text from Cade.

Jet is wheels up whenever you are ready.

"It's time to go rescue one of our own."

THE TEAM WAS GOING in blind. They'd gone in blind on other missions in the past, but this one felt more personal.

Probably because it was. Way more personal.

Zac had stayed behind on the island with his bride to go on their honeymoon. Gavin didn't blame him a bit, especially since the close call yesterday.

And besides, the team on the jet with him couldn't possibly be any stronger. Finn and Aiden had both served with Gavin as Green Berets. Gabe hadn't been in the army, but his years as a Navy SEAL made him more than prepared.

And then there were the final two members of the team, whose arrival just before the plane took off had ensured Zac could stay with his new bride.

Dorian and Ray.

Neither took part in active missions any longer, for reasons Gavin more than understood—Dorian suffered from severe PTSD after being held and tortured in an enemy prison camp for five weeks while they'd been in the army. Ray had her own demons just as cruel.

The two of them were the most lethal trained killers Gavin had ever known. The chances of getting Lexi out safely no matter what the situation had improved exponentially the moment Dorian and Ray—Ghost and Wraith—had stepped on the plane.

Reports from Kendrick and Neo were starting to come in through the plane's Wi-Fi, just in time since they'd be landing in Reddington City in less than an hour. Everyone pored over them.

Gavin answered his phone when it buzzed in his hand.

"Did you all get what I sent?" Kendrick asked. "This shit isn't good, Gavin."

"I know." Gavin was looking through the data on a laptop.

"It looks like her aunt and uncle sold her to this Dr. Hamilton guy—they got two million dollars deposited into an account from an account suspected as his. That can't be right, can it?"

"Her aunt and uncle have been manipulating her for a decade. They stole all her money when she first went to prison. So . . . yeah, I think it could very well be right."

"Dr. Hamilton is bad news. He's on a watch list for damned near every law enforcement agency in the world. No recent pictures, so nobody's been able to arrest him." Kendrick's voice lowered. "And he's got strong ties to Mosaic."

Fuck. Information brokers, weapons dealers, cyberterrorists, human traffickers . . . all available under Mosaic's umbrella. Gavin didn't want Lexi anywhere near them, especially since she'd publicly announced she'd be gone for a year or two.

"We need to get to her before her aunt and uncle hand her over. It'll be a hell of a lot more complicated if she's in Mosaic's clutches."

"Agreed. Neo and I are digging for a time and location of the meet. Hopefully, we'll have something once you're on the ground."

"Thanks, Blaze."

"Ian DeRose is going to have weapons and vehicles waiting for you when you land. He's very interested now that Mosaic may be involved. And hopefully, I'll have a location."

"From your lips to God's ears."

"Side of the angels, man. That's all we can do."

Gavin hung up to read more about Cheryl and Nicholas Adams. None of it was good. He watched the press ambush Lexi at the airport one more time, hoping to catch something he'd missed before.

But all he could see were her sad eyes. Even worse, her hopeless expression when she turned back to say she'd miss the Wyoming redwoods. Miss *him*.

She knew she was in trouble and had no hope that anyone would be coming to help her.

That was his fault.

He picked up the carved keychain she'd given him for Christmas from where it sat on the table, and rubbed it between his fingers. He'd told her it was now his lucky charm, and he was going to keep it with him all the time. But the truth was he'd wanted a little piece of *her* with him all the time.

"You okay, man?" Gabe squeezed Gavin's shoulder as he passed him in the narrow jet aisle and took the seat across the tiny table from him. Finn plopped down in the other row.

"So much makes sense now." Gavin rubbed his forehead with his finger and thumb. "So much about Lexi's behavior. She was scared. I let it go when I shouldn't have."

He thought about that letter incident on Christmas Day. How she'd completely freaked out over something so innocent. Right fucking then he should've pushed to know what was wrong.

He sat back, then let out a breath. "Then when I *should've* let it go—when I found out she was really Alexandra Adams —I didn't."

"Been there, brother," Gabe said. "Almost lost Jordan before we got our start. The important thing is we fixed it."

"Lexi thinks she's in this alone, that no one is coming to help."

"Violet thought that once too," Aiden said, reaching up to scratch at the long scar that marred the cheek of his otherwise almost-pretty face. "I had to leave her behind in an impossible situation. But I came back."

"You show up this time," Ray's feminine voice said from behind him. "Then you show up again and again, every single day in every way she needs you, until she finally defaults to knowing you *will* show up."

Dorian slipped an arm around Ray's shoulder and pulled her up against his chest. "All you have to do is be who you are: steady, solid, unshakeable. Redwood."

36

Consciousness came back slowly, the darkness sticky and clingy, like walking through a spider web, then spending a thousand minutes trying to get it off your skin, your hair, everything.

But it was a familiar darkness as it folded in on her, swirled around her like a deep fog. Or a blizzard. But there was no Gavin this time.

I'm done with this.

The words—the sound of his voice—dragged her closer to consciousness, even though she didn't want to feel the pain she knew was waiting for her. She and Gavin were finished.

And *Mac.* Mac was dead because of her. Another innocent person destroyed because of her choices.

She bit back a sob and forced the darkness the rest of the way back. And immediately wished she hadn't. The pain— physical, emotional—was almost unbearable.

She opened her eyes.

Everything was sideways.

The cobwebs still surrounded her mind, making it hard to

think. She took a breath. She was lying on a couch. That's why everything was sideways.

Cheryl and Nicholas had taken her. Drugged her.

Killed Mac.

They were in some sort of cabin, not very big. Nicholas sat at a small table while Cheryl paced back and forth in front of him.

Lexi closed her eyes against the dizziness. It was so much easier to relax into the darkness than fight it. So much easier to let it numb everything.

Because pain waited outside the numb darkness—that clawing, knifing, biting pain that would rip her apart. And there were pain's companions: loneliness and terror. She couldn't fight all three.

Mac was dead. Gavin wanted nothing to do with her. Oak Creek hated her.

She let the darkness drag her under again.

She had no idea how long she stayed in the black, conscious but not coherent—caught frozen in that moment where she was not quite asleep and not quite awake. But then she reached the fulcrum, the pivot point in the darkness, and couldn't stay there. She was sliding back toward consciousness whether she wanted to or not.

She clawed her way to the surface. Opened her eyes. She was going to have to find the strength to fight through the numbness, to face the pain that waited for her.

She tried to sit up and let out a moan.

"I told you, you gave her too much," Nicholas said.

"She'll be fine. Her system is just a little out of practice with how our game is played."

"Hamilton and his men are going to be here soon. He wants to see her conscious, coherent. And I want to get out of here as soon as possible." Nicholas looked around. "The whole cabin-in-the-woods thing is not our style."

"What are you doing?" Lexi said. The words felt thick and garbled in her mouth. She forced herself to sit all the way up.

"See?" Cheryl said. "She's awake. I told you she would be fine."

"Where are we?"

"Where are we?" Nicholas mocked her tone, then walked over and pinched her chin while he looked into her eyes. "We're in this shitty state you made us track you to, you little bitch."

She pulled her chin back from his fingers and looked around. She didn't recognize anything in the small room. Glancing at the window let her know it was night outside.

"You've been hard to find, Alexandra," Cheryl chimed in.

Lexi breathed through the dizziness. Forced herself to look at her aunt. "I thought I had a stalker, so I was hiding."

Nicholas chuckled. "Craig Isaacson got a little overzealous."

"My stunt director Craig Isaacson?" Lexi blinked at them, trying to make sense of everything. "What does he have to do with this?"

"That's who we hired when you first got out of jail. He was supposed to follow you around, scare you, and then send you running back to us when we stepped in to help out."

"He punched me. Threw me into a wall."

Nicholas shrugged. "I guess he was a little angry over losing his livelihood. When they brought someone in to replace you on the show, she had her own stunt coordinator, so Isaacson lost his job. You screwed over a lot of people when you decided to cry wolf, Alexandra."

Lexi gritted her teeth. They'd killed Mac, kidnapped her, tied her up, forced her to publicly say horrible things about people and places she cared about, but it was hearing them call her *Alexandra* that had her wanting to break through the rest of this ice and rip their eyes out.

It made no sense, but it was something to latch on to. To fight the pull of the numbness.

Because fuck them. She might be alone and in emotional agony for the rest of her life, but she was not going to give her aunt and uncle *anything*.

"I don't know what you want from me, but you can forget it. Even if I could get a job in the entertainment industry, I have no interest in going back there. And as soon as I get out of here, I'm going to tell them what you've done. That you killed Mac."

Nicholas and Cheryl looked at each other, then laughed. Nicholas sat down at the table. "The great thing about you, Alexandra, is that you've destroyed your own credibility without us having to use any of the stopgaps we put in place over the years in case you tried to get rid of us."

"What?"

"We've got years' worth of doctors' notes, psychologists' reports, toxicology screens, release letters from drug treatment facilities, all proving you're a danger to yourself," he continued.

"I never went to any drug treatment facilities."

Cheryl sat down at the table with him. "None of the documents are real, that's why we never attempted to use them—because if you argued their authenticity, we'd have a difficult time getting anyone to believe us. But now, we don't have that problem. You've made sure no one will ever believe you again."

"You can't make me work. You can't make me get in front of cameras. I won't do it."

She fought the dizzying fog harder as they smiled. Smiling wasn't good.

"Of course not." Cheryl shifted closer to Nicholas. "It's too soon anyway. Everyone still hates you. So you'll go away for a couple of years, then you'll come back repentant and contrite. Everyone will be much more likely to forgive you then."

"Are you going to keep me in this cabin for a year? You think I'm going to cooperate?"

"Oh no." Cheryl made a tsking noise. "We found Dr. Hamilton, someone who specializes in . . . *keeping* people. Training them, so to speak. He was very interested in you. Paid a premium that will allow us to live the way we're accustomed to until you return to your career. A lifestyle you ripped away from us with your lies and arrest two years ago."

Lexi sat up straighter, ignoring the dizziness. "You *sold* me?"

Cheryl made a sour face, as if she found the word distasteful. "More like rented. He gave us his assurance that you wouldn't be scarred."

"Physically, at least," Nicholas muttered.

"I need water." She needed to dilute whatever was in her system. She'd thought they'd brought her here to talk her into going back into the business. Not to *sell* her to someone.

She had to get out of here. Had to find a way out herself because no one was coming to help her. Even if Gavin or any of the Linear Tactical guys had been willing to help her, what she'd said to the press today would put an end to that.

She was on her own.

Cheryl walked over and dropped a bottle of water in her lap. "I did hear Dr. Hamilton likes keeping his subjects caged. But honestly, I don't think he's in it for the kink. He's a scientist—working on chemical compounds that will allow some sort of mind control."

Lexi nearly spewed the water. "What?"

"Yes. He and his organization need test subjects—people who've shown an aptitude for chemical dependence and who wouldn't be missed."

Nicholas smiled. "And thanks to your announcement earlier today, that's you, my dear."

Cheryl smiled. "We get two million dollars, and they get their guinea pig. They even cleaned up our clumsy attempts to get you back in the public eye with a 'real' stalker. All police reports gone. The man you bought your ID from . . . also gone."

Her aunt and uncle—the only family she had left—didn't care about anyone but themselves. They had killed to buy themselves financial freedom, and were selling her to further ensure it.

She had to get out of here. Now, while it was just her and them. Her head was still dizzy, her body sluggish—not to mention the shape of her feet. But this might be her only chance.

Because she definitely wasn't going to allow herself to be used for human experimentation—in a fucking cage. She'd rather die.

She stood up. Her feet still hurt, but the drugs were making that pain bearable. She'd have to find a way to run on them. "I have to go to the bathroom. Whatever you gave me is making me sick."

Cheryl pointed at a door in the back corner of the cabin. Lexi stumbled toward it, partly because of the pills and her feet, but mostly to keep up the appearance of being much more under the influence than she really was. She needed them to underestimate her.

As soon as she saw the window in the bathroom, she knew it was her ticket to escape. Evidently Nicholas and

Cheryl were so confident that the drugs would keep Lexi passive that they didn't think to require her to keep the door open.

And why should they? For a decade, she'd been passive. Stupid. Had done whatever they wanted her to.

She made a retching noise to cover the sound of her opening the window, then moaned and poured a little water into the toilet to make it sound even more gross. She needed to buy as much time as she could.

Climbing up onto the sink was treacherous. She could barely keep her balance as she hoisted herself up and through the small opening. She landed with a thump on the cold ground.

Nothing outside provided any clear indication of where she should go. It was dark. It was cold. All she could see were trees and wilderness.

She had a jacket on, but not the new, heavy coat she'd bought. She was dressed for San Amado, not for running through Wyoming in the middle of February. She wanted the hat and scarf and gloves Gavin had given her.

She pushed all thoughts of him away. She couldn't think of him right now, not if she had any chance of surviving this. She would have to deal with her shattered heart later.

The sound of approaching vehicles caused her to start running—away from them. They were in the middle of nowhere. Anyone approaching wouldn't be here to help her.

And it wouldn't take her aunt and uncle long to figure out she wasn't still in that bathroom.

She wanted to sprint, but her feet only allowed her to hobble. And she had to stop every few seconds against a tree to combat the dizziness from the drugs.

She wasn't going to make it. She knew a few moments later when she heard people—at least three men with deep, scary voices—outside yelling. They'd already discovered she was gone, and she hadn't made it far enough.

She kept going, swallowing a sob when she heard someone yell that they'd spotted her footprints.

Damn it, she hadn't thought about covering her tracks at all. And now it was too late. There was no way she was going to be able to outrun them. Not in her condition.

She kept going anyway.

Water rushed somewhere nearby, and she headed for it. She could follow the river and lose them since they wouldn't be able to track her footsteps along it. Maybe this was her chance to get away. Her chance to set the record straight about what she'd said. Her chance to let the cops know what had really happened to Mac.

But as she broke out from the line of trees and rushed forward, she realized she wasn't at the same level as the rushing water she'd heard. The river was in a ravine at least thirty feet down. She stopped at its edge, her sobbing breaths filling her ears. There was no way for her to get down to it without jumping.

And there was no way she'd survive the jump.

The men were still behind her. She glanced over her shoulder as Cheryl and Nicholas shouted her name farther back.

They were going to catch her.

They were going to *cage* her.

The worst part was, in the end, no one would miss her. No one would look for her. Everyone would assume she was off doing her normal selfish stuff. She'd be some human experiment, and when she did come back, she wouldn't be herself.

Lexi stared down into the dark, rushing water, barely discernible in the moonlight.

She stopped fighting the drugs swirling through her system like the waters below. Let the numbness pull her.

It would be over quickly if she jumped. Painful for a second, then nothing.

She'd gotten Nadine scarred. Gotten Mac killed. Lied to everyone who'd cared about her.

She could end it all right here and never do anyone else any damage.

"If you move, we shoot you."

The voice was maybe twenty or thirty feet behind her, right where the trees ended. She didn't look. Whether they shot her or she jumped, the result was going to be the same. She took another step toward the ledge.

She wished she could've gotten one more message to Gavin. Not trying to excuse anything, just to say she was sorry. Sorry for the lies. Sorry that she'd disrupted his life.

And then her brain broke. Her mind snapped. The drugs took over. She knew they had because Gavin stepped out from around a tree on the other side of the ravine and walked toward her.

"I'm going to need you to take a step back from that ledge, Green Eyes. I can't take a chance on anything happening to you."

She shook her head. "You're not here."

He reached a hand out toward her. "I am here. I should've been here sooner. You should've never been on that plane without me. I should've listened instead of running my mouth."

"Boss." That came from one of the men behind her. "We've got an unknown subject across the ravine. What do you want us to do?"

She couldn't hear the answer—the guy was talking into some sort of communication unit—but she knew they weren't going to let Gavin walk away from here. These people had already killed and would kill again.

Would kill Gavin.

"Get down!" she screamed at him, wishing the ravine weren't so wide so she could throw herself across it. Protect him. Save him.

"No!" She closed her eyes and threw her hands over her ears as a gun fired. She was terrified at what she would see when she opened her eyes but forced herself to do it anyway.

Gavin was still standing there. Still watching her. Still had an arm stretched out to her. "Step back from that ledge, Green Eyes, and I promise I'll come around and get you."

She forced herself to breathe. "But . . . How . . ."

He smiled. That smile he only ever used with her. "I'm not here by myself. There are a lot of people who want to make sure you make it back safely."

Gavin pointed to either side behind her, and she looked.

Finn was dragging out one unconscious guy. Gabe was restraining a second guy on the other side of her.

She looked back at Gavin. "The rest of the team have your aunt and uncle subdued. Kendrick got us all the info we needed to know you were here."

"But how . . . All that stuff I said to the press . . ."

"Anybody who knew you knew immediately that wasn't how you really felt. Including me. *Especially* me. Take a step back from that ledge, Lexi Johnson. I can't take a chance on losing the most important person in my life. I love you."

She took a step back, then another one.

"It took me way too long to get here, but stay right there. I'm coming over to your side."

Less than a minute later, she was in his arms, his fingers trailing down her cheeks as he kissed her. "And I'm not leaving you again."

37

The next month was the best of Gavin's life.

For nearly a week after they'd rescued her at the cabin, he wouldn't let Lexi out of his bed.

He tended to the wounds on her feet. He helped her as her body rebelled and then craved the drugs that had been reintroduced to her—a mini withdrawal, complete with muscle pain, nausea, and clammy skin.

Once she made it through that, he made love to her as many times and ways as she felt up for.

He held her as she cried when she saw Mac was alive—and grumpy as ever. Held her as she cried some more as she realized she had no stalker. No more reason to be afraid. Her aunt and uncle would be going to jail for attempted murder. Law enforcement was still trying to find Dr. Hamilton and any other members of Mosaic—hopefully, the men Gavin's team had tranquilized would provide more information.

But mostly, they talked. They talked about all the things she hadn't been able to tell him before. He listened as she explained her reasoning behind what had happened two years ago. And although he would never be able to condone that behavior, he was very well aware that the person who'd made those decisions wasn't the woman he was in love with now.

And when it came to making poor choices, he certainly had apologizing of his own to do.

They talked about her past, about his. She still fell asleep every time he started telling her stories about being in the army.

And he loved it.

They talked about the future. His. Hers. Theirs. Because there was no way he was letting her out of his sight without her realizing that as long as she wanted it, they had a future *together*.

But he also wanted to give her choices. For the first time, she had a lot of options in front of her. No one out to hurt her. No one out to control her. No one else getting the two million dollars that Kendrick had shown her was in her accounts. The money Nicholas and Cheryl had gotten for attempting to sell Lexi to Dr. Hamilton and Mosaic.

For the first time, maybe since her parents had died, Lexi had the freedom to do what she wanted, to be who she wanted to be.

He only wanted her to know that he would be honored to be among those options.

She was no longer trying to hide her appearance, and Oak Creek had accepted Lexi into its arms with no problems as she went back to work at the Eagle's Nest. That was the great thing about small-town gossip—everyone had seen the interview she'd given, but before they could be offended, the rumor mill had provided all the details about what had really happened.

The town wasn't a stranger to protecting its own—even when its own was a celebrity—and everyone had been very careful about honoring Lexi's need for privacy. Since the press thought she was off the grid for a while, nobody had come looking for her.

Good, because Gavin wanted her all to himself. She'd basically moved in with him. Well, more like he'd gone and gotten all her stuff that first week and hadn't let her move it back out again. He wanted her with him, where she belonged.

Their closeness was why he'd realized she was keeping something from him again. Another secret had cropped up the past couple of days, and he wasn't sure what it was she wasn't telling him. Only knew it was *something*.

A huge chunk mourned that they were back to secrets.

And then she'd decided to sleep at her house last night, because she had things she needed to do all day today.

He wasn't going to let them revert back to old patterns and behaviors that would drive a wedge between them. He'd gone to the Eagle's Nest this afternoon to have it out with her.

But it had been closed. Neither she nor Mac had been there. He couldn't remember the last time that had happened on a Friday.

So when he'd gotten her text this evening—from the phone Mac had given her, the phone she still carried with her —asking him to meet her at the Eagle's Nest, he'd jumped into his SUV immediately.

He hadn't seen her in nearly twenty-four hours. That was too long. He didn't want her cutting him out of her life even for a day. And he planned to make sure she knew that.

Surprise hit him as he arrived in the bar's parking lot—it was nearly full with vehicles he recognized, including Lexi's. Evidently, when the sign had said *closed* earlier, that had only been temporary, because there were lights shining brightly and noise coming from inside.

He walked inside and found nearly everyone he knew there—drinking, talking, laughing. Like any given Friday night here. His eyes sought Lexi and found her, serving drinks as usual.

He didn't hesitate. He walked over, slipped an arm around her waist, and yanked her against him. And kissed her.

Not a chaste, we're-in-public kiss. A deep, heated kiss that left nothing to anyone's imagination about what he'd rather be doing with her right now.

"I'm glad you're here," she finally said against his lips when he let her catch her breath.

"I missed you. No more secrets."

She stepped back, those green eyes studying him. She reached up and trailed her fingers across his jaw. "I worried you. I'm sorry. I didn't mean to."

He leaned his forehead against hers. "We've had too many secrets. I don't want to leave room for something to come between us again."

She nodded. "I meant this as more of a surprise than a secret."

That thought had never occurred to him—that her keeping something from him could be for a *good* reason. "Then I'm sorry too. I forget some secrets can be good. Tell me your surprise."

"I've figured out what I want to do. With my money, my time. My life."

His stomach clenched, but he kept his features carefully neutral. He'd spent the past month making sure she knew she had endless options.

He just hadn't thought she'd make a decision without talking to him about it first. But whatever it was, he would respect it. Support it. Even if it didn't involve the two of them being together.

Even if that broke his fucking heart.

"Finally, Redwood is here," Mac yelled from across the bar. "Can we announce it now?"

"Announce what?" he murmured to Lexi.

She smiled at him. "Mac wants to tell it."

"People!" Mac banged a tray on the bar to get everyone to quiet down. "I have something I want to say."

"Go ahead, Mac," Finn yelled.

"Is this going to end with drinks being on the house?" Baby called out.

Mac rolled his eyes. "Maybe."

Lots of hoots and hollers for that one.

"From now on," Mac continued. "I'm not going to kick anybody out of the Eagle's Nest, no matter how late it is."

More cheers.

"Because as of this afternoon, I'm retired."

Now it got quiet.

"You okay, Mac?" someone called out. The question all of them were thinking.

"Never better." He picked up something from the bar and walked toward Gavin and Lexi. "I had someone make me an offer on this place, and I couldn't refuse."

The pieces came together in Gavin's mind, right before Mac handed the small sign in his hand to Lexi. She held it up.

Under New Ownership.

"Meet the new owner of the Eagle's Nest!" Mac yelled.

Lexi was beaming. "Drinks are on the house!"

Everyone cheered. The music got turned back up and the drinks started flowing.

Mac pulled Lexi in for a hug, then reached over and pulled Gavin in too. "I would've given it to you for free, you know. Because you're family."

She kissed his leathery cheek. "I would've given you all the money I had. Because you're family too."

Gavin spent the next couple of hours helping Lexi make and pour drinks. Watched her hug the people who meant the world to him—who well and truly had included her in their ranks. Saw her touch the bar and the booths with the kind of pride that meant she was content with where she found herself.

Saw her laugh and knew he had to spend forever with this woman.

It wasn't until things started settling down that he was able to catch her by the waist and pull her onto a barstool.

"Sit. All those times you made me a fancy-named drink, now I want to make you one."

She laughed but grimaced as he went around behind the bar. "After all the ones I sent you, I'm pretty sure I should be terrified."

He winked at her. "I'm going to make three, and you get to choose."

Gavin wasn't a professional bartender, but he'd been raised by Ronald Zimmerman, so he knew his way around alcohol. Besides, the drinks he was making weren't that complicated.

He finished all three and set them in front of her.

She raised an eyebrow. "Is that a margarita, a Bloody Mary, and sangria?"

He shook his head, tsking. "Now that you're the owner of a bar, you're going to have to learn to be a little more discerning with drinks."

She smiled. "Is that so?"

"Absolutely. These are not just *any* margarita, Bloody Mary or sangria. It's a Marry Me Margarita, a Bloody Marry Me, and Say I Do Sangria."

Her eyes got big as she looked up at him from across the drinks. "Gavin . . ."

"If you're staying in Oak Creek, I want you tied to me in every way possible, Green Eyes. So you've got to choose one. Which is it going to be?"

She stood up, grabbed him by his shirt, and pulled him across the bar. "I choose you. I love you. I want to spend the rest of my life with you."

It was everything he'd ever wanted to hear.

.

ACKNOWLEDGMENTS

This book has been stewing in my head longer than any other of the Linear Tactical books...ever since 2017 when Alexandra Adams showed up in Survival Instinct. She wasn't quite a villain in that book, but she wasn't very lovable either.

I knew making her a redeemable character would be tricky and almost didn't write REDWOOD for that reason. But ultimately the Alexandra found in that book and the Lexi found in this one were two totally different people.

And most importantly: *Everyone deserves a second chance.* I'm glad Lexi got hers and Gavin finally pulled his head out of his ass. :)

As always, it takes more than just me to bring you a Linear Tactical book. A special thanks to my alpha/beta readers, editors and proofers (many of whom read this book more than once to get it as perfect as possible): Susan, Marci, Dee, Marilize, Tesh, Diana, Aimee, Laurie, Jane. You catch things I don't even see and I'm in awe of you all.

Much appreciation to Elizabeth at Razor Sharp Editing. *Thank God you're back.* I'm the only baby you're allow to deal with from now on.

Once again my thanks to Deranged Doctor Designs who not only created the cover for REDWOOD, but have crafted ALL the Linear Tactical covers. I dare say, mine are some of the best looking books in the biz.

It's so difficult to believe that 2021 is the year the Linear Tactical series will wrap up—three years and fourteen books later.

But don't worry, you've still got three more books coming... Wyatt and Nadine's love story in SCOUT, Kendrick and Neo's story in BLAZE (which includes how Dorian and Ray's family comes to be), and Ethan and Jess all grown up in FOREVER. I think you'll love them all, and I can't wait to share them with you.

Believe in heroes,

Janie

ALSO BY JANIE CROUCH

LINEAR TACTICAL SERIES (series ongoing)

Cyclone

Eagle

Shamrock

Angel

Ghost

Shadow

Echo

Phoenix

Baby

Storm

Redwood

Scout

Blaze

Forever

INSTINCT SERIES (series complete)

Primal Instinct

Critical Instinct

Survival Instinct

THE RISK SERIES (series complete)

Calculated Risk

Security Risk

ABOUT THE AUTHOR

"Passion that leaps right off the page." - Romantic Times Book Reviews

USA Today and Publishers Weekly bestselling author Janie Crouch writes what she loves to read: passionate romantic suspense featuring protective heroes. Her books have won multiple awards, including the National Readers Choice and Booksellers' Best.

After a six-year stint in Germany (due to her husband's job as support for the U.S. Military) Janie is back on U.S. soil and loves hanging out with her four teenagers. Sometimes.

When she's not listening to the voices in her head—and even when she is—she enjoys engaging in all sorts of crazy adventures (200-mile relay races; Ironman Triathlons, treks to Mt. Everest Base Camp) traveling, and trying new recipes.

Her favorite quote: "Life is a daring adventure or nothing." ~ Helen Keller.

facebook.com/janiecrouch
amazon.com/author/janiecrouch
instagram.com/janiecrouch
bookbub.com/authors/janie-crouch

Made in the USA
Monee, IL
17 January 2021